MW01134561

BUST ON THE MISSISSIPPI

BUST ON THE MISSISSIPPI

A Mississippi River Novel

Captain Art Wilson

Copyright © 2018 by Captain Art Wilson.

Library of Congress Control Number:		2017919399
ISBN:	Hardcover	978-1-5434-7450-3
	Softcover	978-1-5434-7451-0
	eBook	978-1-5434-7452-7

All rights reserved. No part of this book may be reproduced or transmitted in any form or by any means, electronic or mechanical, including photocopying, recording, or by any information storage and retrieval system, without permission in writing from the copyright owner.

This is a work of fiction. Names, characters, places and incidents either are the product of the author's imagination or are used fictitiously, and any resemblance to any actual persons, living or dead, events, or locales is entirely coincidental.

Any people depicted in stock imagery provided by Thinkstock are models, and such images are being used for illustrative purposes only.
Certain stock imagery © Thinkstock.

Print information available on the last page.

Rev. date: 01/09/2018

To order additional copies of this book, contact:
Xlibris
1-888-795-4274
www.Xlibris.com
Orders@Xlibris.com
772364

Thanks to all of my family, friends, and acquaintances for their encouragement, help, and technical assistance in writing this book.

Special thanks to Fred, Maggie, and Freddy
Peterson, Paul & Marietta Malrick at Pier 4 Cafe,
Hale & Janet Evans at Great River Harbor

These wonderful people kept the spirit alive!

"I'm sailing away
Set an open course for the virgin sea
'cause I've got to be free
Free to face a life that's ahead of me.
On board I'm the Captain
So climb aboard
We'll search for tomorrow
On every shore…"

STYX

"Come Sail Away"
1977
A&M Records

Chapter 1

Another early spring day on the upper Mississippi River!

As Dock Master of a fairly good size, upscale marina on the upper Mississippi River in a small river community about an hour south of the Twin Cities, I am accustom to getting up about the time the sun peeks it's golden glow over the horizon.

This is the time of spring we are really busy at the marina launching boats and I like to be up and about doing the "Jamaican ting." A pot of strong Blue Mountain coffee from Jamaican braced with a healthy splash of Appleton Jamaican Rum, a nice Cubano and a seat on the aft deck of my boat to watch the sun come up. It was a bit nippy this morning but the coffee and rum were warming me.

Nothing is ever taken for granted about the weather on the upper Mississippi River. Minnesota, known as the "Icebox" of the nation, can be dealt some severe winter weather from Mother Nature. This year she was kind to us. On the average, we start launching boats around the first of May to the mid part of May when the ice is out but this year due to a mild winter, we were able to start launching on April 17th.

Back in 2000, we had two back-to-back spring floods that resulted in a late June launch for most boats. Funny! They called the 2000 flood a 100-year flood. It was the forth 100-year spring flood that we have had in the last twenty years or so. Yet I don't feel like I am four hundred years old.

Everyone calls me Captain Art! My real close friends call me Cap. At 58 years young, I have been blessed with good health. My theory is; get a nice big boat and keep it full of good booze and young women and you'll get most all of the exercise you will ever need. My motto, you're only as old as the woman you're feeling.

When I am not carousing young women I keep fit as a 5th degree black belt in Karate. Sporting long hair kept in a neat ponytail and a well-trimmed full beard, people perceive me a modern day Buccaneer. Married women love me and want their husbands to be like me. Their husbands hate me because their wives love me.

At 6'2" and two hundred and forty pounds I can still stand up to the young tough kids on the block. On the river I have a reputation to be one of the first to stand up in a bar room brawl and the last to walk away. My last ruckus at the Harbor Bar in Hager City, Wisconsin sent small group bikers to the emergency room for repairs.

It was a Saturday night and it was Reggae night. A great Reggae band was playing and the dress that evening for many of us regulars were tropical wraps or sarongs. Women, and men without fear of loosing their masculinity, were running around with their tropical wraps, the only item of clothing the majority of us had on.

A small group of bikers had walked out to the patio bar and started to harass some of the women. Being the fun person that I am, I walked over and asked them to chill out and have some fun and ease up on the harassment. One of them reached out to grab my wrap and I caught his hand and did an under hand twist and brought his hand up high enough behind his back so his fingers could touch his neck. That started the melee.

His buddies jumped up and surrounded me. "Come on guys, we don't need any trouble here", I said. About then one of them yelled, "Let's stomp this fucking faggot." I gave a hard rabbit punch to the kidneys of the guy I was holding and he dropped like a wet rag to the ground. A flying kick and took out two more, along with their front teeth and the last received a back hand that he never saw coming, so hard it broke his jaw. It was all over in about fifteen seconds. The ones that could walk picked up their buddies and started heading for their Harleys.

About then, Brad, the owner of the Harbor Bar runs up yelling, "Christ Captain!" "Are you chasing my customers away again? Thank god it was outside this time. Your last fight here cost you forty two hundred bucks in repairs to my inside bar. What the hell was the problem this time?"

I explained to him what had happened. He shrugged his shoulders walked off mumbling something about bikers and boaters but I couldn't understand what he was saying. A crowd had gathered and I told everyone to that it was all over and to head over to the outside bar and I would buy a round.

Chapter 2

I had just returned from a two-week trip in the Caribbean delivering a private mega-yacht to Aruba from Miami. A beautiful 96' custom-built 8.7 million-dollar yacht. As a licensed United States Coast Guard Master, I spend the winter delivering private yachts from my winter haven in Florida all over the world. When the owners of these big yachts pay you a thousand bucks a day plus expenses. …Hey! It's a job but it's fun and someone has to do it.

While I was making coffee I switched on the remote VHF Marine Radio to the weather channel. The marine weather was predicting clear skies and a high of fifty-two degrees with southeast winds at five to ten knots, which is, pretty much normal for this time of year.

There is nothing worse than trying to launch boats when it is cold, windy, and raining and the boat owners are breathing down your neck. Just the boat owners themselves are bad enough. Everybody wants their boat in first.

My boat, Winkin 'Blinkin' & Nod III, aptly named because I was always winking at the women, Anne Marie my former wife was blinking with jealousy and our daughter would nod off five minutes after she got on the boat. She was already in the water tied up to her usual slip at the head of the gangway coming down to the marina. I like it there 'cause I can see who is coming and going on the docks. You never know when some well looking young babe is going to walk down on the docks just to look at the boats. I am always happy to show them around.

Winkin' Blinkin' & Nod III is a 1986 65' custom sport fisher that I had purchased at a bankruptcy auction. A good Auctioneer friend of mine Carl Radde, the top auctioneer in the state of Minnesota at that time called me about the boat and said it was perfect for me. She was weathered, ill kept and hadn't seen the water for three years. The motors were shot and the interior was plain ugly.

With a 21.5' beam I knew with a little time and money I could make her into one of the best boats of her type on the river. With a 5.2' draft she was ideal for the river yet would be a stable platform at sea. I re-powered her with twin unmuffled high-speed 2,000 HP MTU 16V2000TA's diesels with a custom made exhaust ports for each cylinder at the waterline, port and starboard.

She can do a respectable 44 knots on top and cruise all day long at 37 knots. She's a real head turner going across Lake Pepin at wideopen throttle. In landlubber's terms, a knot is 1.2 mph. I added extra fuel storage for extended cruising. At 20 knots I could run nearly 4,000 nautical miles using around 10,000 gallons of fuel.

She has three staterooms of which one I turned into an on board office. The master stateroom is full beam just forward of the engine room. A walk around king size bed and "His & Her heads". The third stateroom I used for rare guests.

The Salon is a work of art. No pun intended. Windy, a longtime lady friend from Red Wing, Minnesota decorated the entire interior of the boat. Windy, a voluptuous thirty five-year-old blond and I were a pair for a while but I think she dumped me for someone who was a little more stable and stayed at home a little more. Still being good friends and knowing that she had an eye for interior decorating I asked her to undertake the project. Using subtle earth tones she maintained a masculine theme with just a hint of femininity. I explained to her that weight was a consideration. What's sense of having a boat rigged to run fast then overload it with furniture to slow it down?

She did her homework! The Salon deck was covered with thick plush Berber carpeting over a 3/4" foam pad. Most of the furniture was made of fiddle back sycamore and black walnut veneer over a lightweight core. On the port side was a wet bar with 4 stools. Down the starboard side was a leather couch and two matching easy chairs. The forward Salon bulkhead contained a 35" flat screen HDTV and was topped off with a Bose surround sound system.

The galley equipment was all polished stainless steel with polished granite counter tops. A three-burner stove with a Jen Air grill allows me to grill steaks inside when the weather is bad. Two Northern Lights 50kw generators supplied the AC power when the boat was not hooked up to shore power.

The most amazing thing about Winkin' Blinkin' and Nod III was her propulsion. The drive units were Komori water turbine drives mounted in modified tunnels at the transom. These drives and the bow thruster were controlled with fly-by-wire technology. A friend of mine who worked for a major aircraft manufacturer was on the F-14 program and had help develop the fly-by-wire system.

After retirement he went out on his own and developed the fly-bywire system for commercial use and with some simple program modifications we installed in my boat. I had three helm stations. One forward of the galley, one on the aft deck and one on the fly bridge. The entire system was run through a shipboard computer.

At each station there were the normal throttles controls and four joysticks. One joystick controlled the bow thruster. Another one controlled the water jet turbine drives in unison and the other two controlled the turbine drives independently of each other. The drive buckets rotated 180 degrees. With that configuration I was able to move the boat fore', aft, port or starboard, or in an oblique direction. In essences I could moor her on a dime and give you 9 cents change.

Going through the lock & dams on the river, I was one of a few boats that they would allow to float through. Once in the lock I could position the boat right in the center of the lock, set my drives and bow thruster and engage the autopilot. I could hold position to one meter even in a fifteen-knot wind. This was great because a lot of times I was the only one on the boat and to try and hold a boat the size of my boat by yourself to the lock wall was impossible.

Equipped with practically every amenity available including satellite navigation and communications, autopilot, and radar, Winkin", Blinkin', and Nod III is my year around home. Summer in Minnesota and winter in the Florida Keys with the Jimmy Buffet crowd. Occasional blue water cruises to the Bahamas to gamble, Jamaica for coffee and rum, and Cuba for cigars. I have to admit it's a good life living on a boat.

Chapter 3

My dock crew was told to be on the dock at 8:00 a.m. to start launching the boats scheduled for the day. On a good day we can splash 10-12 boats if the weather holds. Today we have a couple of the big yachts to splash and will maybe get nine boats done.

With 142 slips and boats ranging from 32' to 95', with no delays we can have them all in the water in two weeks. My technician, Ekim, was already making the boats ready to splash. Ekim is the top boat tech on this part of the river. At 5' 5" he is a perfect size for crawling around in the confined spaces of an engine room. There is a lot work to be done getting these big boats ready to splash. Forget one detail and you could have a mess on your hands and the EPA threatening you with major fines. Alternatively, a multi million-dollar boat on the bottom of the river.

Being the Dock Master I answer directly to the owners of the marina. Nape William's and his wife Doris own the marina jointly. Nape is a funny sort of guy. He is not a people person. I never trust a person that won't look you in the eyes when he is talking to you. I gave him explicit orders not to step a foot on the docks unless he was showing a boat. After all, I am the Dock Master!

Our relationship was strictly business. The one saving grace that he does have is his knowledge of boats. I don't believe that there is another person on the river that knows as much about boats as Nape.

I guess what is most important, certainly to me as the Dock Master, is quality of care and respect that our Dockers receive. They pay handsomely for their slips. Upwards of fifty dollars a foot based on L.O.A. Not cheap but then when you pay a few million for your boat, what's another couple of thousand to pay for dockage.

A few years ago the owner of a large corporation in Minneapolis had a 118' Hakvoort. In the summer he would have it brought up from Florida and dock it in Stillwater, Minnesota. Dockage in that part of the river is about twice what we charge in our area. If you're going to play the game you have to pay the price. What to the hell, the definition of a boat is hole in the water that you throw money into. Let the good times roll!

I went back aboard Winkin' Blinkin' and Nod III for a fresh cup of coffee. Chad, my lead dock boy knocked on the rail of Winkin' Blinkin' and Nod and asked for permission to come aboard. I yelled from the galley for him to come on down and to take his deck shoes off before coming in.

I could hear when his feet hit the aft deck. At twenty-five he was a strapping lad and the most trusted of my crew. Chad came to me when he was just eighteen and still wet behind the ears. What he knew about boats he could write on the inside of a matchbook. I offered him a cup of Blue Mountain without rum. One of us has to be level headed and I would rather it be him. He accepted the coffee and put the cup between both hands to warm them up from the morning chill. He lifted the cup to his nose and inhaled the deep rich aroma.

"Captain! One of these days I am going to own a boat like yours and I promise you will always be welcome aboard for a cup of coffee like this." "Chad, I said, when your well enough off to own a boat like this

I will be long gone as fish food. Chad is 6'3", lanky but very muscular. His long straight blond hair was very typical of the Norwegian heritage in Minnesota. I was proud of him. I had taught him the ins and outs of boating and I knew that if I asked him to do something it would get done in the same fashion that I would have done it.

"What's on the list of things to do today Captain", he asked. I reached over to the galley counter and gave him a list of duties that I wanted him to oversee. "Chad, I want you and three others to work with Ekim launching the boats. Put two people on the fuel dock and one to clean up the boater's lounge and the patio. The patio looks like some of our early birds had a party last night. Damn boaters and their Jell-O shots. There must be a hundred little Jell-O shot containers on the patio deck."

Chad snapped back with a sharp salute and an "Aye Aye Sir." He turned on his heels and headed across the salon to the aft deck. I could hear him walking on the dock yelling out orders to the rest of the crew.

I thought to myself for a moment. If I had been blessed with a son I would want him to be just like Chad but then, I was blessed with a wonderful daughter from a marriage gone sour. My daughter and her husband have blessed me with 3 grandsons. The story on the docks is that I am raising my own Mafia gang. Myself being of Italian heritage and Heather marrying an Italian then having 3 boys and naming them Rocco, Dominic, and Anthony sure sounds like the start of something.

Chapter 4

Then the phone rang. It was my life long friend Tom Turpin. Tom and I were both born and raised in San Diego California. Our fathers were both Career Navy Officers and we opted to take the same route. We went through elementary, junior high and high school together and then had gone through college together. During our high school days we were the biggest beach bums around. We were hot dog surfers. You could always find us surfing at Law Street just north of the Crystal pier in Pacific Beach.

We joined the Navy together and went through Top Gun flight training at Miramar Naval Air Station in San Diego. We served as Pilots aboard the USS Oriskany CVA-34 in Vietnam and strangely enough ended up coming to Minnesota to seek our careers after our tour of duty in the Navy.

I went into the communications and security industry and Ron went to work for a major chemical company in St. Paul. He went up through the ranks and was now the CEO knocking down around 12 million a year with his stock options.

There was something in his voice, by the way it sounded I knew there was something amiss. "Cap, I need your help." I don't know what is was but for some reason, maybe from the tone of his voice, or from past experience I knew it had to be his son "Toad". "Toad" is his son's nickname. Eugene "Toad" Turpin. Toad was the youngest of five siblings and the worst.

Throughout his short life his name in the Turpin family was synonymous with trouble. At twenty-six years of age he has yet to work an honest day in his life. But then why should he? Daddy does everything for him. Daddy gets him out of trouble. Daddy gets him out of jail. How can Daddy be so successful in business yet a miserable failure in raising a son? The rich mans son.

Two years ago Tom bought Toad a new 28' Sea Ray Sundancer. Paid for a slip in a nice marina in Stillwater. Tom knew Toad liked boating because he spent a lot of time with me on Winkin' Blinkin' and Nod III. He knew boating. Not well, but he knew it.

"Cap! It's big time now, Tom said. He is in jail for possession and distribution of drugs." "What kind of drugs", I asked. There was a slight pause and I could hear Tom taking a deep breath. "Cocaine," he replied.

The word was like an electrical shock going through my ear. Cocaine!

Now he was "big time"!

Toad, generally speaking is a good kid. His past brushes with the law were mainly kids stuff. Stuff that we used to do when we were younger but today you get in trouble for it. Drinking under age, joy riding in cars, fighting, simple possession of pot, and stuff like that. Hell, we knew he was doing pot but we used to do it when we were his age.

Anyone, well 99 per cent anyway, that are the age of Tom and I have smoked pot. We came from the age group that cultured it. It was no big deal. Even Minnesota came to grips with it and reduced it to a hand slap for simple possession.

Christ, Tom and I used to get stoned in 'nam and go on flight training missions. Back then it was no big thing. I not saying it was right but it was the thing to do at that time. The big brass knew we were doing it but turned their heads to it.

Now Toad was playing a different game. A big league game for which there was no return. About six months ago Toad started hanging around a motorcycle gang in Minneapolis. One per centers. I know the gang! I know the leaders. I used to do a lot of motorcycle riding and was involved with a good group of motorcyclist that were dedicated to preserving motorcycling and protecting the rights of motorcyclists.

Now Toad was on the other side of the street!

I waited until Tom had calmed down and asked him to meet me at my favorite steak house in Roseville later that afternoon. I paged Chad and told him I had to leave for personal matter and would be back in the morning. I knew I could depend on Chad to get things done while I was gone. Before I left the boat I made a quick call to the Minneapolis Police Department to talk with a friend in the vice squad.

I asked him if he knew anything about the bust on Toad and he said yes but he couldn't tell me anything else because it was a Federal bust. Toad was being held in the Minneapolis jail until his initial appearance the following day.

Chapter 5

I headed up the gangway to the marina parking lot where my truck was parked in it's reserved spot. I got in and started it up. It was another toy. A 1998 R/T 5.9 Dodge Dakota. I had it tricked out at a local hot rod shop in the cities.

The lifeblood of my truck was a 426 Hemi, putting out just over 500 ponies before I hit the NOS switch. Going through a 3000

RPM stall converter to a B & M Hydro Stick to a Dana quick change rear end with Splicer 3.91 gears that feed the power to a pair of 15" Mickey T's Cheater Slicks. Dropped 2" in the front and 4" in the rear she was a mean and lean machine. It was really old world equipment but it was the stuff that I grew up with and I got a good deal on all of it at a swap meet at the Minnesota fair grounds.

I slipped the transmission in to gear and gave it some gas. Just about the time the tach hit 3000 RPM's she started to roll. I could see Chad down on the docks giving me the high sign to light the tires up. For some reason I didn't feel like doing it. I had other things on my mind.

Out of the marina parking lot I head the truck north on Highway 61.

Highway 61 is all countryside driving. The way my suspension was set up the ride was not the most comfortable ride. If you were picking your nose and hit a bump you would probably pick your brains out.

14

You have to also look at the condition of the average Minnesota road. In Minnesota they don't repair potholes. They just move them so you can't memorize them.

Highway 61 turns into Highway 50 and 50 runs into Interstate 52

North. I turned right to the on ramp for the interstate. Looking to my left I was even with an 18-wheeler doing about 70. I was doing 40 and thought to myself, what the hell. I stomped the gas pedal to the floor and those 500 ponies came to life. Even at 40 mph those 15" Mickey T's broke loose. It was everything I could do to hold the truck straight. I hit the interstate at 80 mph about five car lengths a head of the 18-wheeler. I'll bet that driver is still trying to figure out what the hell happened.

I held my foot to the floor for another 5 seconds and the speedometer was showing 140 mph. Okay, I cleaned the engine out and now it was time to come back down to earth. I eased back with my foot and the truck started slowing down. At 75 mph I set the cruise control, kicked back and pulled out one of my Cuban cigars, lit it at relaxed the rest of the way to the cities.

Just as I was coming into the cities I made a call to Siena longtime lady friend. Siena stood by me when I was going through my divorce. It was a hard time for me going through the divorce. Why can't divorces be friendly? If you could keep the lawyers out of it things might not be so tense. It's like they pit you against each other just to keep the clock running and all the while they're making a mint.

Siena is a business owner and sells high quality wedding gifts and the like over the Internet. In the age of dot.coms she has done a terrific job and is very successful where others have failed.

I got here on the phone and told her I was meeting Tom at the steakhouse in Roseville. I asked her to give Wendell, the manager of the steakhouse a call to reserve the back private room for us. I felt all right about inviting Siena along. Tom knew her and Siena has a good head on her shoulders. Besides, I needed a place to crash for the night and Siena is a lot of fun in bed.

Whenever I head up to the cities I always seem to pick the wrong time of day. I got to the Interstate 52 & 94 exchange right at peek evening rush hour. I really think half of the drivers in this city got their drivers licenses out of a box of corn flakes. I've always found that using Kamikaze tactics works best when driving in the cities.

I exited 52 and got on Interstate 94 heading west. I knew that the traffic would be a little lighter going west at least up to Highway 280 then I could get off of 280 at Luerpenter and run the surface streets to the Rosedale Mall where the steakhouse was.

The Backwoods Steakhouse is a premier restaurant. Some of the finest steaks in town at a moderate price. Wendell was at the Hostess stand when I walked in and greeted me like a long lost buddy. Wendell and I had both ridden motorcycles together. He was more into the Jap Crap and I was a dyed-in-the-wool Harley rider.

We exchange greetings and I headed for the bar. The bartender had seen me come in and had already made me my favorite drink.

When you frequent an establishment on a regular basis they get to know you and go the extra mile to make you happy.

Beefeaters Martini, straight up with two olives on the side. All the bartenders at the Backwoods know how to make my Martini. Pour a splash of extra dry vermouth into the shaker, swirl it around and dump it out. Pour in the Beefeaters gin, shake it, not stir it and pour it into a chilled martini glass. Sort of a James Bond approach.

I like the olives on the side until I have about a mouthful of Martini left then I toss those in and let them soak a while.

I decide to drink my first slowly. Normally I slam down three of them back to back and then order dinner. I figured I had better be clear headed when I talk with Tom. I had been there about 20 minutes and Siena walked in. I could smell her before I saw her. Her perfume was not overpowering or over used. It was just the smell of it and her together. The combination of the two sent ripples of excitement through my loins.

She slid up on the barstool next to me and gave me a big hug and a passionate kiss. That's all it took! I was ready to throw her up on the bar and satisfy that animal urge that she always lit up in me. Somehow I don't think Wendell would be as tolerant about that as he had been with some of the other stunts I have pulled over the years.

Siena is in her late thirties and has kept herself in shape. Short dirty blond hair and a knockout body. I could already tell she was scheming on events that would happen later that night. She ordered a glass of Chardonnay and slowly sipped it while looking over glass at me with her beautiful blue green eyes.

We exchange generalities and she filled me in on the latest gossip around town. We use to run in the same circle of friends when I was working in the cities. The usual amount of divorces, who's sleeping with whom and guess which one our mutual friends just came out of the closet.

I ordered another round of drinks. Just as the bartender set them on the bar I saw Tom out of the corner of my eye. I told the bartender to make Tom a sour Brandy Manhattan. Tom's favorite.

He looked a little haggard. The circles under his eyes told me that he hadn't had a lot of sleep. This thing with his son Toad really had him down. I stood up and gave him a friendly man type hug. Then he bent over and gave Siena a little kiss on the cheek.

"If you want to ditch this lug Siena I'll take you home tonight", he said jokingly. Siena smiled and gave him a kiss on the cheek. "I'm sure Marci would appreciate that Tom", Siena said. Tom sat down and downed his drink in two gulps. I signaled the bartender to make him another one right away.

"Tom, I asked Wendell for the private room so we would not be disturbed and I asked Siena to come along. I hope you don't mind." "No not at all", he replied. I caught Wendell's eye and nodded towards the private room. Wendell acknowledged me and grabbed some menus and we followed him. Wendell said he would have the waitress come in right away to take our orders.

"Okay Tom, I said. "This is your show. Fill us in on the details. "I got a call last night from Toad. He said he been arrested in a drug bust. He didn't go into detail but said bail had not been set and he only had a couple of minutes to talk. I called our family lawyer and asked to check into it. According to my lawyer he goes before the judge tomorrow for his initial appearance. He's a little worried that bail might not be set because Toad may be considered a flight risk."

"Cap, can they do that? Not set bail and keep him in Jail?" "Yes they can Tom but I think once they find out he is and who you are they will probably set bail on him. It wouldn't surprise me if the bail were set at six figures or more."

"Six figures! My God Cap, he's not a murderer. He's just a young kid that was in the wrong place at the wrong time." "Tom, let's not worry about the bail right now. Fill me in on the details that Toad gave you."

Tom took a big swallow of his fresh drink and hesitated for just a moment. I could tell this was hard for him. It's not easy knowing that you your youngest child could be sent to jail for a long time.

"Okay, he started. Toad said that he was down on his boat cleaning it up. He saw three bikers pull up in the parking lot in front of the bar adjacent to the marina. He said he recognized them from the Minneapolis gang." "Hang on a second Tom. What gang are you talking about, I asked?

The "Troubled Disciples." I couldn't believe it. There are biker gangs then there are biker gangs. The "Troubled Disciples" are on top of the pecking order of motorcycle gangs. They control all other biker gangs in the state of Minnesota. I had heard rumors that they were trying to expand their turf outside of Minnesota. They started up in the late '70's and got real big, real fast. Now they want to move to other states. Toad really screwed up this time! He picked some bad dudes to hang around with.

"Go on Tom," I said. "Well, he said that they walked up to his boat and jumped on without even asking. Then they all went below. He said a few minutes after they got below all hell broke loose topside. "What do you mean all hell broke loose, I asked "The boat was full of cops. There was lot of screaming and yelling and one of the bikers warned Toad to keep his mouth shut."

"Is that all, I asked? "Yes, Tom said.

"Toad's time was up and he couldn't tell me any more. Wait, he said. There is one more thing. I got a strange call at work this afternoon and they told me that Toad had better keep his mouth shut or there was going to be trouble."

"Do you know who it was, I asked. Tom shook his head no but he really didn't need to answer the question. I knew who it was. It was the biker gang using their typical form of intimidation. If you threaten the family they get panicky and everyone clams up. I've seen it before.

We talked a little bit more about the subject while we ate dinner. The mood was pretty somber. Siena had said nothing during the conversation. I could tell she was taking it all in and her brain was working overtime.

I could imagine how Tom was feeling about right now. All of the money and power in the world could do nothing at this moment to console Tom or help Toad.

"Cap, Tom said as he looked up from his plate. Cap, I want to hire you to find out what happened. I know police will have their version. I need you to find out the real truth for me. I want to know how Toad got mixed up in this."

"Tom, I explained, you can't hire me. Friends don't hire friends.

This one is on the house. There may be some expenses involved or I may need your influence but I am not about to charge you. Toad is close enough to me to be my son. If there is a right answer to this I will find out.

"Thanks Cap. I knew I could depend on you!

As we finish dinner I couldn't help wondering to myself where I was going to start. I could see me going over to the "Troubled Disciples club house and breaking a few heads but I would probably get my own broken. No, that was not the way. I had to get to Toad and find out the whole story.

Chapter 6

Siena and I parted company with Tom. We decided to head over to POETS for a drink. POETS stood for Piss On Everything Tomorrow's Saturday.

When we got inside the place was unusually pack. Mostly college kids because POETS. was near the University of Minnesota campus. Siena ordered a Grasshopper and I could see the bartenders eyes roll back in his head. Bartenders don't like to make ice cream drinks when they are busy. I settled for a snifter of VSOP Cognac. He brought my drink to me right away and said that Siena's drink would be right up.

I turned to look at Siena and our eyes met. In the dimly lit bar her eyes sparkled and their color shown like the sparkling waters of Jamaica. She was a beautiful woman. I could smell the subtle fragrance of her perfume. I had to find out what kind it was. It always drives me crazy.

She put her hands on my face and looked deeply into my eyes, then she spoke ever so softly. "You know Cap, she started out. Maybe in our next life there will be a chance for us. You are a very handsome man and have a lot to offer a woman but your feet need to be more firmly planted in the ground."

She offered a kiss and I accepted. Just as our lips touched the Bartender came up with her drink. I paid for the drinks and included a nice tip with the words to the bartender that we would like to be alone. I looked at Siena and decided to finish the kiss that she offered. We quietly finished our drinks and slid out of POETS. We were headed for Siena's and a night passion.

Chapter 7

I was up bright and early the next morning. Siena, typically is not an early riser but this morning she was up when she smelled the coffee brewing. I always keep some Blue Mountain at her house for my infrequent stays.

I have always said that the real beauty of a woman is how she looks when she gets up in the morning. Siena was one of those women that was just as beautiful in the morning as she was when she went to bed. Her dirty blond hair was barely mussed. Her skin was light and smooth and her lips were still pink even without makeup. I often wondered why I didn't settle down and put my hooks into this woman. She would be beautiful the rest of her life.

We chatted idly for a while and I made a call to Tom's lawyer. He was not in yet so I left a message for him to call me at the marina. I helped Siena clean up and got myself ready to head back to the boat. I told Siena that I would be back later in the week. "Cap, she said, you're always welcome here". I gave her a quick kiss and left on that note.

I made a quick stop for gas. With the way my truck is set up, economy was not one of the considerations. When I drive it as a person my age should, at best I can get around eleven to twelve miles to a gallon. It drops substantially when I put my foot in to it.

I decided to take Highway 61 back down to the marina so I could stop by the ships store in Hastings to get a few things that I needed for the boat. Highway 61 goes through several small towns heading south like Newport, Cottage Grove and Hastings. After you leave Hasting it's all countryside again. The gentle rolling hills now bare but in a few months will have corn growing. I saw a couple of farmers out in the fields working up the soil in anticipation of planting.

There was a temptation to stop by the Casino on the way down but I had more important things to do. Minnesota has a host of American Indian Casinos throughout the state. I've always said this is the way the Indians are getting back at us for taking their land. They are taking our money at their casinos.

This particular Casino is settled just off the Mississippi River in Welch Minnesota. It is a beautiful Casino and it has a large Marina attached to it. On any given weekend the marina has it's nearly two hundred slips full with boaters trying their luck at gambling.

I had to pull hard on my steering wheel to keep the truck from heading in that direction and continued on to the Marina. My cell phone rang and it was Chad wanting to know where I was. I told him I was about 15 miles out and would be there in about a halfhour.

He gave me yesterday's report. All of the boats that had been scheduled to be splashed were in the water. They were going to start launching boats in about an hour and he wanted to know if I had any input as to which boats would go in first. I told him that I was confident that Ekim could make that decision.

He had to tell me that some of the boaters partied again last night and left a bunch of their Jell-O shot cups lying around. I was beginning to get a little irritated with these boaters and their Jell-O shots. My crew shouldn't have to go around after them and do their clean up. I made a mental note to write a memo and post it on the bulletin board in the Boaters Lounge with regards to this particular problem.

Chapter 8

As I pulled into the Marina I could see things really coming together. A marina is not a marina until the boats are in. This last winter we kept about a dozen boats in the water and with those that we had splashed in the last few days we had about half of the boats in. It was beginning to look a like a marina.

I parked in my reserved spot, grabbed my boat parts that I had purchased at the Ships Store in Hastings and headed down the gangway. Nape, the owner of the marina was just coming up the gangway. My most immediate reaction was to throw his ass over the gangway but held back my temptation. He shuffled up the gangway with his goofy sort of walk and we met in the middle.

"Captain, he asked, when are you going to have all of the boats in the water?" For a fleeting moment the urge to throw him over the rail came back but I instead responded to his question. "Nape, we should have everything in by week's end. It would probably go faster if you would keep your ass off the docks." I could tell he didn't like that response and he reminded me that he was the owner of the marina and he could come down anytime he wanted.

I just looked at him and told him to have a nice day and headed on down to the docks. When I got to Winkin' Blinkin' and Nod III, I

25

reached over the aft deck rail and put my gear on the deck. About then Chad was at my back and I turned around to greet him.

"What's up Chad"? "You can't get boats in the water standing around and gawking." "Good morning Captain, he greeted. Here is the list of the boats that we are going to put in today. I just wanted to make sure it was okay." I took a quick look at the list and nodded to Chad with my approval.

"Chad, has anyone called me yet this morning." "Not yet Cap but I'll keep an ear for the phone and let you know if anyone calls."

What a kid! I made another mental note to think about giving him a raise. He's sort of the "Johnny-on-the-spot". Always thinking ahead and is there when you least expect him. I could also see that he had picked up the mess in the patio.

I went aboard my boat and put on a pot of coffee. Mornings on my boat just don't seem complete unless that wonderful aroma of Jamaican coffee beans is wafting through the air. I picked up the phone and made a call to my friend at the Minneapolis Police Department and left message for him to give me a call. I had to start putting some facts together about this situation so I could plan my strategy.

As in many drug cases things are pretty hush. I didn't see this case as being any different. I poured myself a cup of coffee and checked my answering machine for messages.

I was just about to take a walk on the docks and the phone rang. It was Tom's lawyer. We exchange greetings and he started out telling me he was about ready to start looking for a new boat. In my mind that tells me that he had fleeced enough clients and now had the money to buy a boat. I am not necessarily down on lawyers but I always remember the joke that I heard. "It sure was cold last yesterday. How cold was it? It was so cold that I saw a lawyer with his hands in his own pockets."

Hey, I don't make them up, I just pass them on. Besides, it's not my fault that everyone has this misconception about lawyers. They bring it on themselves.

He had spoken with the DEA people this morning and got a scant bit of information. It seems that at the moment, the bust on Toad was a clean bust. They found just over twenty kilos of pure cocaine. That's forty-four pounds of cocaine that would have a street value in the millions of dollars.

Toad would go before the judge tomorrow afternoon to have his bail set. I need to get more information but I needed that information from Toad. I could only hope that he was not so involved with the motorcycle gang that he wouldn't open up to me.

There was nothing more for me to do until I had information on Toads release. I knew I was going to have to go back up to the cities for a few days and decided to take Winkin' Blinkin' and Nod III up river to Minneapolis. I knew the Shackleford tour boats had not been launched yet so I would be able to use the dock at Boom Island to tie up.

I called Siena to let her know that I was coming back up the following day on the boat and if she had time we could get together on the boat. Then I called Tom to let him know also and he said he would arrange to have Toads car at Boom Island for my use.

There was nothing to do now but to get Winkin' Blinkin' and Nod III ready to get underway in the morning.

Chapter 9

Morning came early!

At five in the morning it is very tranquil on the docks. There was no wind and you could hear the soft gentle lapping of the water against the hulls of the boats. An occasional fishing boat would go by and leave a wake that cause some of the boats to gently tug at their mooring lines.

There was a morning fog and all the boats had dewdrops hanging from spider webs on their railings that appeared like little diamonds in the morning light. I started coffee and went below to the engine room to start my check for getting underway.

The engine room is also a piece of work. It is a full stand up engine room and you can walk around both engines to facilitate any repairs or servicing that might need to be done. The generators are forward of the main engines and in between the two generators is the water plant. On a long cruise I can produce a thousand gallons of potable water each day.

I checked the oil in the main engines and the generators. I also checked the cooling level in all engines, as they were all inter-cooled systems. I have this thing about drawing raw water and pumping it through my engines. Most boats on the river draw raw water from the river and pump it directly through their engines to cool them. My system draws raw water through massive heat exchangers to dissipate the heat from the engines.

I turned on the engine room blowers to air out the engine room while I was checking all of the hydraulic levels. After checking the hydraulics I pulled the cover on the port generator and started it up. I knew I would not be using a lot of electrical power so I only needed one generator. I usually let the generator run about a halfhour to let it settle before putting a load on it and disconnecting the shore power. After I was satisfied that the generator was running okay I replaced the cover and went back topside for a cup of coffee.

It was about six and I decided to take a quick shower. The hot water felt good coming from the triple showerheads. One showerhead on each one of the three interior bulkheads. I still use the prescribe method of showering that is used in the Navy aboard ship. Wet down, soap down, rinse down. Even though I carry a thousand gallons of potable water in the on board tanks, when you get a woman or women taking showers you need the thousand gallon water maker.

I put on a pair of light chino pants, a white polo shirt with the Marina logo on the left and my name on the right and a pair of soft leather boat shoes. I didn't worry about a jacket because the fly bridge was enclosed and if it got to cold I could turn the heat on.

Chad showed up around seven because he knew I was getting underway and heading for the cities. I invited him on board for a cup of coffee and to go over the list of things I wanted him to do while I was gone. I didn't know how long I would be gone but I felt sure I would be back by the weekend. I knew that the marina would be in good hands during my absence.

I switched from shore power to the generator power and asked Chad to disconnect the shore power cables and stow them in the aft compartment for me. While he was doing that I started up the main engines.

If you are motor head like me there is nothing more satisfying than to hear the roar of a sixteen-cylinder diesel motor running. I had climbed up to the fly bridge to start the engines. I like to be up there so I can hear the engines when they running. The sound bounces off the dock floats on each side of the boat.

I turned the ignition switch for the starboard engine first. You can just barely hear the starter from the fly bridge. The engine turned over and finally caught. The sound is a rich deep bass tone with each exhaust port at the same pitch. Then I started the port engine and now had 32 cylinders singing the same tune. If you were standing at the stern of the boat the sound was not deafening but it did register eighty-seven decibels and for some tender ears that is too much.

I went over some last minute details with Chad and climbed back aboard. When I was ready I yelled at Chad to start casting off the dock lines starting with the stern lines first. Next were the bowlines, then the aft spring lines and the forward spring lines were last. Like many boaters in our marina I leave my dock lines on the dock. I always carry a spare set of lines on board in case I decide to tie somewhere else or at another marina.

I momentarily pushed the jet drive joysticks forward them brought them back to the neutral position. That was enough to start the boat in a forward direction. Chad gave me a thumb up when the swim platform cleared the slip. Once cleared of the slip I put the port drive ahead and the starboard drive astern so I could do a ninety-degree pirouette right in front of the slip to get the boat heading out of the marina into the main river channel.

Our fuel docks are at the head of the docks, right on the river. After passing the fuel docks I eased the joystick to port and brought Winkin', Blinkin', and Nod III to a compass heading of 320 degrees and eased the throttles up 800 RPM. I was underway!

Chapter 10

The engines responded to the throttle advance. The rumbling at idle now turned into a soft purr...of a tiger. The fog had burned off already so I saw no need to fire up the radar. Beside I was running only one generator and would need both of them to use the radar.

I kept the boat at 800 rpm all the way up to Lock & Dam #3. I gave the Lock Master a call on VHF channel 14 about a half mile below to let him know that I was on my way up there and asked if it was all right for me to float through. They advised me that there was no commercial traffic in the area and granted me permission to float through. The lower lock doors were open when I got the to the Lock & Dam.

I pulled the throttles back to idle at 530 rpm and eased the bow into the middle of the lock. I had already turned on my GPS and computer system. I brought the boat to a complete stand still in the middle of the lock. As soon as I had a fix on my position I engaged the autopilot and sat back to enjoy the lock through.

This time of the year there isn't much of a lift in the locks. Maybe two feet at the most. Lock & Dam #3 holds 1.4 million cubic yards of water and can cycle that water in 7 minutes. In all it took right at fifteen minutes to lock through.

Once the signal was given I disengaged the autopilot and eased the water jet drive joysticks forward. Once I had cleared the rafting wall, which is a "NO WAKE" zone, I started to ease the throttles forward. As this was the first run of the season I decided I might as well give her a shake down and burn some old fuel.

The sound of 32 cylinders coming to life is unexplainable. The high pitch of the turbos became evident as I continued to ease the throttles forward. 1,000 rpm, 1,200, 1,500, 1,700 the roar was increasing. At 1,760 the bow started to rise. With jet drives there is a lack of vibration that you would feel from normal screw drives. The power comes on and the boat goes faster. My knot indicator was showing now me at 27 knots and some change.

I now had 23 miles of river to travel to get to Prescott, Wisconsin. I knew that there was no commercial traffic, maybe a fishing boat or two and the turns in the river for the next 23 miles were soft turns.

I went W.O.T. Wide open throttle. 2,550 rpm is the recommended maximum rpm. It takes a few moments for the maximum rpm to come up but once that happens the boat itself starts react totally different. Steering becomes more responsive and very quick. Within moments the engines had reached maximum rpm. The sound from the exhaust was music to my ears and the turbos were screaming.

I kept my eye on the knot indicator and watch it as the speed creeped up to 40 knots. I eased the throttles back to hold her at 40 knots. 40 knots in statute miles or land miles is right around 47 mph. I made some final adjustments on the drives and sat back for a short 50-minute cruise to Prescott. Actually 23 miles can be covered in 34 minutes but given the "NO WAKE" zones at either end of this leg I calculated 50 minutes to the confluence of the Mississippi and St. Croix rivers.

At 40 knots per hour the boat puts out a fairly nice wake but not nearly as bad as some smaller Carver cabin cruisers that I have seen. I always look for small boats that could be easily swamped from my wake but I'm happy to say there was not one on the river.

I pulled the throttles back just before the Prescott "NO WAKE" zone and held them at 600 rpm. At 600 rpm there is just a perceptible wake from my boat. At the confluence of the two rivers the Mississippi River makes a slight turn to port and about a mile up is Lock & Dam #2. I gave the Lockmaster at #2 a call on the VHF and told him I would be there in a few minutes and again requested to float through. Permission was granted they were waiting for me when I got there.

Once again as in Lock #3 the lift was minimal due to the high spring waters. In about 15 minutes I was on my way once again. I decided against a high speed run on this next leg. I set the rpm's for a moderate 17-knot cruising speed and started watching the waters ahead.

In this area, known as the "Stump Yard", the channel can be full of deadheads or floating logs. On normal screw driven vessels the logs can be tear up a prop, rip out struts or go right through the hull. The beauty of jet drives is the unlikelihood of damaging the drives. The worst that could happen is a 6-inch log going through the hull.

Another 23 miles and you come up right in Downtown St. Paul. I got on the VHF channel 16 and tried to raise a couple of friends that have boats in the St. Paul area. I got a negative response. Poor suckers are probably at work.

I had slowed down to around 10 knots and was getting an eye full of mid morning traffic on the roads. I can't say as I miss it. Some of the yard tugs were pushing barges around. Commercial barge traffic would start in earnest in a couple of weeks. I gave Lock & Dam #1 a call and told them I was about 30 minutes south of them. They responded back that they were currently locking a southbound tow and the locks would not be open for northbound traffic for about an hour and a half.

Doing some quick calculations I knew that even at a minimum speed I would get to the locks 45 minutes early. I decided to pull up to the quay wall right beneath the sports arena in St. Paul. I idled the boat down until I was making zero headway against the current. Waited a few moments for the GPS to get a position fix then engaged the autopilot so I could go down and get my lines and fenders ready to tie up. I opted to put out only a bowline, as the current would keep my stern into the wall. I was using an inch and a half nylon line to tie off the bow from the forward spring cleat.

When I was ready I went to the aft deck control station and disengaged the autopilot and eased the boat sideways to the quay wall. I gently nudged her against the wall and held her steady until I got a new position fix and once again engaged the autopilot. I walked up to the bow and dropped the bowline over the cleat on the wall. Took up the slack and tied it off on my forward spring cleat with one full turn, two figure eights, and two half hitches. I walked back to the stern and disengaged the autopilot and when into the galley for a cup of coffee with a brace of rum.

I switched the VHF to channel 13. This is the working channel that the locks and Barge Captains use when locking through. I could overhear all of their conversations and would hear when the tow was underway heading south my way.

I decided to jump up on the wall to stretch my legs a little. I refilled my cup and set my alarm system just in case someone thought they might want to drive off with the boat. With the alarm system set, nothing can be engaged. The throttles are even electronically locked.

With the water as high as it was it was just a matter of stepping onto the quay wall from the stern quarter of the boat. Once on the wall you can walk anywhere you want. Even downtown if you so desire. I didn't feel that energetic so I started out just walking the length of the boat looking her over with admiration.

I slowly walked towards the bow admiring her graceful lines. Everything was flowing. She had the look of speeding through the water even when she was tied up. When I got to the bow I turned around and looked at her entire 65' of length. I had to admit she was a beautiful boat

Chapter 11

As I was gazing down the hull I was startled by a raspy feminine voice behind me. "Now that's what I call a boat" she remarked. I turned around and I was looking at five foot seven inches of welldeveloped woman. She was dress in white hip hugging bell-bottoms with a soft curve revealing a midriff blue silk blouse. And was it ever revealing her curves.

The slight breeze was gently blowing her thick long flowing auburn hair. She had green eyes, high cheekbones and very full lips that seemed to be begging to be kissed. For a fleeting moment I wasn't sure what to say. In my mind I was thinking of a simple response like, "yep, she sure is", but it sounded too simple. My mouth started working but my brain didn't. "She's sixty-five feet long and has a twenty-one and a half-foot beam," I stammered.

I could see her eyes widen and she pursed her lips in awe. I was about to say something else as intelligent but thankfully she started speaking first. "I don't imagine that there is a chance that one could get a look at the inside of your boat, is there?" My brain went into overtime. A chance......lady I am about to physically pick you up and carry you aboard. I snapped back to reality and said, "I would be happy to show you around."

We walked back to the stern and I jumped aboard and turned around and held my hands out to her. She stepped towards the boat and I grabbed her gently around her small waist. She couldn't have weighed more than 110 pounds. As she came towards me her arms went around my neck and I could smell the freshness of her hair. I lowered her slowly to the deck and for a moment she kept her arms loosely around my neck.

"Thank you", she said in that soft raspy tone. She was wearing leather sandals, which I asked her to take off. Leather soles will hold grit and dirt and will scratch the surfaces of the boat.

Like I was really worried about that right at this moment!

She put a hand on my shoulder for support and bent down to remove her sandals. With a little smile on her full lips and a wink from her right eye she remarked, "As long as that is all that I have to take off." I decided not to respond.

I walked over to the salon doors and slid them open then stood back and motioned her in. She took about five steps in side the salon and stopped. I could see her toes flexing in the soft Berber pile with the 3/4" foaming padding. She took me by surprise when she asked, "do you have a bed or do you sleep on the carpeting? It feels as soft as my own bed," she said.

I chuckled and told her that the boat did in fact have beds to sleep on but that it was not mandatory. At that moment a yard tug went by leaving a fairly good size wake and as the boat rolled she lost her balance. I reached out and grab her inadvertently touching her full breasts. "Excuse me, I stammered, feeling the blood rushing to my face, that was not intentional."

"No harm intended, no harm done and my name is Carmen." "Well Carmen, it's a pleasure to meet you and welcome to Winkin 'Blinkin' and Nod III. My name is Art, Captain Art to many, and Cap to my friends."

"Cap, she asked, can I be your friend?" "Carmen, you can be my friend or whatever you want." I wasn't sure what that statement meant but it sounded like I just had a brain fart.

I offered her a cup of coffee or a drink. She opted for a drink and asked if I had any scotch. I said yes and asked her how she would like it. Her choice was on the rocks.

I poured her a healthy drink and handed it to her and started telling her about the boat. I turned on the Bose sound system. I had a Jimmy Buffett CD in the player and Margaritaville was the first song to play.

I showed her around the galley and the forward helm. She wanted to know what the two TV screens were for at the helm. I explained to her that they were part of the navigation system. One was used to view electronic charts and the other was the radar screen.

I open the door to the main deck stateroom that I had converted into an office. She walked in and looked around the office seeming somewhat impressed. I walked out ahead of her and directed her towards the ladder going below to the staterooms. I told her to go all the way forward, to the rarely used guestroom. She opened the door and looked inside and turned to me and asked me if that was where I slept.

I told her that this was the guest stateroom and that my cabin was aft. I turned around and started walking aft hearing her little feet padding along behind me. We reached my cabin door and I opened it all the way. I could hear the small gasp that she emitted as she walked into the cabin.

"My God! This room is bigger than my bedroom in my apartment and I thought I had a big bedroom."

I could imagine what a person would think seeing a king-size bed on a boat that you could walk all the way around. The bed was covered with a nautical bed quilt that went all the way down the sides of the bed touching the deck. The bulkheads were burled walnut and all fittings and lighting fixtures were brass. A few nautical pictures hung randomly on the bulkheads around the cabin.

On the bulkhead over the headboard of the bed hung a large framed portrait of me sitting nude on my 1991 Harley Davidson Ultra-Glide. It was a non-revealing portrait but it often brought a lot of comments. She looked at the portrait, then looked at me, and then back to the portrait. I smiled but said nothing. She looked at it for a few moments more then turned to me and smiled. I could only imagine what was going through her pretty little head at that moment.

I broke the silence and showed her the "hers head". The first thing she noticed was the Bidet. Her silence was starting to confuse me. I wasn't sure if she was just plain in total awe or if she was a wellbred lady and a bidet was just a part of life. I walked over and opened the shower doors. She walked over and looked inside and then her silence was broken. "Three showerheads? Wow! I am really impressed now. Is it possible that I could take a shower? You could scrub my back for me."

This was a chance of the lifetime and I was about to blow it. I told her she could take a shower on my boat anytime she wanted with the exception of today. I explained to her that I had to get to Minneapolis to take care of some important business. She gave a little frown and I couldn't believe what I had just said. It was like kicking the proverbial gift horse in the mouth.

We went back up to the salon on the main deck and I asked her if she would like her drink freshened. She declined and said that she should be going and that she was meeting a friend for lunch. "By the way, she asked. What brings you up this way?"

I told her that I was going up to Minneapolis to be with some friends that had a son who had been busted on a major drug charge and that I would be tied up at Boom Island while I was in the cities. I took the opportunity to tell her that I would be heading south on Friday and I would be happy to pick her up and take her along for the ride.

She opened her little shoulder purse and took out a card and handed it to me.

I looked at the card. A fancy corporate card. "Carmen Mendoza, Attorney at Law, Senior Vice President, Hewlett, Green, & Canon Law Offices. When I pick them, I pick them. This law firm just happened to be one of the most prestigious law firms in the state of Minnesota.

I made a mental note to tell Tom about meeting her. I exchanged one of my cards with her and began wondering if I had even made an impression on her because she put my card in her purse without as much as a glance.

"Thank you so much for the tour and the drink Cap." Why don't you give me a call on Thursday and let me know what your schedule is. I might be interested in your offer. I have no plans for this weekend."

I walked her to the aft deck and she put her hand on my shoulder again to put her sandals on. We walked over to the rail and I put my hands around her waist and gently hoisted her up to the wall.

I followed right behind her and offered her a handshake just like a gentleman should do. She took my hand and put it up to her neck then with both of her hands she took my head and pulled it towards hers. Our lips met and for a moment you could have knocked me over with a feather. I could feel her hips softly pushing against mine. That tingling feeling was rushing through my loins. Her kiss lingered for about ten seconds. She pulled away and said good-bye. She turned abruptly and started walking away. I stood there dumbfounded. As she walked away she turned her head and told me not to forget to call her on Thursday.

Chapter 12

I broke out of my trance when I heard the Captain of the barge in Lock #1 telling the Lockmaster that he was ready to head south. I watched Carmen for little while longer then turned and headed to the boat. I jumped on board and went to the aft control station. I engaged the autopilot and walked up to the bow and untied the line made fast to the quay wall.

I climbed up to the fly bridge, disengaged the autopilot. I directed the bow thruster and drive buckets to discharge to starboard. This would cause the boat to go to port. I waited until the boat was about fifteen feet from the wall then shut down the bow thruster and directed the drive buckets to forward. I eased up the throttles to 800 rpm's and headed for Lock & Dam #1.

I gave the Lockmaster a call on channel 14 to let him know that I had heard the Captain of the barge saying that he was underway. I told him that I was also underway and should be at the lock in about twenty minutes.

In a little bit I could see the barge heading my way. The barges on the river have always amazed me. These Captains are masters at what they do. The largest hook up that I have ever seen on the upper Mississippi was with 15 barges or containers. One container can hold the equivalent of 190 train boxcars. You're talking about 1,200 feet of barge and towboat. The way that they control these things is awesome. I have always had a desire to get aboard a barge and take a trip down river however I found out that you have to be an employee of the company to get aboard.

I waved at the captain and a couple of the deck hands as I went by. The Captain gave me a short blast on the horn and I gave a return blast. As I passed his stern I could see the water that the barge was kicking up. Many a small boat has erred by passing behind a tow and has ended up swamped by the prop wash. Rule one of boating around tows; never pass close to the stern of a tow. Not only can a small boat be swamped and sucked under, but also the massive props on the tow pick up sunken logs and literally throw them up in the air.

Rounding the bend I could see Lock & Dam #1 also known as the Ford Locks. There is a big Ford manufacturing plant that primarily produces pick-up trucks. I had a buddy that worked there that was going to get me a deal on a new Ford pick-up. Sorry! I am a 100% Mopar Man.

I gave quick call to the Lockmaster and told him I was looking at him and he responded that he could see me, and the gates started to open up. I pulled the throttles back to idle and again eased into the lock. Getting my position fix I locked the autopilot and waited for the lock through.

After Lock & Dam #1 there is only one other set of Locks. They are the St. Anthony Locks. On the land side next to the Locks is the new Federal U. S. Mint. A massive complex in it's own rights. Surrounded by concrete barriers you can't get within a 100' feet of the building with a vehicle.

Once I cleared the lock I radioed the Lockmaster at the St. Anthony Lock & Dam to tell him I would be there in a few minutes. Barge traffic is rare this high up on the river so I knew I would not have a wait locking through. The Lockmaster was an acquaintance of mine and he radioed back that he would be waiting for me.

As promised the lower doors were open and I was locked right on through. After exiting the Lock, Boom Island is about a half mile up river from the Lock. As I had suspected the dock was empty. I nosed the bow to starboard and headed for the dock. When I was near and parallel to the dock I positioned the boat about twenty feet from the dock and set the autopilot. I climbed down to the main deck and started setting fenders and getting the dock lines ready.

With everything ready I went to the aft control station and disengaged the autopilot and started walking the boat sideways to the dock. With a gentle nudge she was against the dock and I reset the autopilot and started tying up the boat.

The bow was headed into the current so I tied off the bow first then walked back and tied off the stern line. I then set the spring lines fore' and aft. Everything looked good and I jumped back down on the boat and disengaged the autopilot. Being satisfied that I was secure I shut down the main engines leaving the generator running.

I wasn't going to be able to get shore power here for two reasons. First this dock is a city dock and arrangements have to be made through the city of Minneapolis for power. The second reason is that the tour boats have two 100-amp shore power hookups and I use two 50-amp shore power hookups. The connectors are also different. There really wasn't a problem with this, as the generator would use less than 50 gallons of fuel in a 24-hour period.

Boom Island, which I cannot tell how it's named was derived has a marina with about 15 small docks. I would guess the largest boat that could get in there would be something around 25' or less. Not a whole lot of room to maneuver and you can very easily put your props into the rocks. I looked up towards the parking lot and as promised I could see that Tom had left Toad's car there. There was a spare set of keys hidden in one of those magnetic key boxes under the left front fender well.

Chapter 13

I went into the salon and started making some calls so I could plan my day's events. It was 12:45 and my first call was to Tom's lawyer. He was out to lunch however his secretary knew me and had information about Toad's arraignment. It was set for 3:30 that afternoon. I left a message for the lawyer that I would meet him in court.

I then called Siena and Tom, in that order, to let them know that I was in town. Siena asked what my plans were and I told her it was too early to tell at this time. I would have to get back with her later in the day.

When I got through to Tom's office his secretary told me he was out for the day but I could reach him on his cell phone. I gave Tom a call on his cell phone but did not get an answer. I left him a voice mail and told him I would meet him in court at Toad's arraignment.

I took a quick shower and put on some business type clothing. Since I retired I had a thing about wearing business attire. I would only wear a tie if it were absolutely necessary. Give me a tropical shirt and a pair of shorts and I was dressed for anything.

I packed my briefcase with things that I thought I would need for the day. Being licensed to carry a gun I thought about putting it on but decided against it. Probably not the wisest thing to do, going to court packing a gun. With all of the terrorist problems the US was having I didn't see a need to add to it.

My trusty side arm was a real beauty. A local gunsmith put it together for me. Jerry Hobbs was retired from the Minneapolis Police Department and was the weapons trainer for twenty years. He opened up his own gun shop after retirement and he knew everything there was to know about guns.

I had Jerry put a custom package together for me that would rival James Bond. He started with a 9mm Beretta machined from pure titanium. Not only was titanium strong, it was light.

It carried 12 rounds. Not legal, but if I had to use the gun they wouldn't know how many rounds that I started with. Jerry, custom loaded all of my rounds. I used three different types of bullets. A full metal jacket with a 125-grain slug that could crack an engine block or go through protective vest like a knife going through butter.

My second type was hollow point also using a 125-grain slug and could stop a full-grown man dead in his tracks. The last was a tracer round in case I got into problems at night. All of the rounds were hot loaded using a fast burning nitro-based powder. When I loaded the magazine I would alternate each type of load starting with the hollow point first.

There was no need to remember which round was coming up next. Any one of the rounds would put a man down at 25 yards, which was the maximum effective range of the piece. Jerry had modified the chamber to release 35 % percent of the gases at ignition to minimize the recoil effect.

He fabricated a laser light that fit snugly in front of the trigger guard and was barely noticeable. At 25 yards it put a two-inch red dot on the target. I used an Uncle Mike's Pro-pak Undercover shoulder holster that weighed a mere 5.3 ounces. It carried the gun in the horizontal position and was lightning fast coming out of the holster. The entire rig was very compact and when I wore it, unless you knew that I was carrying a gun you could not tell it.

Chapter 14

I had my briefcase packed and was set to go. I took quick walk through the boat to make sure everything was secure. At the last minute I had decide to shut down the generator. It certainly wasn't the cost of running it, it was just that it served no purpose to keeping running. The refrigerator and freezer worked on a combination of electricity or LP. If there was no electricity they switched over to LP automatically.

I set the alarm and walked out the salon door locking it behind me. I sprung up to the dock and headed for the parking lot. Toad's car was easy to spot. I was at Toads birthday party when he got the car as present from his father.

It was a 1999 Chevy Monte Carlo. Black over black with custom wheels and tires and $3,000 stereo system. It had one of those obnoxious subwoofers in the trunk that you could hear coming two blocks away if it was turned up. I reached under the left front fender well and found the hidden keys.

I hadn't had anything to eat yet so I figured I had better get some food in my belly or the judge might get me for contempt of court from my belly growling. I headed out of the parking lot and took the Lowery Street Bridge across to Washington Ave. and headed down Washington towards downtown.

It had been a while since I had been in downtown Minneapolis to eat and I knew there were hundreds of places to choose from. I decide on the Pickled Parrot on 1st Ave. North. They have a wide variety of foods on their menu and the food is always good there. I thought it was best that I keep lunch light so I had a chef salad with ice tea to drink. I took a quick glance at my watch. It was nearly 3:00. The courthouse was just a couple of minutes away. I caught the waiter's eye and signaled for my check. I paid the waiter and left him a nice tip.

I used underground parking lot of the Federal Courthouse. Generally it is easier to find a parking spot there than at a meter or one of the many parking lots around the courthouse. I took the elevator to the street level so I could check the docket to find out which courtroom Toad's arraignment was being held in.

The hearing was scheduled in Federal Courtroom 512, which would be on the fifth floor. I grab an elevator and rode it up to the fifth floor. I stepped off the elevator and turned towards room 512. I had walked about ten paces and I saw Tom, his wife Marci, and the family lawyer.

They all turned about the same time as I walked up. Marci was the first to respond and gave me a big hug and a kiss on the cheek. I knew there was going to be a big set of red lips on my cheek so I made a mental note to make sure I wiped it off before going into court.

Tom stuck his hand out and I grabbed it and pulled him to me giving him one of my man type hugs. He didn't look much better than he did two nights ago when we had dinner together.

The family lawyer, Bernie Goldsmith offered his hand and I accepted it. Typical of many lawyers his grip did not convey a true meaning of greetings. I would put his handshake about one-step above being limp wristed. Even dressed in stereotype fashion, a dark blue pinstriped vested suit, black wing tips and a Harvard tie, there was something greasy looking about him.

Bernie was in fact a very successful criminal defense lawyer but it didn't alter the way that he looked. His reputation in drug defense was unparalleled in the Twin Cities. I was still trying to figure out how a leading drug lawyer came to be Tom's family lawyer. I made another mental note to ask Tom about that.

It was 3:20 and we all walked into the courtroom. Bernie walked up to the counsel tables in front of the bench and Tom, Marci, and myself sat in the first row right behind Bernie.

Two Deputy US Marshals were escorting in Toad just as we were sitting down. Dressed in bright orange jail coveralls and shackled by his hands to a belly strap and ankle shackles he looked like a real criminal. He saw us and tried to wave but his hands were attached to the belly strap and could only managed to wave his fingers.

They sat him the seats normally used for the jury with a deputy on each side. I took a quick glance around the courtroom recognized a couple of the DEA agents and an agent from the local FBI office having a discussion with the Federal Prosecutor.

About then the court bailiff asked everyone to stand as the judge walked in and sat at his seat behind the bench. The judge was Henry Haines. He was not known for his leniency. I started to nudge Tom and tell him but I had second thoughts about it.

Judge Haines was a key supporter in the Minneapolis's D.A.R.E. program. He was out to stop the drug traffic and didn't care whose toes he stepped on. The outcome of this hearing was going to be real interesting.

The judge went through the normal routine of calling the case. The US Attorney stood up and requested that bail not be allowed because of the severity of the violation, the amount of cocaine that had been seized, and that Toad was a potential flight risk.

Bernie, Toads lawyer stood up and objected. Bernie explained that Toads father was a recognized pillar of the community and CEO of a major Minnesota Corporation and that Toad would not be a flight risk.

The judge asked the US Attorney a few more questions then announced his decision. Toad was to surrender his Passport and Drivers License. He was to be fitted with an electronic ankle-monitoring device at his parent's home and was to make daily phone checks with court.

Bail was set at $2,000,000. The judge ordered that Toad be remanded in custody until such time as the bail was posted. Toad's preliminary hearing would be set for 9:30 in the morning five days hence in this courtroom.

Bernie turned around and looked at us. By the looks on his face it didn't seem that he was surprised by the judge's orders. He asked us to go out to the hallway and said he would meet us out there shortly after he spoke with the US Attorney.

We went out to the hallway and the mood was rather somber. Tom was comforting Marci and I didn't have anything of any importance to say. Ten minutes later Bernie came out of the courtroom. He asked Tom to go with him to take care of the bail. I told Tom I would take Marci with me and we would meet him at Maxwell's on Washington Ave. Marci and I headed for the underground parking lot. Once in the car Marci broke down and started crying. I put my arms around her to comfort her. I handed her my handkerchief so she could wipe her eyes. "Cap, she said through her sobs. How could this happen? We have tried hard to raise Toad right. How could he possibly be involved in a situation like this?"

Chapter 15

I headed out of the parking lot and headed in the direction of Maxwell's just a couple of blocks away. I found an open meter right along side of Maxwell's and we got out. I stopped at the meter and put in, as many quarters needed to give us two hours of parking. The parking meter raised another issue about my dislikes of downtown Minneapolis, no free parking anywhere in the downtown area.

We went inside and selected a table right in front of the windows. At least if there was not going to be any conversation we could look out the window and watch the cars going by. The waitress came and asked if we would like some drinks. I looked at Marci for a response and she said that she would have a tall Windsor seven with a twist of lime. That being one of my favorite drinks, I ordered the same.

I looked at Marci. She was a beautiful woman. At 55 she still had firm facial features and a trim body. Tom had met her while we were in the Navy. The aircraft carrier that we were on was in the shipyards in Bremerton Washington for repairs prior to our deployment to Vietnam. She was the manager of the Officers Club at the Bremerton Naval Shipyards.

Tom met her by happenstance as the result of an altercation that him and I got into with a couple of pilots from another air squadron aboard the USS Oriskany. We were young Lieutenant JG's at the time. Pilots have a reputation for getting crazy and out of hand when they have been drinking. The naval code of an Officer and a Gentleman does not always hold true. The argument started over an incident that had happened on a flight-training mission off the coast of San Diego during carrier qualifications.

This younger pilot sitting next to Tom at the bar was making some brash statements about his flying ability and Tom got fed up with it and told him that he was blowing smoke and couldn't fly his way out of a wet paper bag. That's about all it took. He threw his drink in Tom's face and Tom reached over and grabbed his uniform tie from under the bar and yanked it down until this kid's face met the bar.

There was instant blood from his nose and he yelled in pain, screaming that his nose was broken. I stood up to make sure that none of this guys buddies would get involved and I was going to let Tom and this kid have it out. The bartender had other ideas. He called back to the manager's office and told Marci what was going on and she was at the bar in a flash.

Without any fear she jumped between Tom and this kid and with the voice of a Marine Drill Sergeant she told them to stand down. In simple terms that means to knock the shit off. No one moved. Tom sat down on his stool and the kid was wiping his nose with a bar napkin.

"Who in the hell do you two think you are, she chided? This is an Officers Club and not some back room gym that you can tear up into a junkyard." She was hot under the collar and no one was about to say anything. She asked who had started the fight but true to the unwritten rule of officer's camaraderie, there was total silence.

She took down Tom's and the other pilot's names and told them that the incident would be reported to their respective Air Group CO's. In the mean time both of them were "86" from the club for the remainder of our stay in Bremerton. It could have been worse but then we only had another week before sea trials and then we would be leaving for Vietnam.

As the request of our Air Group CO, Commander John Olsen, Tom called Marci at the Club and apologized for the incident. I don't know how he did it but talked her into a date before the ship left and that's how the relationship started.

They wrote constantly during the nine months that the ship was deployed. Tom and I took an R&R trip to Hawaii and he asked her to fly over for the week that we were there on R&R. Being married then, my wife Marie was already planning to come over which meant we could all spend some time together. I'm not sure that it was a good idea on Tom's part but we made arrangements for the girls to meet in San Francisco and fly together to Hawaii.

It was a fun but very short week. Marci and Tom hit it off and about the only time that we saw them was at dinnertime. Tom wasn't about to let any moss grow under his feet.

Chapter 16

Tom finally showed up about an hour later. He ordered a drink and began telling us about getting Toads bail posted. Everything had been taken care of and the paperwork would take a few hours and Toad would be released and brought to Tom and Marci's home by the US Marshals in the morning. They had to deliver him and set up the electronic monitoring device.

Tom had not had a chance to talk with Toad but that would come soon enough. We had a couple more rounds and decided to go have nice dinner at Manny's Steak House in the Hyatt Regency Hotel on 12th & Nicollett.

I gave Siena a call and invited her along. She accepted and I told her to pack an overnight bag 'cause she was going to stay on the boat with me. She asked if that was an order or if she had a choice in the matter. I told her that the only choice she had was whether or not to bring an overnight bag. She chuckled and said okay. It was nearly five so I told her to take a cab and we would meet her in Manny's bar at six.

We finished our drinks and I picked up the tab. We went out to our cars and I took the lead. I headed up Washington to 3rd Ave.

South and hung a left with Tom & Marci following me. I drove down to 12th and turn right then a few blocks to Nicollett into the Hyatt Regency parking ramp. I found two parking spots together on the 4th level and we parked the cars and walked to the service elevators. Once inside the elevators I pushed the button for Manny's Steak House and in a flash we were on Manny's level.

Manny's Steak House is to steaks like Rolls Royce is to cars. We are talking the best of the best. Everything on the menu is Ala Carte and prime. I used Manny's as a place to impress people or just to get the best steak in town. There is nothing "chain" about this place. It is one of the top independent steak houses in the nation. If I remember right, the last time that I flew they were listed in the flight magazine as the 2nd top steak house in the nation.

When you walk in you can go to the right to the formal dining room or take a left into the bar where dinner is also served. It is also a cigar friendly atmosphere and well ventilated with electronic smoke eaters to keep the smoke down. I always say if you don't like the smoke you can go eat in the non-smoking formal dining room.

We slid up to the bar. The bartender knew me and asked if I wanted my usual Beefeaters Martini. I said yes and then he asked Tom and Marci what they would like to drink. Before he walked away I asked him to bring me the private humidor so I could pick out a nice before dinner cigar. I asked Tom if wanted one but he declined.

I picked out a nice Te Amo Cheroot. Te Amo's are made in Mexico and have a terrific taste. I was going through the ritual of getting the cigar ready to light up when Siena, "Miss it's not fashionable to be late", showed up. She must have anticipated that I was going to call her for dinner. She must have been already dressed and waiting for my phone call. I made a mental note to ask her about that.

I ordered Siena a glass of Chardonnay, which the bartender brought right away. Tom, Marci and Siena started talking about the events of the day and I kind of went into a mental wonderland and enjoying my cigar.

Tom had to shake my arm to bring me back to reality. He asked if I was ready for another drink and I said yes. I asked the bartender to tell the Maitre'd to have one of the booths in the backset up for us and asked that Joe be our waiter. Joe has been with Manny's for many years and is about the best that they come. He has a sense of humor and a manner that some people find offensive. I find it refreshing.

A few minutes later Joe, our waiter came up to the bar and looked at me and said. "Well blow m' down mates, the Captain is on the bridge. Captain Art, I haven't seen you since the last Nor'wester came through. How in the heck are you, you ol' Sea Dog?" I accepted his offered hand.

"Joe, it's good to see you again you no good excuse for a sailor. Are you still running your blow boat on Minnetonka?" Blow Boat was what power boaters called people who had sailboats. In turn the sail boaters would call us smudge pots. We both laughed and he said our booth was ready and we could go over to it anytime we wanted. He said he would be there all night so there was no rush.

Rush is not what you do at Manny's. This is a place that you can eat at your leisure. Just tell the wait staff how you want to eat and you'll be taken care of. We finish our last round of drinks and I told bartender to make another round for us and have Joe bring them over to the table.

We walked back to our reserved booth, which was in the very back of the bar against the right wall. Siena and Marci slid in first and Tom and I followed. Joe delivered our drinks right away. I asked Joe to bring the selection cart over so we could take a look at today's feast.

Joe wheeled up the diner cart, which takes place of an actual menu. A sample of each cut of steak, lamb, veal, pork, fish, and whole Maine lobster are laid out on the cart in a decorative manner, along with the vegetables of the day.

I never cease to be amazed whenever I see the fresh asparagus. Each piece is about nine inches long and about the diameter of the average mans thumb. Believe me it is fork tender when it's cooked. The potatoes are also on the large side measuring five inches in diameter and about seven to nine inches long. Joe left us alone and we sat and stared at the food cart. No one was in a hurry to order.

Tom quickly filled me in on the details of posting Toads bail. He was still somewhat mesmerized by the amount of the bail. I guess I was too but not surprised. To and I started talking about Winkin', Blinkin', and Nod III while the ladies talked about things that ladies talk about.

Joe stopped back to check on us and I asked him to give us about ten minutes then we would be ready to order. He departed with a smart salute. We turned our attention once again to the food cart. Everything looked so delicious. Siena suggested that everyone order something different and we could all share. Marci thought it was a great idea and it appeared that Tom and I had no choice in the matter.

I actually despise having dinner and knowing that I may have to share it with someone. I can put up with it in a Chinese restaurant but not in the best steak house in the nation. I bit my tongue and decided that I wouldn't spoil the mood, as Tom didn't seem to have a problem with it one way or the other.

Siena chose the lobster and all of a sudden I thought maybe the sharing thing wasn't such a bad idea. I knew I going to have the 24ounce sirloin tip cooked medium rare and a piece of her "shared" lobster sounded good. Marci couldn't make up her mind between the lamb chops and the veal steaks. Tom was no help there because he opted for the Alaskan Salmon steak.

I saw Joe and gave him a slight nod and he threw me a salute letting me know that he that he would be there as soon as he could. Marci still hadn't made up her mind by the time Joe arrived to take our order. I let Siena order first then told Tom to go ahead. I was just about to give Joe my order when Marci blurted out that she had made up her mind and was going to have the lamb chops. I gave Joe my order and suggest that we get the Asparagus on a common platter and a platter of the house hash browns. Everyone agreed and I asked Joe for another round of drinks and to open up a bottle of Gewurz-Tramminer wine so it could breathe before dinner.

I was beginning to feel a little loose from my Martinis. No wonder I thought to myself. The martini glasses here are twice the size of martini glasses in any other bar or restaurant. I had a sneaking idea that Siena was driving back to the boat tonight.

Until dinner came we kept the topic of our conversation to generalities. I think we all felt that talking about Toads situation would put a damper on the evening. I sneaked a quick look at my watch and was surprised that it was only 7:15. My God! I'm half in the bag and we still have half the night to go.

I decided to start sipping very slowly on my Martini or I'd be out of it before dinner arrived. Siena with her uncanny women's intuition leaned over and nibbled on my ear and whispered for me to take it easy as I had other duties to perform later that evening. I was sure that Tom and Marci could not have heard what she said but I could still feel the blood rushing to my face. At least…I think it was my face.

It took about a half-hour for dinner to be prepared and we were ready for it. By the time all of the plates were on the table there was not an inch of room left for anything else. Joe poured each of us a glass of wine and placed the bottle in the wine cooler beside the table. The wine that I had chosen was a semi-dry white wine. According to my tastes, it goes with everything.

Dinner went by uneventful. We were all hungry and good food and wine would take our minds off of the problems at hand. We shared our food; well at least I had some of Siena's lobster. The food had taken some the edge off my high and was beginning to feel a little more like myself.

Joe brought up the desert cart and for a moment I thought I would have a slice of their famous New York cheesecake. But only for a moment. I was full to the gills, as were all of us. We still had food left and Joe asked if we wanted it packed in a "People Bag". I told him yes and to give it to Tom. I knew Toad would be hungry when he got home tomorrow and they could feed it to him. I chuckled to myself. I didn't feel the least bit bad about sending left over food home with a man that makes 12 million dollars a year.

Tom suggested we go into the bar and have an after dinner drink. I knew without asking what was coming. Tom had this thing about a hundred year old Grand Manier. At $50.00 a shot it still tasted like the stuff my mother tried to get down my throat when I was sick.

After we all had our required two shots of the hundred-year-old Grand Manier, that was it for me and I knew Siena would back me up. I told Tom and Marci that I had had it for the evening and Siena and I were heading for the boat. I let Tom grab the check for the evening's festivities. I had already made a mental note to consider it as part of my expenses. Besides, Tom was better able to fork out the $572.54 dinner and bar bill.

Chapter 17

I tossed Siena the keys to Toads car and asked her if she remembered how to get to Boom Island. She said she thought so. I was okay with that answer because I was going to shut my eyes and check my eyelids for leaks.

It seemed that I had no sooner shut my eyes and Siena was shaking me to wake up. We were at the boat. I shook my head while she walked around the car to open my door. I guess the excitement of the day wore me out. Surely it wasn't the booze. She grabbed her overnight bag and we headed for the boat.

There was a slight breeze blowing off the river and it was a little chilly but it felt good in my nearly drunken state. I put my arm around Siena and as we slowly walked to the boat. Everything looked to be secure and normal. I got on to the boat first and helped Siena down. There was a little dew on the deck so I didn't expect Siena to take her high heels off. I knew that she would do it on her own as soon as we were inside.

I unlocked the salon door and slid it back and I walked in first. I immediately reached for the alarm to disarm it. Siena was right behind me. Something was not right and it made the hair stand up on the back of my neck. I reached behind me and pushed Siena back with my hand. Then I reached above the salon door where I keep a small 32 cal. automatic pistol.

I reached to my left and hit the DC light switch. I did a quick visual of the salon and the galley. Nothing seemed to be out of place but I still was feeling that something was wrong. There was a smell in the air that I could not associate with my boat. I motioned for Siena to stay where she was and I slowly walked towards the galley. I peered over the galley counter maybe expecting to find someone crouching behind it. Nothing!

I walked through the galley towards the forward helm station. I flipped the forward lights on but still did not see anything out of the ordinary. I was about to open the upper stateroom door and Siena called out my name.

"Cap come here" she beckoned. I walked quickly to where she was standing. She pointed to the lamp on the end table in the corner near the wet bar. There was a note hanging from the lampshade. I walked over to the lamp and pulled the note off the shade.

It read:

You are in a part of town that you don't belong in.

Get out and mind your own business. nothing here concerns you.

That was all there was to the note. I began to feel a little uncomfortable. Someone had breached my security alarm, entered my boat and left a note. I made a mental note to get a hold of my buddy that put the alarm system together to find out how someone could breach the system.

Siena was nervous and rightfully so. She and I both remembered what Tom had told us at dinner the other night about the phone message he had received and the warning for Toad to keep his mouth shut.

Siena's a smart gal. "It's from the biker gang, isn't it?" "That would be my guess, I replied. "But how could they know who you are and what you were doing already", she asked. I couldn't answer that question. For once I didn't have an answer. I looked at her and said, "Siena, I don't know. I can't figure out they got in here and I can't figure out how they know about me already."

Siena was shaking a little from the cold. I shut and locked the salon door. I told Siena to mix herself a drink if she wanted while I went below to the engine room to start one of the generators. When I came back up I went to the control panel behind the wet bar and turned the heat on high. I knew it would take just a few minutes for the boat to warm up.

Siena had already made herself a drink and I decided I would have one too. I poured myself a couple of straight shots of J. Walker Black. I sat down next to Siena at the bar and put my arm over her shoulder. I gave her a light kiss on the cheek then took a healthy swallow of my drink.

"Siena, who are the only people that knew I was coming up to the cities, and for what?" She looked at me quizzically. "Tom and Marci, and, and me I guess". "Right, I said. Don't forget my dock crew, but they only knew I was coming up here. They didn't" know why. Then there was my friend at the Minneapolis Police Department. He knew I was coming and why." I made a quick mental note to find out why he never got back to me.

I didn't like this. I suppose someone at Toads arraignment could have seen me with Tom and Marci and either recognized or ask someone who I was. But then, that doesn't explain how anyone knew about my boat and where I was docking it.

I asked Siena if she still wanted to spend the night and she said yes. I told her to go ahead and go below and I would be down shortly. I switched on the AC power switch and reset the alarm and turned the sensitivity adjustment up a little higher. I knew that if the wind picked up and caused the boat to bang against the dock that it would probably set the alarm off but I had to take that chance. I also knew that if Siena and I rocked the boat, it would cause the alarm to go off. I checked all of the windows to make sure that they were closed and locked. I rechecked the salon door to make sure it was locked then started to go below.

I had put my 32 cal. in my pocket but thought that it would not be enough firepower if someone were gutsy enough to break in tonight. I put it back in it's hiding place and went to my on board office to get my Berretta. If someone was going to mess with us tonight at least I had some stopping power.

I shut off the salon lights and headed below. When I got to the lower deck I remembered that there was a hatch in the guest stateroom that opened up to the bow. I can't remember when anyone or I used it last but just for securities sake I would go and check it.

I opened the guest stateroom door and turned on the lights. I walked over to the bed. The hatch was right over the bed. Bingo! I found out how they got inside the boat. The hatch was still ajar.

It was the only access on the entire boat that was not hooked up to the alarm system. I was beginning to sweat. I pulled the receiver back on the 9mm and injected a round. If someone was still around they were fixing to get hurt. I climbed up on the bed and slowly raised the hatch. I stuck my head and the 9mm out at the same time.

The bow was empty. I stood all the way up and could see footprints on the deck in dim light. One question had been answered. I now know how they got in. There were still questions to be answered. I secured and locked the bow hatch. I knew that at least they would have to break in to get in the boat again. I walked back to the master stateroom. The lights were still on and Siena was fast asleep. Damn! I now had another reason to kick the shit out of the "low life son of a bitch" that broke into the boat.

I got undressed and went into the head to brush my teeth and splash some water on my face. When I came out of the head I reset the thermostat to a comfortable 65 degrees. I headed for bed and put the 9mm under my pillow.

Siena was laying on her side with her back to me. I rolled over and slid one arm under her neck and the other across her breasts. Then I slid my body up to hers in the spoon position, gave her a kiss on the back of her neck and went to sleep.

Chapter 18

I woke up at 6:40. Siena was still sleeping. She was now on her side facing me. She looked so peaceful and very beautiful. I was getting some ideas in my head but decided against waking her up.

I carefully slid out of bed and headed for the shower. I gently closed the head door as not to wake Siena up. I open the shower door and adjusted the automatic temperature control to 95 degrees. I turned the shower on a waited just a moment for the thermostat to adjust the water temperature. When it was ready I climbed in and shut the door behind me.

The water felt good! It was hot but not scalding. With three showerheads you are virtually surrounded with spraying water. I maintained a 55-pound water pressure throughout the boat and the spray from the showerheads creates a nice tingling feeling all over. I was standing there with my eyes shut, relaxing and totally disregarding my policy on taking a shower.

Then I heard the shower door open. It startled me and I opened my eyes and spun around. It was Siena in her…well…. in her nothing. My eye dropped to her breasts, then down to her midriff, then every inch from there on down. She had a coy little smile on her lips. "Want your back scrubbed, she asked. I was thinking something other than my back, but I answered, "yes!" There was time enough to get my back scrubbed.

I gathered her into my arms. Our wet skin created a wonderful sensation. I put my lips to hers and she respond in like. I let my hands wander down to the middle of her back. I rubbed that special little spot in the middle of her back that sent quivers through her body. I slid my lips down her neck making her quiver even more. Her body was responding to my every move.

I kissed her gently and I kept going lower. Her nipples were engorged and seemed to be begging to be kissed and sucked. A flash back went through my head remembering an affair that I had with an older woman when I was around nineteen years old.

She taught me that there was only one way to properly suck a woman's nipples. She taught me to peel a large table grape using only my tongue and my teeth. When I had reach the point to where I could peel the grape without crushing the meat of the grape I was there.

I put my lips around her right nipple. There was a new wave of shivers through Siena's body. She wrapped her arms tightly around my neck and I could feel her lifting her body up and her legs wrapping around my hips. She gently lowered herself to me. Her passion was uncontrollable.

I knew the boat was rocking!

I finished taking my shower and left Siena to her own. I stepped out of the shower and grabbed a towel and dried off. I wasn't sure what my plans were for the day so I put my thick terry cloth robe on and went up to the galley and put a pot of coffee on. The thought suddenly entered my mind that the alarm didn't go off while we were in the shower. Com' on Cap, did you think you were moving mountains, I thought to myself.

Just about when the coffee was ready Siena came up from below. Her hair was still damp and her cheeks were flush. She walked up to me and gave me a hug and a kiss then said, "Cap, I'm sorry I fell asleep last night." I told her not to worry about it because this morning more than made up for it. I poured us both a cup of coffee and gave us both a brace of rum. We deserved it. I turn the TV on to get the morning news on Kare 11. It was almost 8:00. I had missed the news but got a recap on the weather. Mostly clear and a high 68 was being predicted. That made my spirits soar.

I knew I had to go by Tom's house to talk with Toad. He was supposed to be home sometime this morning. I got Siena's attention from the TV and asked her what she had planned for the day. She said she had to go home and check for orders from her Internet business. I asked her if she minded taking Toads car home and Tom could send someone to pick it up. I knew Toad wouldn't need it for a while. She was okay with that and went back below to get dressed. I grabbed the phone and called my buddy at the police department again. He was out for the day on an investigation. I left a message and told him he didn't have to call me unless he wanted to.

I filled my coffee cup and went below to get dressed. Siena was almost dressed when I got below. I picked out a colorful tropical shirt from the closet and a pair khaki shorts. It was the weekend and the Turpins could care less how I was dressed. Siena was finished with dressing and went up to the galley. I followed her shortly. She was putting her things in her bag when I came up. "I suppose you're just about ready to head out", I asked. It was more of a rhetorical question and she did not answer. She was looking at the business card that Carmen had given to me on Wednesday. I had left it on the galley counter.

She held the card up and asked, "Business?" I could detect her catty intuition. "Not yet", I responded and we both left it there. She picked up her bag and gave me the "come here" gesture with her finger. I walked over to her and put my arms around and gave her a soft lingering kiss. We walked out to the aft deck and I helped her up to the dock. She blew me a good-bye kiss and told me to be careful. I wonder how she meant that.

Chapter 19

I went back into the salon and poured another cup of coffee. Carmen's business card caught my eye. I looked at and for some reason I felt a little strange. Maybe it was because Siena had seen it. I remembered that I was supposed to call her on Thursday about her riding down south with me.

I picked up the phone and called her office. Her secretary said that she out for the day and would not be back until Monday. I asked if there was anyway to get a hold of her. She told me that she could not give out any more information. I told her what the situation was and asked her if she would please call Ms. Mendoza and ask her to call me on my cell phone. She said she would.

I decided to take the boat back down river to Willie's Hidden Harbor. just south of St. Paul. If Carmen called back I could tell her to meet me there later today if she was still interested in going. Then I called Tom at home and told him what my plans were. I also told him that Siena had taken Toads car to go home. He had no problem with that and said he would send his limo driver to Willie's to pick me up. I told him I would be there around 10:30 as long as I didn't hit any tows in the locks.

I went below and went through a quick modified checklist. The generator was already running so all I had to do was start the main engines. I decided to start them while I was in the engine room and they could be warming up while I was making everything ready to get underway. I flipped the power switches for the engines and hit the starter for the port engine first. It fired right up. It was really loud when you where standing right next to the engine. I checked the pressures on the port engine then fired up the starboard engine. It caught right off and I check all of the pressures and went back up to the galley.

I cleaned the coffee cups and glasses from last night and put them away. I went down to my stateroom to make sure all of the doors were secure. When got back up to the galley I switched on the remote VHF and called the St. Anthony Lock. I gave them my situation and they said they would be ready for me when I got there.

Satisfied that everything was secure I headed out to the aft control station. I had a position fix and engaged the autopilot. I started casting off my dock lines. I didn't worry about the fenders because I knew I would have time to take care of them while I was locking through.

I disengaged the autopilot and directed my thrust to push me away from the dock. When I was far enough away from the dock I headed the boat forward to get into the stream. Once I was in the stream I gave her hard left and switched the port drive bucket to the reverse position. The boat responded immediately. The bow swung to the left and the stern to the right. When the bow was about 10 degrees from the direction I wanted it in I switched the port drive bucket to the forward position and brought both drives too amidships.

I added a little power and the bow stopped swinging right when she pointing right at the Lock. Sometimes I amaze myself. The lock gates were just swinging open and I stayed at 800 rpm's until I was about 500 feet from the lock. At 500 feet I pulled the throttles back to idle and put the bow to the middle of the lock. Once I was stationary and had a fix I set the autopilot and went down to the main deck to stow the fenders. By the time I was done with the fenders the down river doors were opening up. I went back up to the fly bridge and waited for the signal to clear the lock. I disengaged the autopilot when the signal sounded and put the drives to forward.

I idled out until I well clear of the wall and started putting the power on. I set my rpm's for twenty knots and sat back to watch the view. It was going to be a good day!

I made a call to Lock & Dam #1 to let them know I was coming down and I should be there in about 20 minutes. The Lockmaster said they would be waiting for me. I got through #1 in record time. I still hadn't heard back from Carmen. I guess I was just going to have to write this one off.

I was still heading south at twenty knots. I saw the entrance to Willies Hidden Harbor about a half mile ahead. I started easing the throttles back to slow the boat down. I didn't want to hit Willies with a wake behind me. When I reached the entrance to Willies I was at idle speed. Willies wife told me to take the first slip coming into the marina as it would be easier for me.

I had just enough room in the harbor to turn my boat about so I could go in stern first. That was my preferred way of docking. Using the bow thruster and drive units together it was easy to turn the boat right on her own axis. I was at the aft control station so I could see everything that was happening.

I slowly slid the boat into the slip and made sure she was at a dead stop before I got of the boat to tie her up. I had already retrieved my dock lines from the storage locker and they were on the deck beside me. I threw half them on the dock on the port side and the other half on the starboard side. I jump off the port side and grabbed a line to use as an aft spring line. This would keep the boat from going aft and hit the dock. I went around to the starboard side and attached the aft spring line there. With that done I could leisurely make all of the other lines fast.

After getting the boat tied up I pulled out the shore power cables. Shore power was available so I wouldn't have to run one of the generators. I connected the shore power cable to the dock receptacle and went back aboard to hit the switch from generator to shore power mode. Then I shut the generator down followed by the mains.

I didn't know when the limo was going to pick me up so I thought I would be constructive and clean the boat up. I went below and changed the linen on the bed then wiped down the shower. I threw the soiled linen in the laundry cabinet and realized that I was going to have to do a load of wash when I got back to my marina. I took the 9mm that was under my pillow and took it back up to the office and put it away in a secure place.

I cleaned out the coffeepot and I was done. I was about to on deck when the phone rang. It was Carmen. She was sorry for not getting back to me earlier but she had been in Minneapolis visiting. I told her it was no problem and that I was also sorry that I hadn't called her on Thursday as promised.

I told her where I was and said that she was more than welcome to come down. I told that I had to go to Woodbury to see my friends for a short while but she could come down and wait on the boat if she wanted. She asked me what time I would be back to the boat and I took a guess at around 3:00 that afternoon. She said she meet me there at 3:00.

Well now you scurvy pirate I thought to myself. It appears you are going to get lucky again. I had to chuckle to myself. My sex life was like salt… when it rains, it pours.

Chapter 20

I heard a knocking on the aft deck.

It was Tom's driver. "Good afternoon Captain Art, are you about ready to go, he asked. "Yes I am Brandon. If you'll wait while I grab my brief case I'll be right with you. I grabbed my briefcase that was still lying on the couch from last night. I set the alarm and walked out lock the door behind me.

We walked up to the parking lot and there stood the gleaming corporate Mercedes Limo. What a piece of machinery. Brandon opened the rear door for me and I slid in. He went around to the driver's side, got in and told me there was some J. Walker Black in the liquor cabinet if I wanted a drink.

It was just a little too early to be hitting the J. Walker. I thanked him and sat back to do some thinking on trip to Tom' and Marci's. I put my head back on the soft leather seat and shut my eyes. The ride was way too comfortable and I dozed off. I woke up just as we were pulling into the Turpin's lane.

Tom and Marci's house always reminded me of a castle. The best way to describe it was, It's big as hell! Three stories high, five car garage, and separate quarters for his house staff and a separate guesthouse for special friends. The house was built on the bluffs overlooking the St. Croix

River. He had 40 acres of land that the house sat on. It was a beautiful place but just didn't fit into my life style.

Brandon stopped the limo at the front door and I told him stay put and would help myself out. Jeeze, it's the least I could do. I got out with briefcase in hand and walked towards the front door. Tom opened the front before I got to it. I gave him a handshake and we went inside.

When you walk into the Turpins house you enter a huge foyer. The floors were made of Italian Marble and there were oil paintings hanging on all of the walls. It would take a day to explain to someone all about the house. Like I said, it was big as hell.

We to the back of the house to the all seasons' room which let out to a large deck that had a perfect view on the river. It was very peaceful out here and it was warm enough to not have a jacket on. Marci and Toad were sitting at a table off to one side.

I walked over and gave Marci a hug and turned to Toad. He didn't stand up until I turned to him. I looked at him and asked, "are you going to shake my hand or do I give you a cuff up side the head?" He stuck his hand out and I took it then he sat back down. He was nothing like his father. At 26 he was still wet behind the ears and sometimes I wanted to beat the hell out of him just to get his attention.

Toad and Marci were drinking beer and Toad asked me if I would like one. I said yes and Toad got up and walked over to the bar. I could see the electronic monitor on his ankle. He grabbed me a beer, opened it and brought to me.

When he sat back down he sat with a flop. I was about to say something to him and Tom beat me to it. "Toad, I've asked Captain Art to help us with this situation that you are in. I expect you to treat him civilly and tell him everything you can."

I looked at Tom and thanked him. I looked back to Toad and gazed at him for a few seconds. I could tell that it made him uncomfortable. He looked away until I spoke. "Toad, I know Bernie, your lawyer told you what you were looking at if you are convicted. You may not see the outside until your fifty years old. I know you don't want that and I know you don't want to put your parents through that. So that means you are going to have to tell me everything from the beginning up to now."

Toad just sat there but I could tell he was taking it all in. I knew he was in a hard spot. He had been threatened like his parents, not to talk. Something told me he wasn't about to give up fifty years of his life.

"Look Toad, I said. Let me begin by asking you some questions. Is that okay?" He shook his head yes.

"Toad, were you selling drugs?" "No, he replied. I was just a mule." A mule is a person that carries the drug from one place to another, sort of a delivery boy. "Who hired you to be a mule?" "It was the president of the "Troubled Disciples", Tony Mendoza." He offered me $2,000 plus gas to go down to Davenport, Iowa to pick up a package from another boat."

When he said Tony Mendoza the bells and whistles started ringing and honking. Mendoza, Carmen Mendoza. Who was the only other person that knew I was going to Minneapolis on my boat, where I was tying the boat up, and what I was doing...Carmen Mendoza.

Could this be a mere coincidence? One is an apparent top notch Attorney and the other is a scumbag 1%'er. 1%'er is a biker term meaning 99 % of all bikers are basically good. The other 1% you can throw in the trash. If there was a relationship there I made a mental note to move very cautiously around Carmen.

I turned my attention back to Toad. "Okay Toad, how did this work. Did you just take your boat to Davenport and meet someone, pick up a package and come back? "Sort of, he said.

"They, Tony, gave me a boat letter pennant. It was the letter "D". When I got to Davenport I put the pennant on my bow Flagstaff. I guess it was a signal to the other boat. I was told to drop anchor in a little cove just off the river, north of Davenport and to stay on the boat."

"This was last Tuesday. I anchored out like I was told to and waited for the other boat. Around 7:30 that night and small fishing boat came up to the side of my boat. There were two men in the boat." I asked him if he could see them and he said no because the sun was already down and it was dark.

"Okay Toad, go ahead." "They told me to get in their fishing boat which I did and they put a blindfold over my eyes. We took off from my boat and rode around for about 15 minutes and when the fishing boat stopped we were at my boat again. I asked them what this was all about and one of the guys told me not to worry about it. They told me to weigh anchor and head home. That's all."

"That's all, I asked. "Yes, that's all Captain." "Toad weren't you the least bit suspicious if not curious of what was going on." "No, he replied. I was scared shitless. I got back on my boat and pulled my anchor and was out of there as quick as I could safely go. I guess I figured that there was a snag somewhere and the deal didn't go through. Or, maybe they didn't like something or me. I don't know."

"What did you do after you got underway?" "I went about twenty miles up river and got out of the channel and anchored for the night. I was tired."

"When you went down to the cabin did you see anything that appeared out of the ordinary?" "No, nothing. I just climbed up on my bunk and went to sleep. The next morning I got up and started heading north again."

"Did you have any kind of a schedule to keep, I asked. Were you supposed to be at certain place at a certain time?" "No. I did just what they told me to do. I had no time schedule. When I got back to the marina in Stillwater I was suppose to call Tony and let him know that I was back. That's all."

I was having a hard time swallowing this story. Knowing that Toad does not operate on all cylinders at times I felt that there was something that was not being said. Right at that moment I couldn't put my finger on it.

I looked at Tom and Marci. They had nothing to say. It would seem that Toad was a pawn in this deal but nonetheless was culpable. I guess if it were proven that things happened as he said they did he might get off with a lighter sentence. I'm not a lawyer so I was just guessing.

I said good-bye to Toad and Marci and Tom and I walked back into the house. I looked at Tom and said, "Tom, this is like a number painting. Until you have all the numbers painted you have no idea what the picture is." I told him I would call him if and when I had any more information. I decided not to tell him about Carmen Mendoza. For the time I thought it was best that he not know about it. We walked through the house to the front door. When we went out Brandon was already there with the limo waiting for me. I shook hands with tom and got into the limo.

On the drive back to Willies I tried to put what information I had into perspective. It couldn't be done. There were to many parts missing. I opened up the liquor cabinet and helped myself to two fingers of J. Walker Black. No ice thank you.

Chapter 21

It was a little after 3:00 when Brandon got me back to Willies. I thanked Brandon and slipped him a twenty. I grabbed my briefcase and got out of the limo. I walked around the bar and restaurant down to the boat. I made a quick visual inspection and everything looked okay.

I climbed on board and unlocked the salon door and went in. I turned off the alarm and went straight to my office. I pulled my shoulder holster and grabbed the 9mm from its hiding place and put it in the holster. I grabbed a lightweight windbreaker and put it on. It was loose enough to visually hide my rig. Unless someone touched me they would be none the wiser.

I felt a little more comfortable knowing that I was now meeting Carmen Mendoza and I would be looking at her through different colored glasses. I walked up to the bar to get a drink.

Willie and his wife were in the bar. Being Friday afternoon the happy hour crowd was starting to come in. Bonnie, Willies wife saw me first. She waved at me and yelled at Willie. "Willie, look who's here!"

I walked up to the bar and gave Bonnie a hug careful not to let her grab me around the waist. I sat down and ordered a J. Walker Black straight up. Willie was behind the bar and came down to say hi. I asked him what I owed him for the slip and he asked if I was interested in doing a trade out.

He said him and Bonnie were coming down my way next week and if I would let him stay overnight at no charge there would be no charge for me today. I agreed and told him when he got down there if I was not around to get a hold of Chad and he would take care of him. I made a mental note to tell Chad.

It was about 3:45 when Carmen walked in. She had a small bag hanging from her shoulder. It was probably things for her overnight stay, if she was staying over night.

She saw me and smiled and gave a little wave. I stood up and waited for her to get to the bar. I grabbed her hands before she could touch and bent down to kiss her cheek. I pulled out a barstool for her and made sure it was a stool that was opposite of my 9mm. I asked if she wanted a drink and she said she would have Gin & Tonic. I called Willie and gave him the order.

Carmen was a very sexy looking young lady. She had on pair of shorts that appeared to be painted on and a sleeveless v-neck sweater that revealed some very nice cleavage. She had a clean and fresh smell about her.

I asked her if she had any problems finding the marina and said no. Then I asked her casually if she had gotten her business done in Minneapolis. She must have forgotten that she told me that she was going to Minneapolis because she acted a little surprised when I mentioned it.

She asked what our plans were and I told her that I hadn't made any plans as of yet. I asked her what she would like to do. She said she was open to anything and didn't have to be back to St. Paul until Monday morning. I thought for a moment and suggested that we finish our drinks and head down river to Hastings. We could spend the night at Kings Cove then down south on Saturday morning. She liked that plan.

She excused herself saying that she needed to make a quick phone call and she would be right back. Red flags jumped up in my head. If she was making a phone call to let someone know where she would be I was going to make a phone call myself. I made a quick call to Leo's Landing in Prescott, WI.

Dick, the owner of Leo's Landing is a good boating friend of mine. His Dock Master answered the phone and I told him that I would be coming for overnight dockage. His Dock Master knew who I was and knew my boat. He said the only spot he had available for my boat was the fuel dock and I would have to be underway by 8:00 in the morning. I told him that it was fine with me and asked if Dick was around. He said he would be around later that evening.

Carmen came back to the bar and I purposely neglected to tell her about the change in plans. I was going to try and stay one-step ahead of her just in case my suspicions were true. We finished our drinks and I left enough money on the bar on the bar to cover the cost of the drinks plus a nice tip. We walked out the back door going to the marina. We got on the boat and I told Carmen to make herself at home. She wanted to go up on the fly bridge to watch me get ready to get underway. I pointed towards the ladder going up to the fly bridge. It was a nice view watching her go up the ladder.

The first thing I did was go to my office and take off my 9mm. I felt reasonably safe at this point. I went through the normal procedures of getting underway. I started the starboard generator to get some hours on it. I switch the power switch to generator and went back topside. Willie was on the dock and said he would get the lines for me.

I asked him to disconnect the shore power cables and hand them to me so I could get them stowed. Then I went up to the fly bridge and started the engines. Everything seemed to be okay and I signaled for Willie to start tossing off the dock lines. When the boat was free I eased the joystick forward and slid out of the slip.

I turned around and waved to Willie. Carmen sat there watching the whole show saying nothing. It was a straight shot to the river be cause I had backed into the slip. When we got into the river channel I pushed the throttles forward to make 20 knots. It was a little faster than I really wanted to go but for the moment I thought I would throw caution to the wind.

Carmen looked excited. I asked her if she needed a jacket or anything and she said she was fine. With the enclosed bridge you don't have the wind blowing on you and if it got really cold the enclosed bridge had heat and air.

I asked her to make me a drink and pointed to the small bar on the fly bridge. She went over and made us a couple of drinks. I asked her if she would like to take command. She was a little hesitant but said yes if I would tell her what to do and not to leave her alone. I gave her some quick instructions and told her to keep her eyes open for deadheads, which I had to explain to her what deadheads were.

She sat in the Captains chair and put her fingers around the joystick. For a fleeting moment she looked the part of a Captain. I grabbed the VHF and called Lock & Dam #2 and told them we would be there in about 25 to 30 minutes. The Lockmaster said there was no traffic so bring it on down.

As we neared the lock I asked Carmen if she wanted to take it in the lock. I kind of knew she would decline and least I hoped she would. The lock was open and we motored right in. I set the autopilot then asked Carmen if she had ever been through the locks before. She said no so I explained to her what was going to happen. I was walking around the fly bridge and she wanted to know how the boat could stay in one position by itself. I told her how the autopilot worked and I could tell that she was genuinely impressed.

In a matter of minutes the drop in the lock was done. The down river doors open up and the signal blew for clearance. I eased the joystick forward and we headed out. Once clear of the wall I eased the throttles forward to indicate rpm for 10 knots. We only had about a mile to go to get to Leo's Landing. I made a mental note to make sure to watch Careens expression when she realized we were not going to Kings Cove.

As we neared the confluence I brought the throttles back to idle. Leo's was dead ahead of us about a quarter of a mile. There was another boat at the fuel dock so I got on the VHF and hailed the marina. The Dock Master answered back and requested that I go to channel 9. I acknowledged and met him on channel 9. I asked him how long the boat at the fuel dock was going to be there. He said the boat was ready to get underway and I could come right in.

I headed down river so I could come back up river against the current to make my approach to the dock. I was landing starboard side to. This is the easiest approach with a boat my size. When you are near the dock you just have to make sure that you have little or no forward motion. Then give a little right rudder and the boat slips right up to the dock like a feather landing on a pillow.

I had been watching Carmen out of the corner of my eye. She hadn't given any indication yet that anything was amiss.

Leo's fuel dock has permanent fenders attached to the dock and there are also all of the necessary dock lines to tie up a boat. All I had to do was get the boat up to the dock. The Dock Master tied us off and I shut down the main engines.

Then Carmen asked how long we would be here fueling up. I looked at her and said we weren't fueling up. I told her that we were going to spend the night here. When you know body English a body can tell you a lot about a person. Carmen's body was telling me something but I couldn't put my finger on it.

The Dock Master had already pulled out my shore power cables so I switched over to shore power and killed the generator. Carmen and I went down to the salon. It was after five and Leo's fuel dock closes at five until the boating season really gets going. Then he stays open until dark.

I felt reasonably safe in that Leo's had a chain link fence with bob wire on the top around the marina on the landside. The only way to get to my boat was by water or by climbing the fence, or using the card to open the electronic gate.

Chapter 22

There appeared to be a fairly good afternoon crowd for Happy Hour. A few people were out on the verandah. I asked Carmen if she would like to go up to the bar. She smiled and thought that would be a good idea.

We climbed off the boat and walked up to the bar. There were about twenty people in the bar. I saw and empty table by the window looking out over the verandah and the river. I guided Carmen over to the table and pulled out a chair for her. I went to the other side of the table at sat down.

The waitress came up and took our order. I asked her when Dick was going to be around. She said that Dick was here and in the office. I asked her when she had time to let Dick know that Captain Art was here. Dick is a big man. He's about an inch taller than me and about fifty pounds heavier.

I met him right after he bought Leo's Landing. The way that we met was by chance. Lock & Dam # 2 is right above his marina, maybe a mile. I was a Sunday morning and I was coming down the St. Croix River returning from a party up in Stillwater. As I neared the confluence of the St. Croix and the Mississippi Rivers, I noticed about 20 boats ahead of me that appeared to be rafted up together. I thought this was kind of odd.

I didn't pay any more attention to it until I got closer. When I was close enough to see what was happening I was flabbergasted. There were 20 boats still tied up in their slips. The whole thing, boats and slips were heading up river against the current. A few people were out walking around on the slips.

I pulled my throttles back and eased up to the side of this armada. I yelled over to a man who turned out to be Dick and asked him what was going on. The story that he told me was unreal.

It seems that the Lock & Dam had inadvertently opened all of the roller dams at the same time. This resulted in a six-foot wall of water coming downstream. When this wall of water hit Leo's Landing it rip the entire north side of his out along with his fuel dock and store. The shear force of the water sent boats, slips and all up stream on the St. Croix.

I had just happened not minutes before I had arrived. Dick asked if I would throw a line over and try to hold the slips and boats from going back downstream. I suggested the he get on the boats that were pointed up stream and drop the anchors from the boats. He agreed and he got a couple of other men to help him. They dropped 3 anchors and all three grabbed the bottom sand and held.

With the boats and slips now secure I got on the VHF radio and notified the US Coast Guard and Lock & Dam # 2. Lock & dam #2 sent down their little pusher barge to assist in getting the mess cleaned up. In all, the inadvertent opening of the roller dams cost the Army Corp of Engineers well over a million dollars to repair Leo's Landing.

I was thankful that I had taken pictures of this catastrophe, as no one would ever believe me that it really happened. With everything being under control I bid Dick a fairway and wished him good luck. I told him if he wanted copies of the pictures to get a hold of me at my marina.

Carmen and I had just ordered another round of drinks along with some snacks. Dick had just come out of his office and I could see him looking around for me. I gave a little wave and he walked over to our table.

"Captain Art, he exclaimed. What bring you up this way?" I told him I had been taking care of some business in Minneapolis and was on my way back to the Marina. I introduced him to Carmen and he shook hands with her. He couldn't resist telling her to watch out for me.

I let out a chuckle and said, "come on Dick. You know I'm harmless." He laughed and asked we minded if he sat with us for a while. I slid out a stool with my foot and he sat down. His waitress was right there and he ordered a drink and told her to fill ours up also.

Together, Dick and I brought Carmen up to speed about our chance meeting. Like many she had a problem believing the story so Dick went to his office and brought back the pictures that I had sent him at his request. After looking at the pictures she was totally amazed and now was a believer.

We talked for a while about some mutual boaters that we knew and swapped some sea stories. I'm not sure which one of us was trying to out do the other with our sea stories but it started getting pretty deep. You can always tell when you're about to hear a real yarn. It's like the difference between a Nursery Rhyme and a Sea Story. A Nursery Rhyme starts out with; "Once upon a time... a Sea Story starts out with, "Now this is no shit".

I'm not sure that Carmen was impressed with our stories but then I wasn't really worried about it. A couple of other boaters had overheard us talking and now they were right in there with us telling their Favorite Sea Story. We were having a good time swapping our experiences. Drinks started flowing and in a little while there was around 12 boaters sitting around our table swapping stories. I started to ask Carmen if she was okay but decided against it. I figured she was a big girl and if she didn't" like it she could get up and leave. I don't think I was being macho by thinking that I just felt that what was happening was a pretty normal event with boaters and she should see how it really is.

This story telling went on for about an hour. During that time several other boaters that I knew came in for drinks. When it slowed down there were eight of us at the table including Dick and his wife whom had shown up. Someone started talking about dinner and I suddenly realized that I had nothing to eat but the snacks we ordered over an hour ago.

I had to assume that Carmen was also hungry. I looked at her and she understood my questioning look. She said that she was open for anything. Ideas were being tossed around and we settled on a Bar-b-Que.

Dick's wife said she would run to the store and I asked Carmen if she would go along with her to help. Carmen didn't appear to have a problem with that. The ladies got up to leave and I slipped Carmen some cash and told her quietly not to let Dick's wife buy everything.

I actually had an ulterior motive for asking Carmen to go with Dick's wife. I wanted to talk with Dick about what was going on, as I knew I could trust him. We excused ourselves from the table telling the other two couples that we were going down on the docks to get the grill ready. When we were outside I quickly brought him up to date about the events of the last few days.

I told him of my suspicions about Carmen and he asked if he could help in anyway. I told him that for right now I would be okay. I mentioned that I did have a small concern about the possibility of Carmen contacting someone to tell them where we were.

Dick understood and said that he would give some thought that evening to minimize my concerns. I thank him and we busied ourselves getting the grill ready.

I always believe that timing is everything. The charcoal was glowing nicely when the women got back from the store. I asked Carmen to take Dick's wife on aboard Winkin', Blinkin', and Nod to get things prepared.

The women had opted for chicken to grill. They picked up all of the trimmings to go along with the chicken. While they were in the boat getting things ready the other two couples came up with their arms loaded with contributions. This really when boating get to be fun.

With boaters an impromptu gathering can turn into a major event and this gathering had every sign of becoming an event. There was already enough food to feed a small army and knowing what I know about the boating community, more people would be joining us and more food would be brought forth.

We set up a makeshift bar against the wall of the ships store. I went aboard my boat and grabbed a few bottles of assorted booze. I filled up a small ice cooler with ice from my icemaker and carried it all to our "bar on the dock."

More boaters were arriving to the marina for the weekend and Dick kept inviting select people to join us. Within a very short period of time we had better than twenty-five people that assured that this was going to be an event.

Chapter 23

The grill was now going full bore. Chicken, steaks, rib, pork chops, you name it and it was probably on the grill. The sun was down and there was a little nip in the air. I pretty much knew that Carmen had not brought along warm clothing for this type of affair. I asked Dick's wife if she would fix Carmen up with something warmer as they were both about the same size.

The two of them walked down to Dick's boat and went aboard. Dick came up beside me and smiled saying, "I don't think you are going to have to worry about anyone messing with you or your boat tonight. I think this will turn into an all nighter." I smiled back at him and lifted my glass to his in salute.

Dick was right! What had started out as a Bar-b-Que. for eight turned out to be a major event for about forty. The night air had turned colder and everyone had their nautical fleece on. Carmen seemed to be enjoying herself and was spiritedly talking law with another lawyer.

She had come up to me a few times during the evening to let me know that she was still around. I could tell that the alcohol was getting to her and she wouldn't make it through the night. I told her to be careful and not to "make like the sailor that fell of the starboard side from to much port."

Sea stories were flying and everyone was having fun. It was a little after mid-night when Carmen came up to me and said that she couldn't keep anymore. She asked if I would mind taking her below and putting her to bed. I excused myself telling those in the near that I would be back after tucking her in. I gave Dick a wink and gently grabbed Carmen around the waist and headed her for my boat.

I helped her aboard and took down below. I asked if she wanted to sleep in the guest stateroom or in the Master's Quarters. She looked at me with her sexy eyes and pressed her body against mine and asked, "where would you like me to sleep Captain?" I headed her towards the Master's Quarters.

I gave her one of my T-shirts and let her go into the head to change. She came back out wearing just the T-shirt that I had given her. It hung nearly to her knees. I had already pulled the covers down and was sitting on the edge of the bed. She carefully walked over to me and pushed me back onto the bed and fell on top of me.

She let her full weight rest upon me as she snuggled her face between my neck and shoulder. In about a minute she was out. I rolled her over and lifted her up then placed her in bed. I pulled the covers over her and gave her a little kiss then headed for the dock. On my way out I made sure that my on board office was locked.

By the time I got back up on the dock the party had thinned out to about twenty people but they were still going strong. I saw Dick and walked over to him. He looked at me questioningly and I told him that Carmen was out…like a light bulb. He smiled and shrugged his shoulders then we saluted with our drinks.

I was about to say something to Dick when his wife walked up arm an arm with a little fox. She was red headed and immediately I wondered if she was a true red head. Dick's wife did the introduction. "Tammy, this is the infamous Captain Art. He'll break your heart but you'll enjoy it at the same time."

I laughed and thanked Dick's wife for the good words and shook hands with Tammy. In the dim light I could tell that she was very fair skinned which told me that she might be a true red head. I asked her if she was ready for another drink and she replied yes. I motioned towards the makeshift bar and winked at Dick as we walked away.

She was a tall girl. I was guessing around five-ten and well put together. Even with the thick fleece I could tell she was built to my specifications. We got to the bar and I asked her what she was drinking. She looked at me and said, "I want... she hesitated for just a second for impact and finished her sentence, Sex on the beach."

I looked at her suddenly and started to respond then realized she was talking about a drink. Okay, I thought to myself. I can see you're going to be a game player. I fixed her a "Sex on the beach" and we slowly walked back towards the main group.

She told me she was from Alma, Wisconsin about two hours south of Prescott. I knew the community. It was a small river community right at Lock & Dam # 4. Several times during the summer I'll take a lady friend down on the boat and spend the week-end at the Great River Harbor Marina and Campgrounds just south of Lock 4.

I always stop there for a week when I head south for the winter. The population is around 900 or so people. Several nice places to eat and drink. Two couples that were friends of mine in the cities went down to Alma and purchased restaurants. Mike and Marie bought the old historic Burlington Hotel and Paul and Marietta bought the Pier 4 Cafe.

The Great River Harbor Marina is about a mile off the main river channel. The thing that I really like about the marina is the limo that is available to any boaters that want to go into town. Hale & Janet have owned the Marina for years and if you want to go into town for breakfast at the Pier 4 or dinner at the Burlington Hotel all you have to do is ask. They will take you to town and pick you up when you are ready to come back to the marina. And what's more? No charge!

Outside of the Great River Harbor Campgrounds & Marina one of the best nightspots in town is the Red Ram Saloon. I have partied many a night at the Red Ram.

I was surprised when Tammy told me that she was from Alma. It was hard to believe that I had never run into her all the years that I been going down there. She must live a sheltered life.

When we got back, Dick and his wife were taking with another couple. Dick's wife looked at Tammy and said, Well Tammy what do you think about the Captain?" Right at that moment she sounded like a pimp trying to get the customer to pay some money for my services.

"I can't tell, Tammy said as she looked up at me. I haven't picked his brain yet." I caught myself trying to figure out what her meaning was by that statement. Deciding that there was no real meaning in it I shook it out of my head. Tammy pointed towards my boat and said, "I understand that's your boat. Would you like to show me around?"

Would I ever I thought to myself but reluctantly I told her about Carmen and I didn't think it would be the right thing to do at the time. She understood and grabbed my arm and told me the next time I come down to Alma that I should look her up. I told her in no uncertain terms that she could expect to see me and it might be sooner than she thought.

The time seemed to be flying by. It was now around two and I felt like I was drinking myself sober. I spoke out to whomever was listening and said that I was going to have one more drink and call it a night. I walked over to the bar and poured myself a couple of fingers of Cognac.

I walked back over to where Dick, his wife and Tammy were standing. I told Tammy that is was nice meeting her and looked forward to seeing her again in the near future. I bid Dick and his wife good night and thanked them for the fun time. Dick told me not to worry about a thing and I knew he meant it. I headed for bed.

Chapter 24

When I woke up I pretty much felt like a truck had run over me, backed up to see what he had run over, and decided that it was nothing and drove off. I couldn't remember coming to bed and just for a moment I forgot that Carmen was on the boat. I rolled over to look at her and I saw the bed empty on her side. I sat up with a jerk, wishing that I hadn't, and started to get a little nervous.

I relaxed and lay back down when I heard Carmen making noise in the head. I got up and went into the "His" head to take care of business and to scrape some of the night before out of my mouth then took an Alka-Seltzer hoping that it would relieve some of the pain in my head. I climbed back in bed and shut my eyes while massaging my head. After a while she came out still wearing the T-shirt that I given to her last night to sleep in. Her breasts were pushing sharply into the fabric and gave me cause to stare. She caught me staring.

"Good morning my Captain, she said making it sound possessive. Do you like what you see?" I nodded affirmatively. She reached down to the bottom of the T-shirt and slowly pulled it over her head. "Now how do you like it?", she asked. Not many things will cure a bad hangover. The exception being when you are looking at a beautiful, thoroughly naked woman. I'm not sure that I was being cured but at the moment I wasn't feeling anything in my head.

She walked to the bed and slid in next to me. I could feel the chill on her skin but it felt good. Her firm breasts were pushing into my chest as she nuzzled my neck. I put my arms around her and pulled her on top me. I looked deeply into her eyes and said, "This where we stopped last night. Shall we continue?" She didn't answer in so many words. Her actions answered my question!

When God gave man and woman the ability to have sex for creation it was a step in the right direction. When Masters & Johnson gave man and woman the ability to have sex for recreation it was like putting the icing on the cake.

Carmen was not satisfying me. She was satisfying herself and she was using me as a means to achieve that satisfaction. Thrusting her hips into mine, moaning with each thrust. Her breath was short. I held her close as if we were climbing a mountain, both of us striving to get to the top together. With a sudden explosion we reached the pinnacle at the same time. Then slowly, ever so slowly we slid down the other side.

Neither of us spoke. We just laid there, her still on top of me. Her body still trembling. The sensual smell of sexual sweat hung in the air. After a while I gently rolled her off of me still holding her close to me.

My hangover was back! I told her that I was getting up and heading for the shower hoping that it would help. The Alka-Seltzer I had taken the edge off but the deep throbbing was still there. She got up with me and said that a nice massage while taking a shower would also be beneficial. Who was I to argue?

My shower taking rules were being broken again and it didn't even bother me. By the time we got out of the shower I was beginning to feel a lot better. When we walked out of the head she playfully grabbed me and pushed me to the bed.

She looked at me coyly, "want another go at it Captain?" I told her that I was not as good as I was once before, but I was good once as I ever was. I'm not sure that she understood what I meant but she backed off without a word.

I flipped on the VHF to get a weather report for the day. The report was good. They were expecting a record high today of around 80 degrees. That helped put a little more wind in my sails. I asked Carmen if she was hungry and she said she was famished. Exercise always made her hungry. I made a mental note of that. I've never considered sex as an exercise.

We got dressed and went up to the galley. The first thing I did was to put on a pot of coffee. I walked back to the salon doors and opened the curtains. It was already a beautiful morning. I waved to a couple of people walking down the dock. I went back to the galley and started digging around for some breakfast fixings.

Carmen came up and her hair was still wet. She had on a pair of blue shorts and a very small halter-top. She was ready for the day. She stepped in and was helping me cook breakfast. I poured us some coffee and put a splash of rum in both of them.

Using some of the leftovers from last night we ended up having a fantastic breakfast. Sort of a, put it all in and let's see what we end up with for a meal.

I had a momentary feeling of guilt because I was not making any progress on Toad's problem. I shook my head and wrote it off as this being the weekend it was my time to play. Besides, I didn't have any new information and I was still working on the Carmen angle.

We cleaned up after breakfast and walked out to the aft deck. It had really warmed up and boat owners were walking around the docks getting their boat ready to go out on the river. I could see Dick in the ship's store. I decided to go in myself to see how he was feeling from last night.

I told Carmen I was going to the ship's store. I got off the boat and walked into the ship' store. Dick looked up at me and smiled. He didn't appear to have had much sleep last night. "Good morning Dick and how was your night?" I asked. As I had suspected he had not gone to bed.

He and five others stayed up all night making sure there were no problems. I thanked him then kind of scolded him saying that there was no need for him to do that but I did appreciate it.

I asked Dick what was on the schedule for the day as it was going to be so nice. He said about eight boats were heading for Treasure Island to spend the night. I thought for a moment then told him there would be nine boats going now.

I went back to my boat and informed Carmen what we were going to do and she was okay with it. Her only other choice was that I could have someone take her by up to Willie's and she could go home. In a way I was happy she was coming along and it would give some more time to try and figure her out.

At 1:00 Dick walked by and said that the group was getting underway around two. He had already called Treasure Island to reserve slips for the group. I told him we were ready anytime. Carmen had helped me give the boat a little wash down ands she was sparkling in the sunlight.

In a little while I knew I was going to have to make the boat ready to get underway. I decided to go ahead and do my pre-check to get that out of the way then all I had to do was start up a generator then start the mains about fifteen minutes before we were ready to leave. I went to the engine room to start my pre-check.

When I went down to the engine room, Carmen was sitting on the aft deck with her feet up on the rail. She was really taking it in. I finished my pre-check and came back topside. Carmen was nowhere around. I got off the boat and went to the ship's store. The Dock Master was behind the counter. I asked where Dick was and he said that Dick was on his boat taking a nap.

I asked him if he had seen the Carmen, the young lady that was with me on my boat. He said yes and that she had gone up to the bar to use the phone. That funny feeling came over me again. I made a mental note to tell Dick about it.

I was walking out of the store and Carmen was just climbing on the boat. I startled her when I walked up. "I thought you were down below Captain, she said stammering. I didn't respond to her statement but asked if she had made her phone call okay. She hesitated slightly before answering then said she had.

It was getting close to 2:00 so I went below and started up the starboard generator. I came back up and Carmen was sitting in a deck chair again with her barefoot up on the rail. I told her that I would be starting up the mains in a few minutes and we would be heading south.

She smiled and said that she couldn't wait. I asked her if she wanted anything from inside and she said she would have a glass of water. I fixed her a glass of water and made myself a drink. I was back to normal from last night and it was Saturday and time to start the party again.

I walked to the aft deck and gave Carmen her water then stepped over the aft control station and fired up the main engines. They both came to life with a roar. I checked all of the gauges and everything checked out normal.

I could hear the others boats starting up their engines. In a matter of minutes, nine boats had their engines running and the crews were running around doing last minutes things that boat crews do. One of the other boat owners came up to my boat and said that we were all going to monitor channel 72 on the VHF radio. I acknowledge him and switched my remote to channel 72.

Carmen and I were ready to go. We were just waiting for the word from whoever was leading this flotilla. Carmen volunteered to handle the dock lines for me and I gave her a quick run down on what to do. All of the other boats had to come out of their slips. All I had to do was untie four lines and walk the boat away from the dock, do a 180-degree turn and head down river.

Dick was first to come on the radio and say that he was pulling out. Then one by one the other boats announced their intentions. I waited until all of the other boats were out of their slips and heading south before I had Carmen untie the lines.

I was just about to tell Carmen to cast off lines when I saw Tammy, the tall redhead from last night running down the dock. She yelled up to the fly bridge and asked if she could go along. I was taken by surprise and wasn't sure how to answer. Carmen broke the ice by looking up at me and saying, "it's your boat Captain." I yelled down to Tammy and told her to help Carmen with the lines. Tammy got the two forward lines while Carmen got the two stern lines. They both go on the boat and I walked the boat to port away from the dock. When I was clear of the dock I put the jet drive amidships, reversed the port drive and put the starboard drive ahead. I used the bow thruster to swing the bow to port and the she swung sharply on her own axis and made a clean 180-degree turn.

When my bow was heading south I turned off the bow thruster and put both jet drives in forward. The other boats were already starting to clear the no wakes buoys and I could see them starting to get up on plane. It would be about five minutes before I was past the buoys before I could throttle up. I pushed the throttle forward to indicate 600 rpm's.

Carmen came up to the fly bridge and sat beside me. She said Tammy had gone below to change clothes. I could see a look in her eyes and I knew she wanted to ask me who Tammy was. I beat her to the draw. "I met her last night after you had gone to bed. She is a friend of Dick's family and lives down in Alma", I told her.

She smiled and replied that she did not have a hold on me and it was my boat. Besides she said, she wanted to see how I was going to handle two good-looking women. I was already thinking of the possibilities. About then Tammy came up to the fly bridge. I had to bite my tongue in fear of saying what I was thinking. As I had suspected, Tammy was a full-breasted woman. She had put on her Bikini...well I'm sure the ladies would call it a Bikini. I thought it was about two sizes larger than a cork and two band-aids. What body! What a fox!

I took my mind off of Tammy and put it back to the task at hand and that was getting the boat safely down river. I heard Dick on the radio asking me where I was. I radioed back that I was just clearing the no wake buoys. He said they were in a line running at 35 knots. I told him I would be up with them in a few minutes. Tammy slid into the seat on the other side of me and I took a quick peek at her. I put my hand on her knee and on Carmen's at the same time and said, "hold on ladies we're going to start flying." With that I pushed the throttle forward and the engines started to roar.

There was not a lot of boat traffic out as it was still early in the season so I let Winkin', Blinkin', and Nod run out at full throttle.

She came up on plane and I watched the knot indicator crawling higher. 30, 35, 40, 44 knots. Her top speed. I told the ladies that we were now doing 50 mph. They both had a look of awe on their faces and both of them had a hand on each one of my legs...squeezing.

We round the first bend after leaving Prescott and I could see the rest of the Armada about a mile ahead. At the speed that we were making I figured I should be on them in about 7-10 minutes. I radioed ahead and gave a general announcement to all and told them that I had them in my sight and to keep to the starboard side of the channel 'cause I was fixing to blow their hatches off.

Right at about 10 minutes I came on the last boat in the Armada. I gave long blast from my ship horn to tell him that I was overtaking him on his port side. I couldn't hear if he had responded but I kept on going. As we passed the boat Carmen and Tammy both stood up and waved. I was hoping my wake didn't upset him too much but then I was a 100 feet to his port and was well within the Rules & Regulations of Navigation on Inland Rivers, concerning overtaking another vessel.

As we came up on each boat I would give long blast on my horn to let them know I was passing them. We were blowing by them and Carmen and Tammy were having fun waving at them as we passed. We were about to pass the last boat, which was Dick's. I called him on the radio and told him I was passing. Dick has a newer 45' Magnum, which he says, will do and easy 50. We were about to put it to the test.

I eased back on the throttles until I matched Dick's speed. I stood up and waved at him then motioned for him to go ahead and give it what he had. I could see him push his throttles forward and I did the same. I could hear the roar of his engines exhausting through the transom as he started to ease away. I could hear the scream of my turbo's kicking in and we started picking up speed again. Tammy and Carmen were jumping up and down in their seat cheering me on. Both of them about to fall out of the tops.

Dick's boat was about 50' feet ahead of us and we were both running full out. It appeared that our boats were running at about the same speed. Dick came on the radio. "What's the matter Cap? Are you out of power?" I didn't respond.

The normal Max rpm on my boat is 2550 rpm. There are mechanical lock forward of the throttle handles that when removed will allow the engines to get up to 2800 rpm's. I pulled the locks up and eased the throttles forward. I could feel the boat surge forward and the distance between Dick' boat and mine started closing. At 2800 rpm's the scream of the turbo's and the roar of the engines was almost deafening. The girls were still jumping up and down with excitement.

We slowly caught up with Dick's boat and I gave him a long blast on the horn to tell him I was passing. We slid past his boat at about 5-mph faster. As we went by he called me on the radio and begrudgingly admitted defeat. The girls stood up and cheered and I radioed back to Dick to tell him that I was backing out of the throttles and was going to slow down to 35 knots. He acknowledged and I could see him start to drop back then I eased my throttles back. The girls were still jumping for joy and I said it was about time for a drink. They went below to fix some drinks.

Chapter 25

We were just passing Diamond Bluffs Wisconsin of to the port. That meant we not far from the Treasure Island Casino channel. I called Dick on the VHF and told him I would go ahead and call the Treasure Island marina to let them know we were arriving. He said okay and I switched channel 9 on the VHF. I knew the marina monitored channel 9.

"Treasure Island Marina, Treasure Island Marina. This is the Motor Yacht Winkin', Blinkin', and Nod III, over." I waited just a moment and the marina came back. It was Lisa the Marina Manager. "This is Treasure Island Marina. Good afternoon Captain Art, over." "Hi Lisa! Just wanted you to know that we are about a mile from your channel and I have 8 boats behind me. We have reservations for the night, over." "We have been expecting you Captain. I would like to put you on "A" dock behind the Island Princess and the others on the other side of "A" dock so you will all be together, over." "Understood Lisa and we'll see you in a few minutes. This is Motor Yacht Winkin', Blinkin', and Nod clearing channel 9 going back to channel 72."

When I got back to channel 72 I gave a broadcast to all of the boats and told them where we were to dock. One at a time the acknowledged and about then the Casino channel came up off my starboard bow. I slowly started to ease the throttles back and made a gentle starboard turn into the channel. I pulled the throttles back to idle and stay just to the right of the center of the channel.

The channel is not a very wide channel and when towboats are passing you need to be careful. The boats behind us started to space themselves out to allow the boat in front to have sufficient time to maneuver once we got to the marina. There is a moderate southerly current in the marina during spring high waters. If there is a wind it can be tricky docking your boat.

When I got to the marina I eased the bow towards "A" dock. When I was around 20 feet from the dock I stopped the forward motion of the boat and went down to the aft deck control station. I was going to swing the boat around so my bow would be pointing out to the channel. I used the bow thruster to swing the bow around to starboard. I need to swing just over 90 degrees. Once the bow came around I used the jet drives to walk the boat to port. Carmen had gone up to the bow to man the bowline and Tammy was manning the stern line.

There were three dockhands to help us tie up. I brought the boat right up to the dock and with a gentle nudge the girls threw the lines to the dockhands. They made the lines fast and I started shutting everything down. Lisa, the Marina Manager was standing there when I stepped off the boat. I sign the overnight slip and she went about her business. The other boats were starting to come in. It took about 25 minutes for all of the boat to get tied up.

I already had the shore power hooked up and the air on the boat running. It was getting warm. The girls had made fresh drinks and we walked across the dock to the other side, one on each arm. Like I said, my sex life is like salt. When it rains it pours.

As people got their boats secured they got themselves a drink and we all started gathering on the dock near my boat. Somehow there always seems to be a crowd around my boat. It's always the gathering spot on the docks. A few of the people were chattering about the race that Dick and I had. I noticed a couple of the guys were having trouble keeping their eyes of Tammy and Carmen. I couldn't blame them.

All of the women had their bathing suits on or a derivative of a suit. Most of the men had pulled off the shirts including me and we were getting our first sunburn of the season. We started getting a loose schedule together so we could keep everyone involved. Dick's wife said that Dick was taking a nap again so don't plan on anything with him in mind. It was nearing 5:00 and the discussion came up about food.

We had two choices. Cook on the boats or eat at the Casinos. The Casino has a regular sit-down type restaurant or a great international buffet. No one was in a hurry to get to the casino to gamble. Most of us were agreement that to win or loose it didn't take long. We decided to do a potluck Bar-b-Que. again. Between 9 boats no one was going to go hungry.

The women got together and started planning the dinner. I had told Carmen to take a look on my boat to see what I had to throw in. The temperature was starting to fall and shirts were going back on and the women were also covering up. What a shame. I was just getting to like the view especially Tammy. I was wondering to myself if I was going to have to wait until I got to Alma before having some fun with Tammy. Actually I wasn't sure about her at all. She suddenly became a third wheel as we were leaving Prescott. I had no problem with her staying on my boat tonight and I certainly was not worried about what Carmen thought. We are ships passing in the night.

The dock was all hustle and bustle. Small little hibachi grills were popping up along with tables and deck chairs. I had brought three deck chairs from my boat. I never used charcoal grills on a boat as I thought the two didn't mix. Besides that's why I put a JenAir grill on my boat.

Lisa had given us the used of a six-foot banquet table, which became our bar. Interesting about boaters. Give me the Liquor concession in any large marina and I could make a mint. Booze and fuel are the two commodities always purchased in gallons.

I had made up my mind to sit back and enjoy the evening. I was going to let someone else worry about cooking and both Carmen and Tammy said that they were going to wait on me hand and foot and I was to want for nothing. I jokingly questioned them about the "nothing" and the both of them at the same time said "nothing." I began to let my mind wander. Sort of a "dirty old man" syndrome but then…dirty old men need love too.

Chapter 26

Dinner was another festive occasion. Just the amount of food that had been prepared was out of this world. I altered my earlier thought about having the liquor concession. I wanted the liquor and the food concession at a large marina. The booze was flowing freely and everyone was in a party mood. Even Dick was up and about after having taken a nice nap. Our festivities had attracted other boaters and we had quite a crowd on the dock. My stereo was going full blast with tunes of Jimmy Buffett blaring out the salon doors. Ah! The life of a boater.

Around 9:00 or so everyone started heading back to their boats to get cleaned up for our trip to the casino. Carmen and Tammy pulled me out of my deck chair and headed me towards the boat. They were ready to go gamble. We went aboard my boat and I told the girls to use the heads in the Master stateroom and I would use the one in the guest stateroom. What a shame I thought to myself. At one time during the rebuilding of the boat I had considered making a single double size shower. Oh well…

I told the girls that they use all the water they wanted. I had hooked up to shore water when we docked and my boat has "on demand water heaters." As long as the hot water is turned on you get hot water. After showering I put on a pair of dark gray pleated slacks and my brightest Jimmy Buffett Parrot head tropical shirt. As I walked out of the guest stateroom I could hear Carmen and Tammy giggling in the master stateroom. My first thought was to pop my head in but I honorably went up to the salon. I mixed myself a drink and walked out on the aft deck. Some of the other boaters were starting to gather around our bar and making themselves a drink. I jumped over on the dock and walked over to the table. I started talking with a couple of guy about boats.

Pretty everyone was there ready to go but the girls. I walked back to my boat and yelled through the salon door for them to step it up. I heard one of them yell back that they were on their way up. In a minute or so they walked out on the aft deck. Both of them were looking good enough to eat. The guys that I had been talking to became suddenly quiet and I noticed that they were staring at the girls as they got off of the boat. "Cap you are one lucky son of a bitch one," of them exclaimed. I turned to them and winked.

We were all there and headed up to the dock head to wait for the shuttle bus to the casino. The casino knew that we had a large group and they had sent one of their larger buses to pick us up. The ride to the casino form the marina only takes about five minutes. We pulled up to the hotel entrance and piled out. I asked Carmen and Tammy if they had ever been here before and they both said no. We went inside to see if Lady Luck was on our side that night.

Both of the girls said they were not into gambling so they just wanted to stay with me. I had no problem with that. Two beautiful women hanging at my side. I could think of something worse. Besides, it put me on an ego trip. We wandered around the casino so they could see the layout. I showed them where the bars were because I knew before the night was over that they would be getting my drinks for me.

We were walking by a pull-tab machine and for grins and giggles I put in a dollar and pulled the lever. A pull-tab slid into the tray and I took it out. I pulled the first tab. There was a red line going through a bell. I looked on the front of the pull-tab to see what I need to win. If I got four bells in a row I could win $500.00. I pulled the next tab. Another bell. The girls were cheering me on. The next tab revealed yet another bell giving me $50.00. I put the pull-tab up to Carmen's mouth and told her to kiss it for good luck and again with Tammy.

I slowly pulled the last tab and Lady Luck had appeared! Four bells in a row with a redline going through them. I was a $500.00 winner and spent only one dollar. The girls were jumping for joy. We walked over to the cashier's window and I trade the ticket for 5 one hundred-dollar bills. I gave one to each of the girls and told them to have fun with it.

I asked them what they wanted to do now and they said whatever I wanted to do was fine with them. I had always wished that Treasure Island would get a Caribbean Stud Poker game in the casino. It was my most favorite card game. Craps was my favorite. We walked over to one of the bars and I let one of the girls buy a round of drinks. Hell, they had money to burn.

I pointed over towards a Blackjack table and said let's go play. We sat down, one of them on each side of me and I placed a bet while they watched. It was a ten-dollar table so threw the dealer a hundred and asked for ten-dollar chips. I made a ten dollar bet and I was the only player on the table. The dealer gave two Aces down. It looked like Lady Luck was about to strike again. The dealer had a 7 showing meaning the best he could have was 18 if he had an Ace in the hole. With me having two Aces already I thought his chances were slim of having an Ace and I split them and went double down.

I explained to the girls what I was doing and if I won I would win $50.00 on each hand plus my bet. The dealer flipped his cards over. His hole card was a five. That gave him twelve. He needed a 9 to get 21. He dealt himself a King. Busted. The dealer stacked up $50.00 on each of my $10.00 bets. I reached down and picked it all up except for one chip and slid it over to the dealer saying thanks. We walked away, me being another $100.00 richer. Now I was up $599.00 less the hundred each I had given the girls. I could tell already that is was going to be a nice night.

We were thirsty but then boaters are always thirsty. We went to the restaurant bar to have a drink and relax. I told the girls this was the way to do it because we would probably be here a while. Go slow. That's the way I do it. We sat down at the bar that had dollar poker machines built into the bar. I gave the bartender our orders and took out one of my hundred dollar bills and put it in the bill receiver. Click, click, click and I had a hundred credits. I started playing with the girls watching. I explained how the machine worked and told them that poker was a game of odds.

I was not hitting any big hands. I was betting Max bet, $5.00 on each hand. I thought to myself wouldn't it be ironic if I hit a Royal Flush. I doubted that Lady Luck was going to be that good to me tonight. I played the machine for about fifteen minutes before it ate my money. Easy come, easy go! That's what gambling is all about.

We ordered another round and I paid the bill. I ask the ladies if they wanted to do anything special. They answered no and that they were having fun watching me. Okay I said, "let's go gamble." We ran into some of the other boaters and the girls had to tell them about my good fortune. I responded saying that I would probably loose it all before the night was over. I'm not much of a slot machine player but I thought it would be fun and all of us could be involved.

We walked into one of the newer sections of the casino that had all slot machines. All you could see were rows and rows of slot machines. We walked down the isles and Carmen pointed to a machine and said let's play this one. It was a $1.00 Chinese Fortune Cookie Machine. We sat down pulling up two other stools one on each side of me for the girls. I put a hundred-dollar bill in the receiver and bet the Max bet. $45.00. Holy shit! Two pulls with no wins and your hundred dollars was gone less $10.00. I looked at the girls and they both rubbed the machine. I pulled the handle. The screen flashed then each row started stopping one at a time. A little bell rang from inside the machine. I had just won $150.00. The girls were screaming and jumping. I pulled the handle again.

The screen flashed and once again, one row at a time they stopped. Ka-ching, Ka-ching and the bell went off again. Another $150.00. By this time the girls had drawn a crowd with their excitement. The odds of this happening three times in a row were not good. I pulled the handle slowly down and released it. The screen was spinning. They start stopping. Ka-ching, ka-ching, ka-ching, ka-ching. The bell went off again and a red light on top of the machine started flashing. I had gotten five fortune cookies in a row, which paid $2,500.00.

The girls were beside themselves. Even the crowd that they had attracted was cheering. I had to admit I was a little excited myself. I knew the odds of getting three $150.00 wins right in a row were slim. I didn't say anything about the third roll being a $2,500.00 win.

It seemed like ever for them to bring me my winnings. After signing all of the withholding forms for Uncle Sam, they counted out 25 new, crisp $100.00 bills into my hand. I gave the floor attendant and the cashier each a hundred-dollar bill. I hoped it might make them a little faster if I won big again. I gave each of the girls $500.00 which they wouldn't take at first. They said they were my winnings and I told them that we were in this together. Like a partnership. I fronted the money and they gave me moral support. Or was that immoral support.

I was happy and the girls were elated. Time for another drink. We found a bar and ordered a round and the bartender said it was paid for. I asked whom to thank and he said management. I told him to thank them and gave him a twenty for a tip. Hell it was only money and it was the Casinos money anyway. Carmen and Tammy wanted to rest for a while before going back out on the floor. I couldn't believe that they were tired from sitting and watching me gamble.

It was a roller coaster night. My winning went up and down. By two in the morning we decided to call it a night. We went to the hotel entrance to wait for the shuttle back to the marina. All in all it had been a god night. I was walking out of the casino having won clear $6,270.00 in my pocket. Plus Carmen and Tammy each had a $1,000.00 that I had given them. In all, $8,270.00 in winnings. Nope! Not a bad night at all.

Chapter 27

There were still a few people up when we got back down to the boats. Dick and his wife were two of them. Carmen and Tammy couldn't wait to tell everyone about "our" luck. I didn't want to steal their thunder. Dick cam e over and slapped me on the back and said, "Captain, you are one lucky son of a bitch. Girls, he looked at Carmen and Tammy, every time we have come down here and the Captain was with us, not once has he ever lost. Not once. Do you think I could get him to go to Vegas with me? No! He won't go."

I was gloating. I could tell. Dick was right. I have never lost at Treasure Island. Don't ask me what it is but the fact is when I walk in the doors they know I am walking out with their money.

We all laughed and made some drinks. It was party time on the docks!

I knew I wasn't going to last much longer. I told Carmen that I was headed for bed shortly and she and Tammy could do what they wanted. Carmen asked which one of them was going to sleep with me tonight. I looked at her and asked her if she was serious. She said yes she was and wouldn't be hurt if I chose Tammy. I thought about it real quickly and decided to be honorable and told Carmen that I wouldn't think of sleeping with anyone else tonight. Am I glad I had my fingers crossed. I gave her a kiss and said good night. I said good night to everyone else and headed for the boat.

I felt sure that a fling with Tammy would come soon enough. I cleaned up and went to bed. I heard the girls come on the boat. They were still giggling and they seemed to be getting along just fine. I could hear them walking down the ladder to the staterooms. I heard Tammy going forward and Carmen heading for my room.

She walked in and went to the head then climbed in bed without her T-shirt when she came out. I slid over to her side and snuggled up to her and started to doze off. I was just about asleep and I could feel the covers being lifted up behind me. I rolled over suddenly and in the dim light it was Tammy. I started to ask her what she was doing but she beat me to the draw. "Captain, I'm scared. Can I sleep with you guys tonight?" Carmen giggled and Tammy didn't wait for an answer. She climbed in and got up next to me and we all three went to sleep.

Waking up in the morning between to absolutely beautiful women is an experience. They were both sleeping when I woke up. Before I had fallen asleep earlier and had put two and two together and figured out the reason why they were giggling when they came back on the boat. They were scheming. Sly ladies, real sly. Now all I wanted to do was get up without waking them up. Like many men they have a fantasy to be in bed with two women at the same time. I am not one of those men.

This situation is like the story where the guy picks up a girl the night before and when he wakes up in the morning she is laying on his arm and she is so ugly he chewed his arm off so he would wake her up. Only these girls were not ugly. I slowly sat up and got me feet from under the covers. Tammy was sleeping closest to the head that I had left my clothes in. I slowly stood up and stretched a leg across her and put it to the floor.

At that moment I was in a very compromising position. If Tammy were to wake up now she would discover my complete manhood right at her face. I slowly pulled the other foot off the bed and made for the head. I shut the door behind me giving myself kudos for pulling my escape off without a hitch. I got dressed and walked to the forward stateroom to use the head.

I was making coffee when Tammy came up. I said good morning to her and she looked at me and asked, "Should I feel bad about what Carmen and me tried to do with you?" I smiled at her and said, "Nice try dear but I'm not that type of man. I am strictly one on one!" She looked a little embarrassed and asked if I was mad. I assured her that I was not mad and actually thought it was kind of funny. About then Carmen came up and the coffee was ready.

Tammy looked at Carmen, "Carmen he figured out our plot." Carmen's eyes open wide and I could tell she was blushing. "Sorry Cap! You know when women like us get together you better watch out. I hope you're not mad at us." I gave Carmen the same response that I given to Tammy and left it at that. I poured us some coffee and asked who's cooking breakfast. The both of them spoke up together. "Great you two girls cook and I'll relax." I thought to myself, the maid service sure is getting better.

I went to on the aft deck. The sun was up and is was around sixty degrees. Boat were starting to pull out and head for their homeports or wherever they were going. I looked across the dock and no one on any of our boats appeared to be up. What a party crowd. Party all night and sleep all day. I went back in to fill up my coffee cup.

Carmen and Tammy were quietly talking and fixing breakfast. I walked over to the galley counter and pour myself a fresh cup of coffee. "What's for chow ladies. Did you find anything good to make?, I asked. Carmen responded, "Omelets, with fresh mushrooms, onions, bell peppers, with bacon and sausage on the side. Oh, two slightly embarrassed but still horny ladies if you don't fill up with breakfast." They both giggled. They just wouldn't give up.

We sat at the bar to eat. It was good and I was hungry. The girls cleaned up while I went out to see if anyone from our group was awake. A few were up and looked like they had also eaten breakfast. The girls came out on the aft deck and sat down on the deck chairs. They were chattering away like two lost friends and I was beginning to wonder how I was going to get them back up river. It didn't make much sense in taking the boat all the way to Prescott to drop Tammy off and then through Lock #2 to get Carmen back to Willies. That would be an all day run and I had only three miles to go to get to my marina.

A few of our group walked over to my boat and bid us all a good morning. We said good morning and I asked immediately who from the group was heading to the cities when they got back to Prescott. One of the guys said that Rick & Kim lived in the cities. I asked him let them know that I wanted to talk with them if they saw them first. We stated talking about my luck last night in the casino. I had almost forgotten about my good fortune.

Everyone seemed to be pretty low-key this morning. I could tell that a couple of them were sporting hangovers. Bloody Marys in the morning are a dead give away. Dick showed up about then also carrying a Bloody Mary. He looked pretty bad. It's really funny how we abuse ourselves in the name of fun. I made the comment to the group and everyone laughed.

I told Dick I was looking for Rick and why. He said no problem. He knew they would be happy to help. I thought I had better inform the ladies so it would be a surprise and they could also be ready to go when Rick & Kim were ready to pull out. They looked a little disappointed when I told them but they understood the reasoning behind it. It was getting to close to 11:00. It was really warming up. A couple of the guys were sporting early season sunburns. That's what they make sunscreen for.

Chapter 28

Rick and Kim were fine with taking the girls back up river and dropping Carmen off at Willies on the way. They wanted to pull out as soon as they could because they had kids at Grandma's. The girls grabbed their belongings from below and I gave them both a kiss and a hug before they got on the boat with Rick & Kim. I told Carmen I would give her a call and I told Tammy I might see her in a couple of weeks in Alma. Everyone on the dock helped get lines and pull fenders off of Rick's boat and he pulled it out of the slip. He gave a short blast on his horn and we all waved.

Those of us that were left stood around a while and chatted. I decided to get my boat ready to head for the marina. I excused myself and went to get the boat ready to leave. I stopped by the Marina and gave them some money for my overnight dockage and left them all a nice tip with their boss's money.

I was ready to head out and went around to all the boats and said good-bye. I thanked Dick for his help and told him I was glad that we had no problems. I asked if I was still worried about Carmen and I told him I wasn't sure. I really wasn't. I walked back to my boat and climbed up on the fly bridge. When I gave the signal the dock crew cast off my lines and lifted my fenders up. I gave a long blast followed by a short one to signify that I was leaving the dock. I waved to everyone and headed for home. Or at least my marina. I was already at home.

As soon as I cleared the marina I switched my VHF to channel 14 and called Lock & dam # 3. They said they were moving recreational vessel and there was no commercial traffic in sight. The next southbound lock through would be in about 20 minutes. The timing was perfect. I could be there in 20 minutes without pushing the boat. As I turned the bow to starboard in the main river channel, I eased the throttles up to a 1000-rpm's. It was a short run to the lock from where I was. As I neared the Lock I could see about fifteen boats waiting to lock through. I figured I would stay in back of the pack. When they open the down river gates to let boats out everyone wants to be in the front of the pack. One of these days there is going to be a bad boating accident there. Mark my words!

When the down river doors open I waited until all of the hot dog boats were completely clear of the Lock before getting out myself. I eased out of the Lock and when I was passed the rafting wall I eased the throttles up a 1000-rpm's. I t was still early so I though I would stop by the Harbor Bar and see my friend Brad, the owner. I got on the VHF radio and called for Island Fantasy, which is the name of Brad's boat. He answered back and I told him I was going to stop by and say hi.

I asked him if there was any room in the slips that he had at the bar. He said the slips were open and he would have some people down there to help me when I got there. I cleared the channel and headed for the Harbor Bar. I hit the Red Wing no wake zone and brought the throttles back to idle. It's about a half-mile to the Harbor Bar from the beginning of the no wake zone.

When I got to the Harbor Bar I went on by so I could approach the slips from the down riverside against the current. Because of the high waters and the current associated with the high water you had to go in to the slip under power. It was a tricky maneuver in any boat, but more so in my boat. At the right moment I turned the bow towards the slips and eased the throttles up to 800 rpm's to maintain a straight coarse. Once in the slip I had to back down and make sure that the current didn't catch my stern and turn me sideways in the slip.

Using the bow thruster and the drives together I brought her in without a problem. As promised, Brad had some people on the dock that grabbed my lines and tied me off. I shut down the mains and left the generator running as he didn't have any shore power. I climbed down from the fly bridge and jumped on to the dock. Brad was standing there and we shook hands. "Ya Mon!", Brad said in his typical manner. How goes it Captain?" I told him everything was cool and it was good to be back out on the river. I asked him his weekend was as we walked up to the bar. He said that he had a packed house but not many were boaters. Still a little early for the boat traffic.

The Harbor Bar is the premier place on the river for boaters. Anyone who is anyone on the river stops at the Harbor Bar for a drink or a good Jamaican meal. Brad has a house down in Jamaica and goes down there several times during the year. During the summer he brings up several Jamaicans to work in his restaurant as cooks and wait staff. The Harbor Bar has quite a history behind it. Back after the turn of the century it was a Brothel and men would row boats across the river all night long to get serviced. The business has been in the family for many years.

The day was still warm and we sat down outside. I brought him up to date about what had happened the week before. Brad also filled me in on some latest details on what was happening around the Red Wing area. One of the waitresses brought us out some ice-cold Red Stripe beers, the national beer of Jamaica. We sat there enjoying what was left of the day.

I was getting full of beer and decided to head to my marina. I'm Chad was still there and waiting for me to get back. I finished up my beer and bid Brad good-bye. I asked him when the patio bar was going to open and he said in a couple of weeks. His Jamaican staff was coming up next week and he was going to have them clean the place up. I told him I would be back in a couple of weeks or so to party. He walked down to the dock with me and I jumped on and fired the engines up.

Brad threw my lines off and I put the jet drives in reverse and backed out into the stream. When I was well clear of his slips I put the drives in forwarded and headed for the Marina. It took just a couple of minutes to get to my Marina. As I had suspected Chad was still there. I backed into my slip and Chad grabbed my lines for me. With the boat securely tied up I shut everything down. I pulled out my shore cables and hooked them up then switched from generator to shore power. Chad started filling me in on the events of the weekend. It sounds like it was a pretty good weekend on the docks. A lot of the boaters were down cleaning up their boats and getting them stocked up for the season. I asked Chad if I had any messages and he replied yes, just one. It was from Tom Turpin.

I made sure my telephone and cable cables were connected and went back on the boat to call Tom. When I called Marci answered and said Tom was gone for a while but would be back for dinner around 7:00. I asked her to let Tom know that I was back at my Marina and would be on the boat all night. I went down below and took a nice long hot shower.

When I was done with my shower I went back up to the salon and flipped on the TV. I thought I had better catch up on the news. I made myself a drink and went to the galley to see what I might have to eat on board. I made a mental note to go do some grocery shopping in the next couple of days.

There was nothing of any importance on the news and the weatherman said we could expect rain in the next couple of days. Fine with me. I had no plans at the moment. It was getting close to 7:00. Chad had finally gone home and I told him not to be back on the docks until 9:00 in the morning. I went to the galley and started pulling stuff out of the "fridge for dinner. I was in the middle of frying up some bacon for BLT"s and the phone rang. I hit the button for the speakerphone and said Hello. It was Tom. I excused myself for using the speakerphone but I told him I was cooking myself something to eat and I needed both hands to cook.

Tom asked me if anyone else was there. I told him no! "Cap, he started out, Toad came clean last night. He knows more about this drug thing than he eluded too when you were here the other day. He thinks he knows the whole "Pony Trail" coming up the river." I asked Tom why Toad suddenly decided to open up. He said that Bernie; the family lawyer had come by on Saturday and told Toad that he might be looking at 20 years prison. After Bernie had left Toad started telling me more about his involvement.

I told Tom to stop right there and not sat anything else over the phone. Not that I was worried about his phone being tapped and if it were it was too late now. I told him I would be up first thing on Tuesday morning. He said okay and he would just go in late to work that day.

While I was finishing up the bacon I started thinking to myself. I wish I knew if there was a connection between Carmen and Tony Mendoza. Ate my two BLT's and took a walk on the dock so I could think a little bit. I went back to the boat and got a full night of rest.

Chapter 29

I was up bright and early as usual the next morning. I felt good. A full night of undisturbed sleep can do wonders for a body. I was on my second cup of coffee when Chad hit the docks. He stopped by the boat for a cup of coffee and to see if I had any special duties that I wanted done. Things looked pretty shipshape when I had taken my walk last night. I asked him to check all of the gin poles on the fingers as the water was going down. I wanted them painted with fresh paint as the water went down. We still had about 20 boats to splash so things were looking pretty good.

I told Chad I was going to do a grocery store run later in the morning. I asked him if we needed any supplies for the boater's lounge. He said he would check. If anything we needed coffee. I cleaned up the coffee cups from Chad and myself and decided to take another walk on the docks. We have very good security lighting at night but you can see so much more during the daylight. I went up towards the fuel docks. Generally we don't get a lot of boat traffic on Monday. Maybe a fishing boat or two or a retired couple out for a days cruise. You still have to have regular hours and someone to man the fuel docks. It's just one of those things. During the week we opened the fuel docks at 10:00 and stayed open until 5:00. On weekends we were open from 8:00 until 9:00.

Everything looked shipshape. I was proud of my dock crew. They were all hard working, personable and ready to help a boat owner. We paid them good and they knew it. In exchange they represented the marina when they were on the docks or off the docks.

I saw Chad down at the other end of the marina and started walking that way. As I was walking past my boat, my phone rang. I jumped aboard real quick and picked up the phone. It was Carmen Mendoza. She wanted to thank me for a wonderful weekend and she hoped that I wasn't mad about the stunt that her and Tammy tried to pull. I told her not to worry about the fun and games and I was glad she enjoyed herself.

She asked if I was going to be around on the boat later this week. I told with the exception of Tuesday morning, I had nothing on my agenda. She asked if she could come down because she had something important to talk with me about. I told her to give me a call before she came to make sure that I was there. We said good-bye and I stood there for a while letting little details go through my head.

I didn't have to walk to the other end of the marina because Chad was done with whatever he was doing down there. He told me he was getting some paint out of the paint locker for the gin poles. I smiled and told him I was heading to the store. I wasn't sure when I would be back but he could expect to have lunch with me on board. I knew it would be at least a couple of hours. I took my time going through the grocery store. I had to plan out everything that I bought. I really enjoyed it. Besides, Monday mornings around this area are when all the housewives go to the store. You never know what could come up.

Chapter 30

Another full nights rest and I was feeling fit as a fiddle. I was up around 5:30 and had coffee going. I took a shower and dressed business casual. I was heading up to Tom's for the morning to meet with him and his son Toad. I left the boat at 7:00 and thought it would be nice to drive up the Wisconsin side of the river on WI. Highway 35. The rain that the weatherman had projected still had not appeared.

It was around 9:30 when I got to Tom's house in Woodbury. Tom was standing on the porch when I drove up. He greeted me and we went inside. Toad and Marci were sitting in the All Seasons Porch. Tom offered me a seat and I sat down next Toad. Marci asked me if I would like a drink or something and I told her if she had coffee made that I would have a cup.

When she walked away I looked at Toad and said, "Toad, I understand you held back on some information when I was here the other day." "Captain, he started, I'm really sorry that I didn't tell you everything. I was scared and I am still scared but after Bernie told me how long I could be in jail I knew that I had to come clean so to say." Marci had come back with a cup of coffee for me and Toad looked at Marci then Tom and asked them if they would mind if he spoke to me in private.

I looked at Tom and Marci and gave them a look of approval. They said they would be outside if we needed anything.

"Okay Toad, let's hear it, I said. Toad said he wasn't sure where to start so I told him to start at the beginning. He told me how he met Tony Mendoza, the president of the biker gang. Tony and some of his members would come down on the weekend and pretty much hang out on Toads boat. There were always a lot of girls there as well as booze and drugs. When he said drugs and I asked him if he meant cocaine. He said yes.

"One day, Toad continued, Tony asked me if I would like to make some money. I asked him how much money and he told me $2,000.00. I said sure and asked him what I had to do."

Toad explained to me about Tony wanting him to take his boat down south, each time to a different place and meet some people and then come back. "Bring back Cocaine?, I asked. "Yes, he said. Cocaine." What I told you the other day was sort of true. Tony would tell me where to anchor my boat and then I would wait. Someone would always pick me up in a fishing boat and drive me around for a while then take me back to my boat. Then I would leave and come home."

"What about the drugs, I asked." Toad looked at me at me and said, "Tony said if I didn't know that there were drugs on the boat then I wouldn't be nervous and do something stupid on the way back home. When they picked me up in the fishing boat another boat would come up and they would put the drugs on my boat when I wasn't there." I couldn't believe what I had just heard. Oh, I might have believed it if it had come from a nine-year-old but not from Toad.

"Toad, I said. You do you honestly believe that if you were caught and they found the drugs on your boat that you could convince them that you knew nothing about them?"

"Well yes, he responded, until I got caught the other week and now I know I am in deep shit." Deep Shit wasn't the word for it. Not only did he have the Law to contend with he had to worry about what retaliation the biker gang might take.

I told Toad that there had to be more to this than what he was telling me. There was! He said that his boat was not the only boat that would make these trips. He thought there might be upwards of ten or twelve boats going south every week picking up cocaine. I did some quick calculations in my head and if Toad was right they were bringing up over 400 pounds of cocaine a week. At the street level that meant after they cut it, they were knocking down over three million dollars a week selling that junk.

I asked Toad if he knew any of the other boats. He said not for sure but he might know a couple of them. "There's more, he said. I over heard Tony talking one day and he was kind of bragging about his connection in Mobile. I heard him say that a ton of the stuff was coming up the river every month, all by private boats and the cops were none the wiser."

"Toad, I asked, Do you know what Mobile is? Is it Mobile, Alabama?" He said he wasn't sure but he thought it was. "Toad, Mobile is the start of the Tom Bigby Waterway, not the Mississippi River. Are you telling me they bring this stuff up the Tom Bigby?" "I'm not sure but I think so, he said.

Well now, I thought. Here's a new twist. Load private boats up with drugs and bring them up north using the inland waterways. I could see where that would be so easy. I knew that on the Ocean you could be stopped at anytime by the US Coast Guard and they could inspected or search your vessel whether you liked it or not. That was the Drug Interdiction Program.

Now Toad is telling me that there is a slew of private boats running right under the noses of the Drug Enforcement Groups. I have been up and down the Tom Bigby Waterway dozens of times and I know for a fact that unless you are doing something wrong, your chances of being stopped by any law enforcement agency is slim to none.

I asked Toad if he knew how it was distributed in Mobile. He didn't have an answer for that question. If I were to hazard a guess I would say that it was broken up in 1-kilo lots and a large shipment would start in Mobile leaving a trail of "keys" as the bulk of it traveled north. Again I could see how easy this could be done. Then I started wondering how it got to Mobile.

I asked Toad if there anything at all that he knew and hadn't told me. He said no. I reached over and gave him a hug and shook his hand. I told him that giving me this information was the right thing to do. I would get it to the right people. Hopefully it would get him a lighter sentence.

I walked out to the deck and Tom and Marci were sitting there talking. They looked up as I came out the door. I looked at Tom and said, "Tom; I don't want you or Marci to ask Toad anything about this for now. He told me what he knew and I will see that the information gets to the right authorities. Have you said anything to Bernie about this?"

"No, Tom replied. "Don't, I said.

I told them I was heading out but I would stay in touch. Toad still had a week or so before his Preliminary Hearing. I told Tom and Marci I would find my own way out.

Chapter 31

The information that Toad had given was still sinking in to my brain as I drove back to the marina. His information was surprising in one sense but in reality it sounded like it was almost fool proof. If what Toad said was true, that they were moving a ton of cocaine each month up river, I couldn't help thinking that it was just the tip of the proverbial iceberg. Hell they could put it on a "Mom & Pop" houseboat and the law enforcement groups would probably never stop them for a search.

The more I thought about it the more I felt that one ton a month was just a minimum because at Cairo, IL one can go up the Illinois river to Chicago and I'm sure the market for cocaine is far greater there than in the Twin Cities. I also knew that getting large quantities of cocaine through the Gulf was a very chancy operation. The Coast Guard and other drug enforcement groups pretty much have the Gulf pretty much tied up.

With radar, planes, and boats they do a good job policing the Gulf. A good friend of mine was in the Coast Guard and he told me about the surveillance techniques that were used in the Gulf for apprehending Drug Traffickers. He convinced me that I wouldn't want to try to smuggle drugs into the US. It's not worth it for the ordinary man. Whoever was running the drugs up the river must have a very sophisticated network to elude the law. My brain was in full gear trying to imagine how this was being done.

I made a stop at the liquor store near the marina to restock my liquor cabinet on the boat. I had gone through some booze over the weekend. This particular liquor store that I went to gave a 10% discount to boaters. He was doing 90% of the liquor business for boaters in the area. Yep! Still wish I had the concession for liquor and groceries for boaters. I could probably buy a new boat in just a matter of a couple of years.

One of the clerks in the liquor store carried my purchases out to the truck and put it all in the back. I hoped Chad was around so he could unload it for me. I'm getting lazy in my old age. I pulled into the marina parking lot and parked in my usual reserved space.

There were about 10 cars in the lot that I recognized as belonging to our Dockers. In the beginning of the season a lot of the boaters will come down during the week to work on their boats. Once the season is in full swing they start coming on the weekends only because all of the hard work is done.

I walked down on the docks under the pretense of looking for Chad. I really didn't want to schlep all that booze down to my boat. I was getting too old for that shit. He was not in plain sight so I didn't worry about it. It wasn't going to hurt the booze sitting in the truck and I had enough on the boat to take care of my immediate needs. Not seeing Chad I jumped on my boat and went into the salon.

My message machine was blinking indicating that I had messages. The first message was from Carmen. She wanted me to call her in her office. Having nothing else to do I gave her a call. The receptionist put me right through. She sounded perky. "Hi Captain, she sort of sang, reminding me of a song that Styx' had sung years and years ago called "I'm Your Captain". "You have been busy to day haven't you?" I wasn't sure what she meant by that. I hadn't really been busy but I played along with it.

"Hi Carmen. I got your message the other day and I'm glad you had a good time, I told her." I asked what she wanted to talk about that was so important. She didn't want to talk on the phone and asked if I was going to be aboard this evening. I told that I was going to be on board and she welcome to come on down. I volunteered to cook dinner for her if she was staying. She made it sound like she might stay over night. I thought to myself, I had two good nights of rest and if she was staying overnight I was ready for her… and in the mood. She told me she would leave the office at five and stop by her place to change clothes and with the rush hour traffic she should be down around 7:30 or so.

I'm glad I had gone shopping for fresh supplies. Now I would be able to cook an exotic dinner for her tonight. After I hung up the phone I started thinking about dinner. Chad broke my thought process by knocking on rail. I would have to think about dinner later. Chad said he had been out at the fuel docks cleaning up the store. We had a little store on the fuel docks that carried basic needs of boaters. Things like Ice, Ice Cream, candy and Pop for the kids. Cleaning agents for the boats and general stuff like that. We weren't out to make money on the store. It was more the convenience of our Dockers.

I asked Chad if he would do me a big favor and bring down the booze from the back of my truck. I told him to take the dock cart with him and he would probably have to make two trips. He said he would be more than happy to accommodate me. What a kid!

I started thinking about dinner again. One of the nice things about a bigger boat is the space that you have in the galley. My galley was as big as a normal kitchen in a three-room apartment. With the appliances you couldn't tell much difference. I took a look in the freezer thinking it would help me make a decision on what to cook for dinner.

My eyes spied two Rock Cornish Game Hens. Why not I thought to myself. Stuffed with wild rice and basted with a Red Wine sauce of my own creation, fresh Artichokes cooked ALA Captain Art, and a fresh wild greens salad with a spicy sweet and sour dressing also of my own creation would be fit for a King. Or a Queen, or in this case, a princess.

I put the hens in the Microwave to start the thawing out process and made myself a drink.

Chad had arrived with first load of booze. He carried it aboard and I busied myself with putting it away. I filled up the bottle holders behind the bar then put the rest of the bottles a storage cabinet.

Chad brought the last box and I also put in the storage cabinet. Unless I had an unusually large party I would be good for a month or so as far as my booze needs.

Chad said he was done for the day and he was leaving. I said okay and told him I might be sleeping in late so don't bother me unless it is an emergency. I checked the Hens in the Microwave and gave them another five minutes then busied myself preparing dinner. I love to cook and there is something about being on the water that makes food taste even better.

At 6:30 I put the Hens in the oven anticipating Carmen to arrive right at 7:30. Everything else was prepared or would take only a few minutes to Finnish. When I cook I like to have the main part of the meal out of the way so I can relax talk with my guests, have few drinks and tell some "Sea Stories."

Carmen arrived shortly after 7:30. Her timing was impeccable. She sat down at the galley counter and I asked her if she would like a cocktail. "I would like one of your famous Martinis," she replied. I gave her the usual warning that I gave to everyone when they ask for one of my Martini's. A woman of Carmen's stature would probably be fine with just one.

She kept me company sitting at the Galley counter while I got dinner ready. I checked the Hens and they were just about done. I basted them again then put the Asparagus in the steamer. I told Carmen that dinner would be ready in about 15 minutes. She smiled and looked at me with her sexy blue green eyes. I had already opened the wine so it could breathe so now all we had to do was wait.

I looked at Carmen and asked her if she wanted to tell me what was so important now or wait until dinner and we could use it as a table topic. She didn't respond right away and I didn't push her.

She took a sip of her Martini with a slight wince. I could tell she wasn't used to drinking them. I turned to the stove busily getting dinner ready.

"Captain, she started, I know that you are doing some investigating for Tom Turpins kid, Toad." I almost cut my finger off when she said that and I turned towards her. She got my attention real quick and I was all ears. She knew she had my attention and continued.

"My law firm represents another young man whom was also busted under similar circumstances. We have had two Private Investigators working on the case for about two months. Like the Turpin kid he was a mule for the Troubled Disciples." You could have knocked me over with one finger at that moment.

The first thing that came to my mind was her last name. At this point I seemingly had nothing to lose by asking her. "Carmen", I asked. Your last name is Mendoza and the leader of the Troubled Disciples is Tony Mendoza. What is the relationship there or is there one?" She smiled and replied, "purely coincidental." At that moment I felt as if the pressure of the whole world had lifted from my shoulders.

The only thing about Carmen that gave me any concern was the possible link between her and this Tony character. I didn't say anything but walked over to the bar and made myself another Martini. I looked at her glass and she still had half of her drink left so I didn't bother to ask her if she wanted another.

After she had dropped that bomb on me, I was still having problems coming up with something to say. Carmen must have realized this and started in again. "We, my firm that is, would like to ask you to work with us on this case. We are aware of your reputation and we think we can get to the bottom of this case a lot faster with your help.

For a fleeting moment I thought to myself that my involvement with this whole thing was now getting a little deeper than I wanted to be. I was begging to wonder how I was going to get more involved with this case than I already was. I was about to find out.

She looked at me and said, "Captain, the fact of the matter is that this other kid is also from a very prominent family. He owned his own boat and met the biker gang under similar circumstances.

After he was recruited he began running drugs up to the cities form Iowa." Now I was really getting interested.

"For now she continued, I am going to keep the name of the other family out of it. When time is right and if there is a need I while tell you who it is." I was just about ready to put dinner on the table and motioned her to sit down at the table and asked her to keep talking.

She sat down and said, "We believe that we know where the drugs are coming from and how they are getting all the way up here to the cities." I continued serving dinner, pouring her a glass of Gewürztraminer.

I sat down and questioned her. "Why don't you go to the authorities with the information and let them take it from here?" She shook her head no and said, "We can't because we have reason to believe that there is a person or persons within the system that is a "Mole", a person that leaks out information."

That statement hit a bell in my head with a resounding clang. Others, and I have felt for a long time that there was a possibility of someone within the legal system leaking information too these gangs about planned raids on their clubhouses. When everything went down the clubhouses were clean. Nothing illegal was found.

"How do I fit in the scheme of things," I asked? She looked really serious and said, "We want you to go under cover. We have another person that will work with you and he has some resources that will be beneficial. You don't have to give me an answer right away. I want you to think about it because it will be dangerous and until we have the evidence that we need we can't go the authorities without fear of the investigation being blown."

I was almost dumbfounded. I was being asked to go undercover to get evidence on a gang that would kill you for looking cross-eyed at them. My mind was now working overtime. There was a lot at stake and this was not a game that was being played. I filled our wineglasses and told Carmen that before I committed myself I would need more information. She looked at me and said, "I can understand and at the right time we will set up a meeting with you and the person you'll be working with and along with our investigators.

We continued to eat dinner with very little conversation regarding what she had just told me. We discussed the day's events and she praised my ability as a chef. I hadn't planned on desert but asked anyway when we had finished our dinner. Gratefully, much to my relief she declined. End of subject!

Together we cleaned off the table and put the dirty dishes in the dishwasher. A dishwasher was a must on my boat otherwise I would let them stack up until I either had no more dishes to use or ran out of room. My duties in the kitchen ran short when it was time to do the dishes.

The galley was all cleaned up and I suggested, as it was a nice evening that we take a walk in the park adjacent to the Marina. She liked that idea!

Chapter 32

It was a clear night as we walked through the park. Due to the lack of backlight from the city and no lights in the park we could see the stars high in the sky like millions of little diamonds. The night air comfortable and it felt good. Carmen had a hold of my arm and had her head against my shoulder. We slowly walked along the river enjoying its pristine nocturnal beauty.

We didn't talk much. I couldn't help thinking how Toads situation had taken a twist as of tonight. I was trying to figure out why I was getting more and more involved in a situation that was clearly a police matter. Understandably, with the amount of illegal money that was being made it was possible that someone in one of Minnesota's Law Enforcement Agencies didn't want to see the supply of cocaine stop. They were obviously making good money by warning the biker gang of any impending actions against them.

I was still trying to figure out how I could safely become involved in an undercover operation. My name was to well known in the cities especially when it came to the motorcycle community. Carmen brought me out of my trance. "Captain you seem to be deep in thought." "I am, I said. I was thinking about our discussion this evening." "Look, she said. Let's not discuss it anymore tonight. You have some time to think about it but let's not let it ruin the evening and if you don't mind I would like to spend the night, if that's all right with you."

I didn't need to be kicked by a horse to get my attention. I immediately forgot about our earlier discussion and told her that I was more than happy to have her stay over on the boat. I made a gentle 180-degree turn and headed us back towards the Marina. No way was I going to be responsible for ruining the evening!

It was about 10:00 when we got back on the boat. I turned on the heat just enough to take the chill out of the air. I flipped the television on to see if anything exciting happened in the cities today. Carmen excused herself and went below to take a shower. There was nothing of any major importance on the news other than a drive-by shooting in the Northeast part of town where two people were wounded and the usual assortment of local happenings.

I was about to grab the remote and turn off the television and I caught Carmen's movement out of the corner of my eye. She looked freshened and was wearing a thin sexy blue silk nightshirt that seemed to accentuate every curve in her body. I couldn't help chuckling out loud.

Carmen asked me what was so funny. I told her that if today were Friday or Saturday some of our male Dockers would be having the view of their lives. I don't have curtains or blinds on my port or starboard windows. The windows are electronically controlled and will darken or lighten by using a special remote control unit. It takes about 10 seconds for the windows to turn completely dark so no one can see in or out. I grabbed the remote and hit the button to darken the windows.

Carmen came over to the couch and sat down beside me. I could feel her body against mine. She smelled daisy fresh and her skin was silky smooth. I put my arm around her and gave her a meaningful kiss. I felt a slight shudder, as she seemed to melt into my arms. She slowly unbuttoned my shirt and pulled it off. I looked at her and said, "Why don't we go below where we can be more comfortable?"

She pouted her lower lip like a child being scolded. I stood up and bent down to pick her up. She wrapped her arms around my neck and I headed for the Masters Stateroom. I'm glad when I redesigned the boat that I made sure that the companionways were widened otherwise I would have been scraping her head along the bulkhead.

I walked into the stateroom with her cuddled up in my arms and gently laid her on the bed. I switched off the white lights and turned on the ultra violet lights. Black lights as they are commonly called, produce a light that is very soft and sensuous. I slowly stepped out of my pants and lay down on the bed beside her. There was no hesitation on her part. She rolled over facing me and was all over me with her mouth. Using her tongue she left moist little trails across my chest and every once in a while she would gently bite my nipples. I wanted to hold her but she kept my arms pinned to the bed. Not that I couldn't get away from her hold, I didn't want to.

She was using her mouth and her tongue to drive me into shear ecstasy. She made sure not to miss a thing from the top of my head and the bottom of my feet. I was in seventh heaven. If she was sent by her office to sexually induce me to working with them the answer was yes. In fact! At that moment she could have asked for anything.

I was literally shaking from her stimulations. She knew exactly what she was doing and I think she was enjoying as much as me if not more. She slowly rose to her knees while still holding my arms to the bed and lowered herself onto me.

Two persons became one. We were physically and mentally joined as one. I responded to her, meeting her every undulating movement. Again like the first time we had sex, she knew exactly what she wanted and she was out to get it. Her movements quickened as she gasped for breath. With a sudden thrust she pushed her hips to mine. Then I felt every muscle in her body tighten. She was where she wanted to be. She shuddered and fell on to me still pushing her hips to mine.

We laid there soaking up the warm glow of our bodies. Neither of us having much of anything to say. I had a thought of Masters and Johnson again in my head as the boat gently rocked at her moorings. Sleep came quickly to both of us.

Chapter 33

Night had brought in a cold front and there was a definite coldness in the air when I rolled out of bed. I made sure that the covers were pulled over Carmen and headed for shower. The hot water felt good as the three showerheads pummeled me with their stinging nettles.

I put on a warm fleece sweat suit and went up to the galley. I put on some coffee and hit the switch for the weather radio. The current temperature was 41 degrees. A cold front was definitely here. I rotated the thermostat to 75 degrees. Within minutes it was comfortably warm in the salon and galley.

I opened my daily calendar to see what, if anything I had planned for the day. Nothing was noted so it looked like the day was open. I turned on the news and sat at the galley counter enjoying my coffee with Appleton Rum. I heard the water pump cycling, which told me that Carmen was in the shower. I pulled out a fresh cup and poured her a cup of coffee bracing it with a little rum. We had not talked about her schedule for the day so I took it easy with the rum. She walked into the galley wearing my thick terry cloth robe. She had a smile on her face that seemed to warm the area up even more. She walked over to me and gave me a little kiss on the cheek and said thanks. I knew what it was for.

I asked her what her plans were and she said that she had taken the day off and unless I had pressing business she wanted to spend the day with me. I had no problem with and actually looked forward to it. We discussed a variety of things to do and settled on a drive South down Highway 61. We enjoyed our coffee while listening to the weather report. Cloudy with a high of 47 degrees. Not a nice day but typical for this time of the year. We got dressed and headed south on 61.

Chapter 34

Carmen volunteered her car, a newer BMW and asked me to drive. It was a racy looking car and handled like a dream. We headed down to Lake City. I wanted to stop by the Marina there to see how far along they were with getting their boats in the water. When we got there it was starting to sprinkle. Just a slight mist but enough to stop the process of launching boats.

It looked like they had over half of the boats in. There was still a little ice in their Marina because there is no current to carry it away. It was not enough ice to hinder the splashing of the boat however.

We got back out on the highway and drove to Winona and had lunch. Winona is another River Town on the Mississippi that has a long history behind it. We had a nice lunch at a nice waterfront restaurant. After lunch I suggested that we drive south then cross over the river at La Crosse. Carmen liked that idea, as she had never been to La Crosse.

La Crosse Wisconsin is one of the larger River Towns on the upper Mississippi River. There are a lot of homes and commercial buildings that are the National Historic Register. We stopped at wellknown "watering hole" to have a couple of drinks. We got in a long conversation about La Crosse with the owner.

I was really enjoying our little adventure. Carmen was an excellent conversationalist and had a little something to say about everything. She told about me her background, school and her career as an Attorney. She was born and raised in Indiana. She went to Law School at Harvard, specializing in criminal law.

We were now driving North on Wisconsin's Highway 35. Leaving La Crosse it goes inland a couple of miles then come back on the river in Fountain City. From Fountain City we went through Cochrane and Alma. Driving through Alma I got to thinking about Tammy, the girl that we met at Leo's Landing and went to the Casino with us.

We stopped at the Red Ram in Alma for a couple of drinks. They had a nice afternoon crowd in there and we talked with the Fred, the owner, and his wife Linda. I have known they for a couple of years. Fred used me as a consultant last summer when he decided to get a new boat.

It was getting to be about 5:00 and I asked Carmen if she wanted to eat in Alma or head back towards the Marina and eat when we got there. She said she was still a little full from lunch and asked if it would be all right if we ate when we got back to the Marina. I had no problem with that.

We finished our drinks and said good-bye to Fred and Linda and headed North. We stopped just a few miles North of Alma in a little town named Nelson. There is a cheese factory there, Nelson Cheese Factory that has the best homemade cheese in Wisconsin.

Both Carmen and me stocked up on a variety of cheeses and some local wines. We crossed the river there at Nelson. The River Bridge brings you back into Minnesota at Wabasha. We drove through Wabasha and headed North back to the Marina. We got back to the marina around 6:30. We decided to head to the boat and freshen up a little then go out for dinner.

Carmen asked if we could go the St. James Hotel. She had heard it was a good place to eat. I agreed! I called the St. James and made reservations for two at 8:00.

We got to the Hotel a couple of minutes early and went up to the Lounge. I asked the Bartender to call down to the restaurant to let them know that we were in the building. I ordered a Beefeaters Martini and Carmen had an Old Fashion. We were sitting at the bar when Jim and Cindi walked in.

They were long time boater friends and the current owner of the Red Wing Marina. Jim, a humungous sized man is about one of the most out going people that I know. His wife Cindi is a little firecracker and can keep you laughing with her little antics when she has been drinking.

They came up to the bar and I introduced them to Carmen. "Cap, Jim said while looking at Carmen. Where do you manage to find these absolutely beautiful women?" Carmen blushed a little and smiled at Jim. Cindi was standing beside me and grabbed my arm and said, "This guy is a hunk and he commands the best!" She gave me a little peck on the cheek and we all laughed.

I asked them if they were just having drink or were they having dinner. Jim said they were having dinner and we decided to eat together. Their reservation was for 8:30 so I had the bartender call down to the restaurant again and canceled our reservations and that we would be eating with Jim and Cindi.

I ordered a round of drinks for all of us. Jim and I got engrossed with Marina talk and the girls got to know each other better chatting away in their own little world. Jim told me that he had splashed all of his boats and things were starting to get busy. I asked Jim if he had plans for making diesel fuel available this year. There were only a couple of places on the river in our area that boats could purchase diesel fuel. Jim said he would love to have my business but he didn't think it would happen this year.

When I fill up I take my boat to the wall right in front of the St.

James Hotel and have a tanker truck come down and fill her up. My boat capacity is 10,000 gallons if I was empty. Generally I let the fuel drop to 5,000 gallons then top it off unless I am planning a longer trip then I will top it off before I leave. I get a commercial rate on my fuel because I charter my boat as a business.

We finished our drinks and went down via the elevator to the Restaurant. The place looked to be fairly crowded. The Hostess seated us right away. It appeared that we were all-hungry and ordered our meals as soon as the waiter came. I listened to what everyone was ordering and ordered a couple of bottles of the appropriate wine.

Cindi overheard me ordering the wine. "Cap, she asked. How is it that you always know which wine to order?" She looked at Carmen and said, "This guy has the best taste in wines of anyone that I have ever known. We have had dinner with him many times and he has never ordered a bad wine. I looked at Jim and winked. Little did she know that I had ordered two bottles of Gewürztraminer. When I order wine with dinner, 90% of the time it will be Gewürztraminer.

While we were eating Cindi asked what we had planned after dinner. I looked at Carmen questioningly and told that we did not have anything planned. She asked if we would like to go to their boat for a few drinks after dinner. I again looked at Carmen and she shook her head yes. I told Cindi that we would be happy to visit with them for a while. I got to thinking that there was a good chance that we would end up in a party mode once we got to the marina.

One has to understand the thought process of the average boat or yacht owner. Any excuse to go down to the boat is just an excuse to party unless they have specific plans to get underway.

We finished dinner and had some desert. I let Jim grab the check. Hell! I wasn't going to argue with him. After all he is a Marina Owner. We saw some mutual friends on the way out and stopped at their table to say hi. I introduced Carmen to them and told them that we were going down to Jim and Cindi's boat and they should come down and we could start a party. Jim piped in a second and Cindi a third. It was party time!

We followed them down to their marina. When we walked onto the docks we saw that a party was already in progress. There was about a dozen people hanging out at the ships store on the fuel dock. Music was blaring from one of the boats and a few couples were dancing. I asked Jim if we could borrow some warmer clothing as Carmen and I were not dressed for being outside. The night was a little on the cool side. Jim said he would fix us up.

The folks that we had seen in the St. James came down and now we had a party in full swing. Cindi had taken Carmen on their boat for a tour. Jim and Cindi have a new 56' Gibson Executive House Boat. It's like a home going down the river. Like myself, Jim and Cindi live on their boat during the boating season.

When they got back from the tour the party was really happening. We had started a game of charades and everyone was doing there best. Carmen asked me if it was always like this with boaters. I looked at her and shook my head yes.

Chapter 35

It was nearly 2:00 in the morning when Carmen and I decided to leave and head back to my boat. We were both feeling pretty good. Luckily my marina was not far away and I wasn't really worried about driving to it. If push came to shove we could have walked back.

We got back to the boat and the first thing I did when we got aboard was to turn the heat up. We were a little chilled. Carmen more so than me. I poured us a couple of Cognac's to warm us up and flipped on the weather radio to check the next day's weather.

To my surprise it was calling for a warmer day. A warm front was heading our way from the southwest and they were projecting a high in the 70's. I asked Carmen if she wanted to work on her tan. She said okay and I told her we would head out in the morning and go down to Lake Pepin.

I secured everything then we went below to the stateroom and I was wondering if there was going to be a repeat of last night. No sooner than we got in the stateroom my question was answered. Carmen was definitely the aggressive type of woman when it came to sex. Little time was spent on talking. She was a woman of action and bordered on being insatiable.

I decided not to be passive and took the aggressive role and like her the night before, I pinned her to the bed and let my mouth and tongue wander over her body bringing her a multiple of sensual highs. We fell deeply asleep, exhausted, in each other's arms.

It was nearly sixty-five degrees when we woke up mid-morning. We woke up at the same time and climbed out of bed and hit the shower, together. I started wondering when I was going to have to start weaning her as this relationship could begin to get serious. I made a mental note to have a discussion with her about this matter.

I let Carmen cook breakfast while I busied myself doing a precheck of the boat for our little jaunt down to Lake Pepin. I really enjoy it when someone else takes over in the galley and does the cooking. She made one of my favorite breakfasts, Eggs Benedict.

We ate breakfast and when we were done she when about cleaning up the galley and I started up a generator then fired up the main engines. Chad heard the main engines fire up and came down to the boat. I told him we were going to spend the day out on Lake Pepin and he could get me on the radio if he needed me. He told me that Nafe Williams had been down on the docks yesterday and left a message for me to get a hold of him.

Nafe would have to wait. I told Chad if he saw Nafe to tell him I would get a hold of him later today if I made it back to the Marina before the office closed. Chad unplugged my shore power cable and stowed it for me. Carmen had finished up in the galley and had gone below to put on her bathing suit.

I went up to the fly bridge and Chad started casting off the dock lines. He shout when the last line was off and I eased Winkin', Blinkin', and Nod out of the slip. By the time the boat was passing the fuel docks Carmen was up on the fly bridge sitting beside me in her very brief bikini. It was going to be hard telling her that this relationship was not going to be a lasting one.

Once we were in the channel I headed the boat South for Lake Pepin. Lake Pepin is still part off the Mississippi River but it is about three miles wide and fourteen miles long and forms a very large lake. Lake Pepin also happens to be the birthplace of Water Skiing.

I headed the boat south and at Point-No-Point, and made a 90degree port turn and headed towards the Wisconsin side of the lake. I was heading for a cove off the shore of Maiden Rock. Maiden Rock is a little town on the Wisconsin side of the river. The cove that I was heading for is known as Bare Ass Beach. A lot of naturists come out here to enjoy the freedom of no clothing.

Years ago I used to charter one of my older boats out to dancers from the local strip clubs. They wanted to go out and work on their full body tans the natural way. There is something to be said about having a dozen naked young girls running about your boat all day. And to think, they even paid me to take them out.

As we got closer to the beach I kept an eye on my depth gauge. The closest I could get to the beach was about a half-mile. When my depth gauge read seven feet I stopped the boat and dropped the anchor. I let out about forty feet of anchor rode and secured the anchor windless. In the part of the river there is no current to speak of but the boat will swing around from the prevailing winds. The wind was very mild and the temperature had risen to about 70 degrees.

Carmen was already on the aft deck laying in a deck lounge minus her bikini. She was a sight to behold. I went in the Salon and shed myself of my clothing and went back out to join her. I slid the other deck lounge next to hers and lay down. "You know Cap, she said. I could really get to like this way of life. Are you looking for someone permanent in your life?" Wow! She took a load off my shoulders. She saved me from having to tell her that this was not going to be a lasting relationship. I looked at her, "Sorry Carmen. A permanent relationship is not what I'm looking for at this time." I assured her that when I started looking for one that she would be on the top of my list.

The sun felt good. It was still a Spring Sun but it had warmth. Carmen glistened from the lotion that I had courteously and freely applied to her body. While I was rubbing her down with lotion I couldn't help but to remember when I would take out the dancers for their tanning sessions. They convinced me that it was the Captains responsibility to make sure that they had lotion all over their bodies. Hey! They were chartering the boat and if they felt that putting suntan lotion on them was part of my duties, well, who was I to argue.

It was about 4:30 and a cool breeze started blowing. We both sat up at the same time and decided to call it a day for sun tanning. I noticed that both of us had a slight pink glow on our skin as we walked into the Salon. I asked Carmen if she would like something to drink and she said yes, after her shower. She went below to take a shower and I headed down after fixing myself a drink.

We came out of the showers at about the same time. This woman was so sexy. It was hard not to reach out and grab her every time I put my eyes on her. She had a towel wrapped around her and her hair was still dripping from the shower. She walked up to me and put her arms around my neck and pulled my face to hers. She kissed me, pressing her lithe little body to mine. "Captain, do we have to get dressed"? I said no and she dropped the towel that was wrapped around her.

I was getting the feeling when in the company of this woman that there was going to be little rest for the weary.

A while later we went up to the galley and made dinner. I pulled out some nice T-Bone steaks and cooked them on the Jen-Air. Carmen made garlic-mashed potatoes and a nice salad. I uncorked a nice bottle of wine and we had a very romantic dinner on Lake Pepin.

We were just about to put in a video movie when Carmen's cell phone broke the silence. I tried not to pay any attention to her conversation but I overheard Carmen using my name. When she got of the phone she didn't look the least bit happy. "Bad news, I asked? "She looked at me and said, "Captain, I'm so sorry. I have to go back to Minneapolis tonight. Something has come up in this drug case and it is very important that I be in the office first thing in the morning. My office would also like you to come in."

I thought for a moment then looked at her and asked, "what do they want me for?" She said that their sources got word that a major shipment of cocaine was going to happen in the next two to three weeks and they wanted me and this other guy to try and get involved in Mobile.

I asked her to get things cleaned up in the galley and I would get the engines started and would head back to the marina right away. I was already dark and Carmen wanted to know if it was safe to head back in the dark. I told her some of the best boating on the river was done at night.

My boat was set up to travel the river or oceans at night. With radar, night vision goggles you could navigate anywhere. However, I didn't need any of those in this part of the river. Familiarity is all I needed and I had that.

I fired up the main engines and told Carmen as soon as she was done in the galley to come up to the fly bridge. I was going to get us underway right away. I got up to the fly bridge and turned the anchor windless on and started hauling the anchor in. I knew I would have to wait until tomorrow to clean the "Loon Shit" off the anchor. Once I had weighed anchor we were underway.

Carmen came up about 10 minutes later just about the time we had reached Point-No-Point. I brought the bow around to starboard and eased the throttles forward until we were running at around twenty knots. Normally one would not go that fast at night because of the lack of visibility. When I had revamped the boat I had twin aircraft landing lights built in to the bow. At a million-candle power each I had no problems seeing anything.

In an hour we were back at the marina. Carmen handled the dock lines and I got the shore power hooked up and shut down the engines and generator. She went below and got her things together and came back topside. Carmen grabbed my hand and said, "Captain I am really sorry about this but you know the importance of the case, as you are also involved. Can you be at my office at `10:00 tomorrow morning?" I told her I would be there then walked her up to her car. She gave me a quick kissed and drove off into the night.

I went back to the boat and put on the video.

Chapter 36

I was up bright and early heading for the cities. If Carmen wanted me at her office at ten I knew I had better leave early or I would not make it because of the morning traffic. On my way in I gave Siena a call just to let her know that I would be in the cities. I told her I didn't know what my schedule was going to be but if the chance arose I would give her a call later.

I made it to the Roberts Street parking ramp at 9:30. If I used the skyways I would make it to Carmen's office right on time. I hate being late. At two minutes to ten I walked into the corporate offices of Hewlett, Green, & Canon. I told the receptionist who I was and she directed me to Carmen's office. She was sitting at her desk when I walked in. She stood up and walked around her desk and gave me her hand. All of a sudden she was very business like.

"Thank you for coming Captain, she said. The rest of the people are in the conference room waiting for us." She grabbed my hand and led me down the hallway to the conference room. As we walked in I saw seven other people. Three of them I guessed to be Carmen's partners. One older frumpy looking lady whom I guessed to be a secretary and there were to other gentlemen.

Everyone but the frumpy old lady stood as Carmen introduced me. My guess was right on. Carmen introduced me to her partners one by one, then to the old lady who was taking notes. The younger of the other two was a Para-legal and the last was the Nad Walker, the man that Carmen had told me about on the boat. He was the one that was going to be my partner going down to Mobile.

I was mentally trying to size Nad up. He stood about five-eleven, one hundred and eighty pounds, and was muscularly built. He had short thinning hair and a good tan like he had just come from a cruise.

We all sat down except Carmen. She walked over to a paper easel and lifted the first sheet. Under that sheet was an outline of past and future events as they related to this case.

She began talking bringing everyone up to date. I was listening intently up until she came to the part about Nad and I going to Mobile. Then I was all ears. She looked at Nad then at me and said, "Gentlemen, our investigators have done some preliminary groundwork for you. They have located what they believe to be the marina where the top dogs of this drug ring hang out."

"The marina is in Biloxi, Mississippi, she continued. Our investigators have talked with informants that have told them that a big shipment was about to hit the coast roughly in about six weeks." I interrupted and asked why the drug enforcement agency's or local police were not being used or at least informed of this information.

Carmen asked me to be patient and in a bit I would understand why. She continued to talk and slowly the whole thing started coming together. She was finishing up her outline then said, "Captain, this is where you and Nad come in."

We want you two too take Nads boat down to Biloxi via the Tom Bigby waterway. We want you to make your presence known all the way down. We feel that if you take four weeks to get there and make contact with as many of the people that we think are involved in this whole affair, by the time you get to Biloxi your reputation will have arrived before you."

I was understanding that part okay but I was still having trouble about the local police or the DEA or whomever not being brought into the circle. I was trying to figure out what a bunch of citizens were doing running around making like gangbusters. I was thinking when Carmen got my attention.

"Captain, she said. We have reason to believe that there are some local officials involved in this drug ring. If we were to bring them in on this it could blow up before we even get started." Hell, I was already thinking that me, Nad, and his boat could get blown up.

With the meeting over and still somewhat in the dark, Nad and I went to a local pub near the law offices to talk. The attorneys had given us an assignment. Our assignment was to map out our trip down south using Nads boat.

Nad a 47' Fountain with triple 800 hp motors. It was a virtual water rocket. Its top speed was in excess of 100 mph. The control area was a three-station design. The starboard station was the helmsman station, amidships was the throttle man's station, and the port station was the navigator's station. This boat was a fullfledged open sea racer.

Nad and I talked for a while then parted company agreeing to meet at my marina the following day. I headed for the parking ramp and decided to drop by Siena's on the way out of town. I gave her a call and she was home. She said she would love to see me!

It was right at two when I got to Siena's house. She was standing in the front doorway when I drove up. I got out of the truck and Siena met me halfway down the walk to her front porch. She gave a little leap and was in my arms. By her actions you would think that I hadn't seen her in years.

She had a thousand questions to ask. They came one after the other including, what have you been doing, why haven't you called, where have you been, and did I miss her. I waited until she was done firing all of the questions at me then tried to answer all of them in one sentence. That was a mistake. With a woman like Siena, you must be more implicit.

I brought her up to date on Toad and told her in a round about way the plans for the trip down south, without being specific. It seemed to put her on edge. She was concerned that it was going to be dangerous. Sure it was going to be dangerous but then life by itself can be dangerous.

She asked how the marina was doing and if I had been out on the boat. I told that the marina was fine and all of the boats were in the water. I told her that I had been out on the boat a couple of times and let it go at that. I didn't think that she needed to know what I was doing or with whom.

She asked if I was staying in town over night and I explained to her that I had an appointment in the morning and I really needed to be there early. She understood my drift and asked when I was coming back up. I couldn't give her that answer. I didn't know myself. We talked a little while longer then I told her I wanted to get on the road before the evening traffic rush.

I gave her a big kiss and left her standing on her front porch. She looked a little hurt but I knew she would get over it. She waved as I drove off.

I jumped down on Highway 36 heading East. I thought taking 36 to 35E would be my best bet at this time of the day. I stayed on 35E then onto 494E down to 52S and nudge the truck up to 75, set the cruise control and relaxed all the way back to the marina.

Chapter 37

I was up at the crack of dawn making a pot of coffee. Nad said he would be here in the morning but said nothing about a specific time. I went to my onboard office to do some research on our impending trip south. I wanted to find out where all of the marinas and fuel stops where. Knowing boats as I do, Nad's boat was a guzzler of gas. In fact I was thinking a good estimate would be one gallon per mile per engine. That estimate turned out to be close. A little low but close.

I heard Nad when he was a half-mile down river. His boat was equipped with an exhaust system called, "Silent Choice". You could run through a muffler system or not. His choice, was not. I saw him as he rounded the last bend in the river before the no wake zone. The boat was at a 45-degree port lean with the throttle on. I would have guessed his speed to be around 70.

He pulled the throttles back just before hitting the no wake buoys. I could see the bow raise and the stern settle as the boat slowed. He pointed his bow towards our fuel docks and I walked out to meet him. He was all smiles. Like a kid with a new toy. His hair, what he has had been wind blown in a variety of directions. I helped him tie the boat up and we walked down to Winkin' Blinkin' and Nod.

I invited him aboard and offered him a cup of coffee with rum. He accepted without hesitation. I asked him how his trip up river was and he said fast. An understatement I'm sure. I gave him a quick tour of my boat that left him impressed. He was fascinated with the technology that I had aboard.

We sat down and started work on our voyage south. I had printed out charts of the river all the way to Mobile. The charts showed all of the marinas and fuel stops along the route. I told Nad that I had estimated that the mileage on his boat was about one gallon to the mile. He smiled and said, "Close Captain, very close. Our speed will have everything to do with it. I was thinking that we needed to average just over 60 mph in order to get to Mobile in four weeks.

Running at 60 mph in a straight shot you could cover the distance in about 25 hours. Traveling on the river you have to allow for Lock and Dams, river traffic, and of course fuel stops. I thought 4 weeks would be a good trip. This would allow, were possible, one person to run the boat while the other napped. Like you can nap on a boat slamming through the water at 60 mph.

It took all day to map out our trip minus a timeout for lunch. By the time we were done we had the whole route, stops, and timing all planned. It was nearly five and Nad asked if I wanted to take a quick ride. I wonder if he meant a short ride because any ride on that boat was going to be quick.

I agreed and we headed down the docks to his boat. Chad was on the fuel dock admiring Nad's boat when we walked up. I couldn't help smiling knowing that Chad would give his left nut to go for a ride.

We jumped in the boat and Nad directed me to the Helmsman's station. I looked questioningly at him. He said this was as good of a time to learn as any. He said he would work the throttles. For a moment I wasn't too sure about that. I was at his mercy as to how fast we were going to be traveling. I wrote it off in my mind by rationalizing that there had to be trust between us and it had better start now.

Nad gave me a quick briefing of everything and I fired her up. The sound was deafening but was like music to my ears. I started one engine at a time. Once all three were running I checked the gauges and gave Chad a thumbs-up to cast off the lines. I pulled all three clutch handles back at the same time. There was a resounding "thunk" as the transmissions engaged. I waited until we were well clear of the dock and moved the clutch handles forward.

Again a resounding "thunk" as the transmissions engaged to the forward gear. We idled south towards the end of the no wake channel. As we cleared the no wake buoys I looked over at Nad. He yelled in my ear that I would have better control if I dropped the bolster seat. He showed me were the control button was and I pushed it. The seat dropped down and I was now in a standing position.

He slowly eased the throttles forward. The bow momentarily went skywards the boat picked up speed. In a matter of seconds the bow lowered itself and Nad kept pushing the throttles forward. We were now in the bend that I first saw Nad when he arrived this morning. The power of the motors was awesome. We came out of the bend heading down the channel we call the Narrows. There were no other boats in sight. Nad kept pouring on the fuel.

The narrows channel goes about a mile and a half then goes through a series of sharp "S" turns. I have negotiated these turns in my boat at 45 mph. We were now doing 85 mph. I looked over at Nad. He was grinning from ear-to-ear. We were about a quarter of a mile from the start of the "" turns. I looked quickly at Nad hoping he would throttle back. It wasn't going to happen.

I held the wheel firmly thinking to myself that if I were sitting on the seat my ass would be biting a hole in it. Fountain boats have a reputation for handling at high speeds. I was fine with that but this was my first time behind the wheel of a boat with this much power.

I brought the bow to the starboard entering the "S" turns. I could feel the stern drifting out but Nad also felt it and made some trim and throttle corrections and the hull bit in and grabbed. The "G" force was in the turn was almost excruciating. We made it through the first right turn then I wheeled the boat to port. Nad kept making trim and throttle corrections the whole time. We had one more right turn then the final left turn, which would put us in Lake Pepin.

We were heading for the final left turn and out of the corner of my eye I saw Nad push the throttle all the way forward. Hell, I didn't have to see him. I could feel the sudden burst of power. Even at 85 mph there was lurch forward. I could feel my heart in my throat. I was holding the wheel as if there was no tomorrow. Coming into a turn fast is one thing. Accelerating while in the turn is another thing. I was wrestling with the wheel trying got keep the boat in the center of the channel.

I eased up on the wheel as the turn started to straighten out. I took a quick look at the speedometer and we had come out of the turn at 110 mph. I hoped the wetness I was feeling was from the spray of us going through the water.

We ran about 10 miles at a 110-mph. Then Nad pulled the throttles back and gave the signal for me to come about and head back to the marina. I wasn't ready to go back. I reluctantly started my 180degree turn heading us back to the marina.

Chad was waiting for us at the fuel dock. I eased the bow into the slip and Chad kept the boat from hitting the dock. He tied off the dock lines and I shut the engines down. I was still shaking as I climbed off the boat. My knees were a little on the weak side. and I could still feel the vibrations from the engines.

Nad and I walked down to my boat which when I saw her, for a fleeting moment she seemed inadequate. I went aboard and grabbed a couple of beers while Nad waited on the dock. I handed him one as I stepped off the boat. He grabbed it and said, "Well Captain, how'd ya like it?

She's a mover ain't she?" I told him she all that and more. I admitted to being a little nervous but Nad said I would get over that.

I learned a little bit more about Nad as we sipped our beers. He was from California and was with the LAPD. He had been shot three times during a big drug bust. It ended his career as police officer. He came to Minnesota and opened up an Investigation and Security agency. He was married and had no children. I started to tell him a little about myself and he stopped me saying he knew all about me. Already investigated I thought to myself. No secrets here.

Nad said that he would let the people in the cities know that we were ready to go and had a plan. I suggested that Nad not give out all of the information for security reasons and he agreed with me.

We set our departure for Monday morning. There would be little traffic on the river and our delays at the Lock and Dams would be minimal. Nad said he would be at my marina on Sunday so we could load up and head out first thing Monday morning. I told Nad there would probably be some partying on the docks Saturday night if he and his wife wanted to come up. He said he would let me know. I walked out to the fuel docks with him. When he was ready he gave me a thumbs up and I cast off the dock lines. He was out of sight in minutes but I could hear him for what seemed like forever.

Chapter 38

Saturday night at the Marina! It's party time! Several Dockers were starting to congregate on the patio. I grabbed a fresh beer from my boat, knowing it would be the last beer that I would need to get from my boat. My Dockers won't let me drink my own booze. I was greeted by all when I walked onto the patio. I made a mental note to remind myself of the mental note I had already made about the Jell-O shot cups.

I noticed that Chad had put out a couple more trashcans. Maybe that would give the hint and I wouldn't have to say anything. I always hated to be the bad guy but then, someone had to be the asshole. Hor's Devours were being brought out and I was glad. I realized that I was hungry. Someone mentioned something about grilling some ribs and I knew it was going to be a good night.

It was going to be a mild night. Lows were expected to be in the high 40's. For us that is a mild evening. There was a fire crackling in the portable fireplace and someone had started up the grill. I was on my fifth beer when the first round of Jell-O shots came around. Champaign Jell-O shots. Interesting!

Someone started telling jokes and then it was non-stop. One after the other. I joined in and through in a couple of my own. It's funny! When someone starts telling jokes it's amazing how many you can remember. At my age sometimes it's hard to remember from day-to-day. No problem with jokes.

I could smell the ribs cooking. Everyone but me made a contribution to the feast we were about to have. It was an unwritten law on the docks that I was not allowed to bring food or booze to a dock party. I don't know who made the law up but I was not about to abuse it the generosity of my Dockers.

Dinner tasted as good as it smelled. I had a plate full of ribs, potato salad, beans, and variety of Jell-O shots. I still hadn't seen anyone toss their Jell-O shot cups on the deck. I wonder if Chad had already given them a warning. It wouldn't surprise if he did. I was contemplating going over to the table for some more ribs when my eyes fell on something more interesting.

There was a stranger on the docks. A female stranger. I stood back for a while to see if I could determine who she was with. There are a dozen or so guys that own boats at the marina. I didn't want to step where I shouldn't step. The night was early and I could wait. I went ahead and helped myself to some more ribs and potato salad.

She was of average height and well proportioned. Her brunette hair was pulled back in a tight ponytail. She was talking with the wife of Spike Adamson. They owned a new 60' Searay Sedan Yacht and had been Docker here for about three years. I knew that they had a daughter but I had never met her. I was wondering if this was the daughter. She looked to be in her late twenties which age wise could make her their daughter. I was hoping not.

I didn't have to wait long for an introduction. I had just dumped my empty plate in the trashcan and grabbed a fresh beer. Julie, Spike's wife walked up with the young lady. I was going to say something flattering but held off. Her name was Kim and she wasn't their daughter. I shook her hand and welcomed her to the docks. She was friend of the Adamson's visiting from Michigan.

Bust on the Mississippi

I made small talk with her asking if she was enjoying herself. She said she was. She said she had been told that our dock parties could be quite memorable. Memorable isn't the word I would have used but it worked. She told me that she and the Adamson's were leaving Monday morning for a cruise down to the Quad cities in Iowa. She must have seen the surprise in my eyes because she asked if I had ever been there.

I told her not only had I been there but I was also leaving Monday morning heading south. I explained that we had planned an overnight in Dubuque but that we would be traveling much faster and would probably be gone by the time they got there. I told her about Nads boat and she said right off that she would rather be going with us. I wanted to second her motion but held back.

She asked me which boat was mine. I pointed to Winkin', Blinkin', and Nod and she gave a nod of approval. I knew what was coming next. She wanted to know if she could have a tour. I told her that anytime she was ready to let me know. She said she would. Spike had walked up behind me just as I was telling her "anytime she was ready to let me know."

Spike can be a little stuffy at times. He stood between Kim and I and said, "Captain, do you have to proposition every women that comes on this dock?" I glared at him. I was instantly hot under the color. I hate it when people make mistakes about my intentions especially when they are honorable.

"Spike, what the hell do you have shoved up your ass tonight? I think you owe this young lady an apology." I wasn't worried about myself. Because of my reputation I was used to getting questioned about my intentions, but Spike was out of line on this one. Spike looked a little confused. "An apology for what, he asked."

Kim was not going to stand-alone. "Spike, you make it sound like you are sleeping with me and you're worried that someone else is going to get in my pants." I couldn't have said it better myself. I had to chuckle on that one. Kim put her hands on her hips and looked Spike square in the eyes. "For your information I had asked the Captain if I could see the inside of his boat. Besides, Mr. Adamson, if I want to bang his brains out it is of no concern of yours."

Spike was at a loss for words. His face was beet red and he was starting to cower under Kim's sharp tongue. Very meekly, I mean very meekly he apologized to the both of us and walked away. I looked at Kim and smiled. She was cool. The emotions that she had shown to Spike was now gone. She was calm, cool, and collected. I was impressed.

About 15 minutes later Julie, Spikes wife came over while we were talking and said that Spike had told her what had happened and that he felt really bad about it. "He really likes you Captain and he thinks your going to be pissed off at him, she said." I told Julie that I was not and that she should let him stew about it for a while. It might do him some good. It was just alcohol talking. This was not the first time this had happened with Spike.

I excused myself from the ladies and went to talk with some of the other Dockers. I stopped by the food table and grabbed a couple of Tequila Jell-O shots. H-mmm, not sure that I like those. Jerry Knupps, another Docker called me over to the group he was he was talking with. Jerry owned a 40' Bayliner Cabin Cruiser. He owned a manufacturing plant over in the Faribault, Minnesota area.

He had bought his boat from a former lady Docker that happened to be the first lady boater that I had ever trained. TJ had gone to get her Coast Guard Captain's License and I was very proud of her. She was one of the few women boat owners on this part of the river.

Jerry and the other guys were talking about my boat ride early during the day. I told them the highlights of the ride and they thought I was crazy. I didn't think it was pertinent to tell them what I was going to be doing for the next month because they would have thought I was going insane. I did however mention that I was going to be away from the marina for a while starting Monday morning and if they needed anything to let Chad know.

The party was getting in full swing. Spike must have been over his embarrassment because he came up to me and apologized again for his thoughtlessness and told me that Kim was still waiting for her tour on my boat. I told him everything was okay and if he spoke with Kim before I did to tell her I would find her in a few minutes.

I didn't see any need to rush to give her a tour. Spike had probably blown me out of the saddle with his outburst.

Kim and I met at the food table. We were both sampling the new Jell-O shots. Hot 100 cherry cinnamon. Neither of us liked them. I asked her if she was ready to take her tour. She smiled and said very sweetly, "I thought you'd never ask." We headed for my boat. I gave her a special tour. The kind that just "wow's" the women. She said that she liked my boat better than Spike's because mine had masculinity.

I decided to keep the tour as a tour. I was not in the mood for a one-night stand. Besides, it was party time on the docks and I would be gone for a month. I felt like partying. The word had spread around while Kim and I was on my boat that I was going to be gone for a while. The party suddenly turned into a party with a theme. A Bon Voyage party for Captain Art. A new batch of Jell-O shots. Banana Pudding????

Chapter 39

Kim was a little flirt. She was like a butterfly, flitting around.

She was full of energy and I had to work hard to keep from staring at her. I began to wonder if I was going to change my mind about getting to know her a little better. I shrugged it off and went to the table to taste the next round of Jell-O shots. This batch was bad. It deserved being tossed over the side of the dock. Jalapeno in Lime Jell-O. Someone's taste buds were way out of whack. I started to notice Jell-O shot cups on the deck. I debated about saying something but I could not at the moment think of any conclusive benefit from telling these people to pick up their damn Jell-O cups. I made a mental note to makeup a memo and put it on the bulletin board, someday.

The beer was flowing and the crowd was loosing some of its punch. I was almost two in the morning. There was heavy dew in the air and I suppose that made a few of the people uncomfortable. I casually looked around for the Adamson's and their guest. They were no longer on the patio so I had to assume that they had gone to bed. Well, that was one more that I didn't have to worry about. No one nightstand tonight!

I popped one more beer and started walking around telling folks I was about ready to turn in. I thanked them for the nice party and told them that when I got back we would have to do a weekend boat out. That's when all the boats head out on the river and we raft off and party all weekend. We have had as many fifty boats rafted up to each other at one time. I had worked what I called "Captain Art's Modified Rafting Moor".

Instead of all the boats being side-by-side, we anchored Mediterranean style, backing down on the anchor then tying off stern-to-stern, then side-by-side. All sterns were tied off with 20' lines from the aft cleats. That way we had a calm swimming area between the boats. It took a little bit of practice and a good skipper to get into position. Once we were all tied up together it was like a little city on the water.

I gave a final good-bye to all and headed to my boat stopping by the boater's lounge to relieve myself. I locked the Salon door after me and hit the switch for the windows to darken. I half-heartedly thought about listening to the weather report but decide that morning was soon enough. I turned off the all of the lights and went below.

When you are used to a place you don't need lights. It's like being blind, you know exactly where you are and where to walk. I walked into my stateroom and shut the door behind me. I undressed and climbed into bed…with someone else.

My immediate response was to go into a defensive mode. When I reached out, I felt softness. My mind was registering, "Not Immediately Dangerous". I heard a giggle and a voice asking, "is this Spike's boat?" She was dressed for business… or undressed.

She made no bones about telling me what she wanted and how she wanted it and I was more than happy to comply. She had just set a new record on achieving an orgasm on my boat. Ninety seconds and she was shooting stars. I was still at ready and she was going for it again. I made a concretive effort to pace myself while I let this young filly have her rein. On the third round she waited for me. She wrapped her legs around my hips making sure that I met her every move. We crossed the finish line at the same time. It was an explosive finish. Sleep came quickly.

I have no idea when she left but it was for sure that she was not there now. Her pillow was cold. I gave myself a big stretch and rolled over to look at the clock. It was 9:30. I tried to think about last night. I remembered a beautiful body that was filled with lust. She was like a Florence Nightingale, a ship passing in the sea.

I slowly rolled my body out of bed and headed for the shower. The hot beating water felt good on my back. My mind wandered as the water pummeled my back. I couldn't help thinking about Kim. Women like her are few and far between. I wondered what my chances were of running into her again.

I dressed warmly. I just had that feeling that I would feel better with warm clothing on. I couldn't remember what time Nad was coming or if he even told me. I spent the rest of the morning packing what I thought I would need for the next week or so. I knew it would be chilly until we were south of Missouri then it would gradually get warmer so I made sure that I packed warm clothing.

When we got further south we could do some shopping for the appropriate clothing. I made sure my 9mm were on the top of the bag. I also put in 10 fully loaded magazines just in case.

I went up to my office and loaded up my Captains bag with charts that I figured that we would need. I also put in my hand held GPS and my night vision goggles. Not knowing what Nad was bringing for equipment I also put in two hand held VHF radios with chargers. Thinking for the moment I was pretty well set I sat down at the computer and started making up a list of duties for Chad to do while I was gone. I made mental note to call Nafe, the owner of the marina to tell him I would be gone for a while.

It was around noon when I heard Nad out at the fuel dock. There was no mistaking his boat. I got off my boat for the first time this morning and casually headed for the fuel docks. Nad had already drawn a crowd. A boat like his is always going to draw a crowd.

He was talking with a couple of the Dockers when I walked up. I started to walk up to them and someone grabbed my arm. I turned and saw that it was Kim. I smiled at her and she looked back at me with an all most embarrassed look. I was going top ask here what time she left my boat but there were too many people in the near so I let it go. I did tell her that I enjoyed last night leaving it open in case anyone was listening. I told her to let me know when she was coming down this way again and maybe we could get together.

I turned my attention towards Nad. I walked up and said hi. He tossed me a bag from his boat and hopped out himself. We sort of faded away to my boat as the others were still admiring his boat. We went on board and went into the Salon. I told him to make himself at home as we would be spending the night on my boat until we left in the morning. I showed him where everything was and told him to help himself. He didn't need another invitation. He went behind the bar and made himself a drink asking me if I wanted one. I declined and told him to go ahead. I poured myself a cup of coffee instead.

I asked him if he had eaten lunch yet and he said no. I told him we had two choices. I could make something up here or we cold run into town. I kind of wanted to hang around the boat because we had a lot of planning to do before leaving in the morning. It was bad enough that we were doing this thing on the wing. We had to have some sort of plan and a little organization if we expected to have any chance of success or surviving at all.

Nad said lunch on board would be fine but he wanted to go to the Harbor Bar for dinner because it had been a long time since he had eaten any Jerk Chicken and the Harbor made the best in the area. He said we could go over in his boat.

I sat down at the bar with him we started making our plans. I started to pull out my river charts but Nad said there was no need to. He had already planned out the whole trip south. He reached into his bag and pulled out his chart book. I couldn't help noticing his side arm in the bag. He handed me his chart book. I quickly glanced through them. He had done a professional job in marking up the charts. All speeds, times, and distances were noted on each page of the chart book.

I asked him about his gun. He reached down and pulled it out. It was a 9mm Lock. A nice gun but a little too bulky for me. Nonetheless it was still a weapon that one needed to respect. Its accuracy in the hands of a good shooter was tops. I had brought my bag up to the Salon this morning and went over to the couch and pulled out my gun. I unloaded it and handed it to Nad. He was impressed.

We spent the rest of the afternoon going over the charts and other important aspects of the trip. I asked Nad what he had packed for the trip and he had pretty much packed that someway that I had.

He also informed me that he had a hundred grand in his bag that he had gotten from the Lawyers when we had our meeting. The two families were footing the bill for this venture and he said there would be a bank account set up for us in Mobile by the time we got there. I smiled and said humorously, "do you think the hundred grand will be enough for gas to get us to Mobile?" Nad laughed and said it should.

Nad said he still had a couple of things on the boat to show me but that could wait until later or even until tomorrow when we got underway. I got up and made us a couple of drinks. I held up my glass in salute and we drank to a successful voyage.

I told Nad about last night's party that he had missed. I also told him about Kim sneaking down to my boat and surprising me. He asked me if Kim was the girl on the fuel dock that I was talking to and I said yes. He shook his head in approval. I asked Nad if he would like a little tour of my boat and he enthusiastically said yes.

I could tell he was impressed with my boat. People don't have to say anything when they see something that they like. You can tell what their feelings are by watching them. We finished the tour in the Salon and Nad went to the bar and made us another round of drinks. I suggested that we stow our gear in my office and we could take a walk on the docks after I called Nafe to let him know that I would be out of the marina for a while.

I called Nafe and told him that I had some important business down south and would be gone for about a month or so. Nafe was not surprised because it was not unusual for me to be gone for an extended period of time relocating yachts.

I told him that I had written up instructions for Chad and will give Chad a phone number to contact me if anything came up. I told Nafe to stay off the docks and leave the Dockers alone. I could tell he didn't like that but what could I say. He can upset an apple cart in five minutes. I wasn't about to let him come down on the docks and ruin what had taken me so long to build up. I knew it was his marina but I was the one responsible for making what it is today. He mumbled something and I said good-bye.

We freshened up our drinks and went out for a walk. There were still a few boat owners in the marina including Spike Adamson. I felt a slight twinge of guilt about my clandestine meeting with Kim and how he had gotten a little out of hand last night about her.

The feeling didn't last long.

I introduced Nad to a few of the boaters and made a point of not lingering to long in any one spot. Nad mentioned that he really like it up this way but couldn't convince his wife to keep the boat up here. I told him I would make him a good deal on a slip in he could talk his wife into it.

We headed back to my boat to grab some jackets then we were heading for the Harbor Bar. I knew it would still be busy and we might not have a spot to tie off Nads boat. I called Brad at the Harbor and told him we were on our way up and asked what the dock status was. He asked me to wait while he checked. He was back on the phone in seconds and said there were two boats leaving the north dock and he would have Homey and Atherton, two of his Jamaicans workers go down and hold the spot for us.

Chapter 40

We went out to the fuel docks and Nad jumped in his boat and fired up the engines. I waited on the dock until he gave me the signal and cast off the line s and jumped in myself. He backed out of the slip and headed the boat north. While we were in the no wake zone Nad took the opportunity to show me some of his technology. He reached in a compartment and pulled out two headsets. He gave me one and told me to put it on. He put his on then plugged both of them into a pair of jacks on the dash.

I suddenly and clearly heard his voice. What I didn't hear was the roar of the motors. He explained there was a noise cancellation device built into the system and it cancelled out the background noise. We could talk in a normal voice and be heard. The headsets were small and barely visible. I really liked this technology. I knew I wouldn't have a voice left by the time we got to Mobile if we had to yell at each other to be heard.

Just as we hit the end of the no wake zone Nad told me to throttle up. He said this was going to be the job of the person occupying the seat that I was sitting in so I may as well get some practice. I eased the throttle forward and instantly felt the power of the engines thrusting us forward. The Harbor Bar was 4 miles up river. and I knew we could be there in about two minutes if I went W.O.T. I chose to keep us at 60 mph.

I pulled the throttle back about a hundred yards before the Harbor Bar docks. When you pull the power on a boat it slows down real fast. Nad nosed the bow into the docks and I could see Homey and Etherton standing on the north dock waiting for us. There was a nice crowd at the patio bar and they were now looking at us coming into the dock.

We slid up to the dock and the boys grabbed the boat then tied us off. We took off our headsets and after Nad had shut the engine down we jumped on the docks and headed for the patio bar.

I introduced Nad to the people that I knew there, which was a lot. Brad eventually came out and I introduced him. I told Brad that Nad wanted some Jerk Chicken for dinner and I told him that this was the place to get the best Jerk on the river. If not the only place.

We sat at a table on the patio and one of the Jamaican girls came out to take our order. It was Homsey wife Gracie. Gracie was a portly lady and I have never seen her without a smile on her face. Homsey and Gracie were the caretakers of Brad's property in Jamaica. Whenever I went to Jamaica I stayed at Brads place and I would have Gracie make me some Jamaican Curried Chicken and Rice. There was none better on the face of the world.

Brad came over at sat down with us. We about general things and I told Brad I would be out of town for a while and if he wanted to spend some time on my boat while I was gone he was welcome to it. He thanked me and said he might take me up on it. Brad liked to come down to my boat and just hang out. A place to get away from his establishment and the crowds.

"Hey there handsome", I heard a voice say. I turned towards the voice. It was Windy the lady that had done the interior of my boat. I stood up and gave her a big hug and a kiss. She was looking fine as ever. "Hi Windy, I greeted her. How have you been? When are you going to come down to the boat and visit me?" She shrugged her shoulders and declined to give me an answer. I asked her if she wanted to sit with us and have some Jerk. She thanked me and said that she was with friends inside. Homsey had told her that I was out here and she just wanted to come out and say hi. Brad introduced her to Nad and we all talked a little then she excused herself and walked back inside.

Gracie stopped by the table to see if we wanted another round of drinks and we said yes. She said that dinner would be out soon. Brad had gone off to take care of business and said he would stop by later if we were still here. I didn't see us leaving early and I told him so.

As usual, dinner was excellent. Anyone can go to the store and buy Jerk seasoning and make Jerk Chicken. Only Brad's Jamaican cooks can do it the right way. We washed the dinner down with liberal amounts of Red Stripe Beer. We were both stuffed and I could have lain down and went to sleep. Nad had engaged himself in a conversation with a lady at the table next to us. I didn't know about his married life but I took him to be a man that might look but not touch. My hunch was right.

I paid Gracie for our dinner and drinks and we went to the patio bar. There were about twenty people sitting at the bar and it was a lively crowd. One never knows what might happen at the Harbor Bar. Brads keeps a list behind the bar of special or exciting things that happen. I remember last summer a young couple went down on the docks, got naked and had sex right on the dock.

Then there was the time that five young things asked if they could used my swim platform to dive from and I said okay. When I looked next the five of them were completely nude and diving from my swim platform swimming around the boats. That was another night that I almost had a problem. There was some young punk on a boat that kept shining his spotlight on the girls and it made me mad. They wanted to go swimming, not put on a show for everyone to see. I went down to this guy's boat and nicely asked him to keep his spotlight turned off. He told me to take a hike and I was about to take issue and Brad walked up and took care of the situation. All five of the girls ended up spending the night on my boat. It took about a month before people quit asking me how my Harem was doing.

The crowd at the bar was getting loose. A shapely young lady climbed up on the bar and started a striptease. Nad was all eyes and was cajoling along with the rest of the men for her to take it all off. Brad walked behind the bar and got his special happenings list out and made a new entry.

Then Brad challenged any women to take off their bra and toss it so it would catch on an oar hanging from the ceiling. A free drink to any woman that made it. That's all it took and bras were flying everywhere. A couple of girls complained that they didn't have bra's on and they should be able to do something to get a free drink. Once everyone verified that they did not have bras on they got a free drink.

I was going to ask Nad how long he wanted to stay but I could see he had no intention of leaving anytime soon. He was having too much fun. I was waiting for the next spontaneous event when my eyes met the girl that was one of the first to take her bra off and toss it. She looked to be in her late 20' or early 30's. I smiled at her and she walked over to where Nad and I were sitting.

It was easy to see that she did not have a bra on and clearly didn't need one. She introduced herself as Crystal. She had long flowing blond hair and fair skin. She stood about five-five and she was looking good. I could feel the firmness of her breasts as she leaned against me. I recognized her perfume. It was Tatiana. Very tropical and very alluring. She spoke with a slight Southern accent. I was guessing she was probably from the Missouri area. My guess was right. She was from St. Louis and had just moved here. She was an Orthopedic Surgeon and had taken a position at the Hospital in Red Wing.

"So, she said. You are Captain Art! I heard from some of my staff that if one was going to hang out with boaters that it should be with Captain Art." I wasn't sure if that was a compliment or what, but she did get my attention. Nad had stood up from his barstool and was cheering on another activity so I grabbed his barstool and motioned for Crystal to sit down. I had Etherton get us a round of drinks while we engrossed ourselves with trivial conversation.

She was from a farming family and was the only girl of five siblings and the first to leave the roost. She had attended the University of Missouri and went on to Med School at the University of Minnesota. She was single and loved her work. She had fallen in love with the river while she was in Med School and set a goal to be on the staff of a Hospital that was on the river.

Nad was looking for his barstool and saw that it was occupied by Crystal. He looked at me and winked and motioned his head towards his boat. I knew what he meant and would keep it in mind if the opportunity arose. Crystal had an air about her that seemed to say she was serious but that she could also let her hair down. I was looking for that side of her.

She ordered another drink for the two of us and I asked her if she would like to go down to the boat. The playful side of her came out and she was off her barstool in a flash. I nudged Nad in the back as we walked away and he nodded in a way that signaled to me that he knew I was on a quest.

It's amazing what effect that spring has on people on the Upper Mississippi River. They seem to crawl out of the woodwork. It's called cabin fever. We wormed our way though fifty or sixty people to get to the docks. I pointed towards Nad's boat and she headed that way. When we got up to the boat she asked if this was my boat and I told her no that it was Nads. I helped her get aboard and showed her around the cockpit area.

She wanted to see below so I lead the way down. The cabin of Nads boat is nicely appointed but it is not anything like mine. Crystals drink was empty and I asked her if she would like a refill. She replied yes and I dug through Nads liquor cabinet to find some Vodka. I found a bottle of Vodka and found some orange juice in the refrigerator and made her a nice Screwdriver.

I pulled out a beer and we saluted our drinks. Without hesitation she set her drink down and grabbed me around the waist and planted a wet kiss on my lips. I looked over her shoulder at the VBunk in the forward part of the cabin. It didn't take a whole lot of effort to head her in that direction. We sort of fell into the V-Bunk landing side-by-side. She was already in the process of removing her halter…

We went back up to the cockpit. The fresh night air felt good. I could see Nad standing at the patio bar smiling. We talked a little bit more exchanging phones number then went back to the patio bar. I introduced Crystal to Nad and he ordered a round of drinks. Nad asked Crystal how she liked his boat. She laughed and said, "I love your amenities better." She looked at me and winked. We all laughed.

Crystal excused herself saying that she had to get home because she had the early shift at the Hospital in the morning. I gave her a soft kiss on her neck, whispering in her ear that I would be back in a month or so and would like to get together with her. She looked at me and shook her head in approval. After shaking hands with Nad she was gone.

Nad looked at me as if he expected me to give him the whole story of what had taken place on his boat. I looked at him and said, "Now there's a nice lady, and a Doctor to beat." I left it at that. Nad looked a little disappointed but I'm sure he understood.

We finished our drinks and said good-bye to everyone. Brad walked down to the dock with us and helped us with the dock lines. I told Brad we would see him in a month. Nad backed out and we headed back to my marina. We had put on our headsets so we could talk going back. I told Nad to go into the slip next to my boat as the boat that was normally there was out for repairs.

We slid into the marina and tied the boat up. I told Nad to grab any gear that he needed and he could sleep in my guest stateroom. I didn't need to ask twice. He went below and tossed up two bags and I grabbed one and headed for my boat. Nad followed with the other.

We got aboard Winkin', Blinkin', and Nod III and I showed him where everything was and told him to make himself comfortable. I went down to my stateroom and changed into a pair of Nautica sweats and went back up to the bar and made a drink. I was checking my answering machine when Nad came back up from the guest stateroom. He had a bunch of charts in his hands, which told me we were going to do some more homework.

Chapter 41

Morning came all too early. Nad was already up and coffee was on. I think that is what probably woke me up. I poured myself a cup with a brace of Appleton Rum. It went down way to easy. Nad had been studying the charts and was making some last minute notations. "Good morning Cap", he said. "I've finalized our stops for the trip down and without any unscheduled stops or problems we should be in the Gulf of Mexico by Tuesday next week."

I did some quick mental calculations and my brain was telling me that this was not going to be a slow boat to China. Some fifteen hundred miles in eight days. If you were traveling by land this distance and time would seem trivial. By water it is different. We have Locks & Dams that we have to wait for. No wake areas to go through and one never know what the traffic on the river is going to be like. Notwithstanding, the fuel stops that we will need to make.

When you break it down it is just short of two hundred miles a day. Not mind-boggling but in a boat two hundred miles is a good day. We had planned on traveling in daylight hours only. River navigation can be testy during daylight hours but at night and at the speed that we will be running our chances of mishap increase five fold.

It was nearly 9:00 and we started loading our bags on Nads boat. Nad took charge of stowing everything. At the speeds we would going it was certain that we would be come airborne on occasion. Everything had to be put in a locker or tied down. There could be no loose gear left lying around. It took us about an hour to get the boat ready to go.

Nad took the boat up to the fuel docks to top off and I buttoned down Winkin', Blinkin', and Nod III. I wouldn't see her for a month or so. I patted her on the rail as I got off onto the dock. I had notes for Chad and headed for the fuel docks. Chad was just finishing fueling Nads boat when I walked up. Nad was in the engine compartment doing a last minute check.

I gave Chad my notes and told him to call me with any questions before he went to Nafe, the owner. I knew that Chad supported me there. The less contact that he had to have with the owner, the better he liked it. I told Chad that the best time to call was in the evenings or early in the mornings because my chances of hearing the cell phone ring were slim. Nad interrupted and said that there would be no problem because we could tap the phones into the headsets. That made me feel better. I told Chad to call me anytime he wanted to.

We were ready! Nad fired up the engines and I gave Chad a hug and a handshake. I climbed in the boat and motioned to Chad to untie the dock lines. Nad slowly backed the boat out. He pointed the bow south and we were on our way to destinations unknown. I gave a hand salute to Chad and he smartly returned it.

When we cleared the no wake buoys Nad told me to set the pace with the throttles. I eased them forward until the speedometer was showing sixty. It was a relatively calm morning. Maybe 5 knots of wind that created a two to four inch chop on the water. It was just the thing for Nads boat. She ran straight and smooth. There was no traffic in the Narrows so I pushed the throttles up until went were running at seventy mph. I was going to love this trip in this boat. At 58 there is still a need for speed!

We came out of the Narrows and went into the S-turns then dumped into Lake Pepin. I asked Nad how fast he wanted to go across the lake. He shrugged his shoulders, which told me that it was my call. I eased the throttle forward and watched as the speedometer climbed upwards.

I held the throttles at a hundred mph. Nad made some minor trimtab adjustments and we sat back for a quick fourteen-mile, eightplus minute run across Lake Pepin. The chop was a little bigger on Pepin than in the Narrows. Nads boat took it in stride. I was expecting to feel more jarring than I did but the hull construction of Fountain boats makes the seem like your sitting on a pillow.

About half way across Pepin we could see a Cabin Cruiser in front of us. Nad told me to hang on because we were going to have some fun. He quickly gave me instructions on what to do when he told me to do it. The distance between the cabin cruiser and us closed fast. I estimated the cruiser was travel at around twenty-five knots. Nad was coming up directly behind her in her wake.

"Cap, Nad said excitedly, when I tell you, I want you to pull the port engine throttle back and snap it immediately forward catching the other two throttles on the way up and shove them all to the bulkhead. I knew what he was going to do. It was not an easy maneuver to do but it was guaranteed to be a hair-raiser.

The cruiser ahead of us was putting out about a five-foot wake. The wake was coming off his boat, ever widening at about a 45degree angle. Nads was going to jump the wake head on. That was the first problem. Getting the boat heading into the wake, bow first at a hundred mph. The only way to do it in the short amount of room that we had was to pull the power from the port engine causing the boat to suddenly swerve to port.

As soon as the boat started its swerve Nad would whip the wheel to port also. At the moment he turn the wheel to port I would bring the port engine throttle back up and grab the other two and go W.O.T.

This causes the stern of the boat to swing very suddenly to starboard. Nad would have to catch the stern swing before we went off center or we would hit the wake at an angle possibly causing the boat to roll over as it went air born.

I could feel the adrenaline pumping through my body as I tensely awaited Nads signal to pull the port throttle. We were coming up fast on the cruiser. I could now see the people on board looking at us. We were now a hundred yards from the stern of the cruiser and closing fast. Suddenly I heard Nads shout. "Pull it", he yelled. I yanked the port throttle back and watch him turn the wheel. When the wheel was over I push the port throttle back forward grabbing the other two on the way by and hit them on the bulkhead.

The effect was unbelievable! I could feel the stern swing to starboard and just as if there was a wall there to stop us the keel of the boat did it's job and we were now on a direct course into the wake. We were still accelerating as I felt the bow bury itself into the wake. Then, like a slingshot the bow recovered and went into the air. We were a scant 75 feet from the cruiser when we left the water. I pulled the throttles back to avoid over-revving the engines as we flew through the air.

We had launched this 47-foot powerboat fifteen feet into the air at a hundred plus mph. I waited for the jarring crash as we hit the water. There was no jarring crash. The boat landed by the stern but nearly level and at the moment the boat made contact with the water I jammed the throttle forwards again. We looked back and saw the people on the cabin cruiser giving us a cheer. I gave Nad a high-five and knew right then that I didn't have to worry about Nads abilities to handle a boat. He knew what he was doing.

We were coming up to the south end of Lake Pepin and I pulled the throttle back until we were cruising at about sixty again. The river gets narrow and there are normally a lot of people fishing from their boats in the channel. We rounded the curve at Reeds Landing and sure enough the channel was full of fishing boats. I pulled the throttles back and let the boat slow. We came off plane quickly and I could see the fishing boats scramble to get out of our way.

Nad saw an opening and told me to throttle up again. I eased the throttles forward and we got back on plane quickly. I again held us at sixty mph. In a few minutes we would be in Wabasha, Minnesota. Wabasha's recent claim to fame was the filming of the movie Grumpy Old Men with Jack Lemon and Walter Mathieu.

We had thought about stopping but it was to early for lunch. We decided to wait until we got to Alma.

We hit the no wake buoys at Wabasha and I pulled the throttles back to idle. We had about a mile to travel at no wake. I pulled out my cell phone and called my friends Mike and Marie at the Burlington Hotel to tell them that we would be there soon and asked him if he would pick us up at the Alma City Dock. He said yes and would meet us there.

As we cleared the no wake buoys I throttled up and got us back up to sixty mph. We would be in Alma in a matter of minutes. I called ahead to Lock & Dam #4 and they said they had a southbound barge that would be exiting in about ten minutes. I pulled the throttles back to a speed that would put us at the Lock & Dam just about the time the north lock doors opened up.

Our timing couldn't have been better because we could see the doors opening as we rounded the bend in the Alma channel. I held our speed to 10 knots as we approached the locks. Nad switched the exhaust to silent running. The noise from the open exhaust can be deafening when you are in the locks and some of the Lock and Dam personnel take exception to boat with loud exhaust.

We slid up to the landside wall and we each grabbed a line hanging from the wall and held on while the Lockmaster drop the water. It was a short drop and we were underway in about 10 minutes. The south doors opened up and when the horn blew for us to clear the lock Nad eased the boat out of the lock. The Alma City Dock is a mere 100 yards from the south end of the lock. We could see Mike with his Nick standing on the dock.

We pulled up to the dock and I jumped out with dock lines in hand. I made the boat fast and Nad shut her down. I walked up to Mike and shook hands with him and said hi to Nick. Nad was out of the boat and I introduced him to Mike and Nick. We walked up the gangway and got into Mike's truck. The drive back to the Hotel was a short one.

Marie was standing behind the bar when we walked in and she was all smiles. Marie is the cook for the operation, and a damn good one at that. They had a fairly good size lunch crowd in the restaurant. Nad and I opted to sit at the bar t eat our lunch. I asked Marie what the lunch special was for the day. "Well Captain, she said. You can have anything your little heart desires for lunch but to answer your question, today's special is a half Corned Beef sandwich with a bowl of homemade chicken noodle soup." Marries homemade soup is to die for. I chose the lunch special and Nad ordered a Cheeseburger.

Mike sat down with us and brought me up to date on the latest happenings in Alma. Alma, with a population of about 700 residents, everyone knows everyone and everything they do. After Mike filled me in on the local gossip I asked him if knew Tammy the girl that I had met at Leo's Landing a few weeks ago. Mike looked at me and asked, "does she have red hair?" "Yes she does, I answered.

Mike smiled as he got up from his barstool and walked to the restaurant. In a minute he was back with his arm around Tammy. Tammy saw me and gave a little jump and walked quickly to where we were sitting. I had just barely cleared the barstool when she got to me. Her arms flew around my neck and she squeezed so hard I thought she was going to break my neck.

"Captain Art, she excitedly asked. What brings you to Alma? Are you here for a while or just passing through?" I told her we were just passing through on our way south, I then introduced her to Nad. She pouted her lips in a little girl way showing her disappointment that I was not staying longer. We talked a few minutes then Marie brought out our lunch. I asked Tammy if she was alone and she said she was with some folks from work. I told her I would be back through Alma in about a month and expected to see her when I got back.

She said okay and excused herself and walked back to the restaurant. Nad I busied ourselves with lunch. As usual lunch was excellent. Marie is a cook's cook. She puts her all into it and you can tell it when it's served. Always generous in portions and hot as it should be.

Chapter 42

We finished our lunch and paid the bill. After we gave our goodbyes to Marie I told Mike we were ready to go back to the boat. Back at the boat Nad got the engines running and he shook Mikes hand and then I gave Mike a big buddy hug, cast off our lines and jumped in the boat.

Nad eased the boat away from the dock. As we left the dock we both turned and waved good-bye to Mike. I eased the throttles forward as Nad switched the exhaust to the open position. The rumble of the engines could now be clearly heard. I held us 60 mph and we headed for Lock & Dam #5 only fifteen miles south of us.

In a matter of minutes we were at Lock & Dam #5. We had passed the southbound barge just south of Alma. I had called ahead and the locks were open and waiting for us. We entered he lock and the doors closed behind us. In a few minutes we were on our way again heading for Lock & Dam 5A.

We knew ahead of time that the Lock & Dams were going to slow us down. Our goal today was to make it to Dubuque, IA. which is approximately 155 nautical miles. The good thing was that the barge traffic was minimal and we could zip right through the Locks. The bad things were the Locks. We went through 5A, 6, and 7 with out delay. From Lock 7 to Lock 8 it is about 23 miles and from Lock 8 to Lock

9 it is around 31 miles. These two long stretches would help us make up time.

We hit mile marker 634 right at 4:00 pm in Prairie Duchien, Wisconsin. We had to more Locks to go through and 51 miles then we would be in Dubuque, IA. We decided to make a gas stop at McGregor Marina at mile marker 633.5 on the West channel. I called ahead to let them know we would be stopping for gas.

McGregor is a small historic river town of about 1,000 population. At one time it was the home of the Diamond Jo Steamboat Line, which ran a passenger service on the Upper Mississippi River.

We pulled up to the fuel docks at the marina and the dock crew was waiting for us. I got out of the boat and told the kids to fill it up. For some reason I couldn't wait to see how much gas we had used in 155 miles. It took nearly forty-five minutes to fill the tanks on Nads boat. with 392 gallons of gas to top it off. Doing some quick calculations I figured we got around 2.5 miles to the gallon. I made a mental note to never complain about the mileage I got in my truck.

We paid cash and gave the kids a nice tip and got back out on the river. The sun was starting to wane and neither of us wanted to travel in the dark. As soon as we could we opened her up and headed for Lock & Dam #10. It was a 19-mile stretch and we made good time. Once again I had called ahead and the Lock was open waiting for us. Once we cleared #10 it was a straight 32-mile shot to Dubuque, IA.

We pulled into Dubuque right at 6:30. I had already made a call to the Dubuque Marina, which is located about a half-mile below Lock & Dam #11. I told the girl that answered the phone that we wanted an overnight slip and that we would be getting underway first thing in the morning. She told me we could tie up at the fuel dock and she would be waiting for us to arrive.

We buzzed right through Lock & Dam 11 and headed for the Marina. The Marina is a short distance off the main channel. We could see the girl standing on the fuel dock as we approached. We pulled up to the dock and she helped tie the boat off. I asked her what the charge was going to be and she said if we would take her for a ride there would be no charge. I looked at Dan and I could tell he was going to veto her option. I smiled at her and told her that we had been traveling gall day and we wanted to have a good dinner and a few drinks then hit the hay. She looked at me with her eyelashes batting. I told her I was sorry but maybe the next time through we might be able to take her for a ride.

I asked her to top off the fuel then I would pay her in full for the slip and the fuel so we wouldn't have to wait for her in the morning. We had burned up almost 85 gallons of gas since our last fuel stop in Prairie Duchien. I could tell now that it was going to be an expensive trip to the Gulf just for gas alone but then… it was all being paid for and who was I to complain.

Chapter 43

With our fuel topped off we got cleaned up, which in boater terms that means we put on a clean shirt and some cologne and headed for the restaurant in the marina. The lounge in the restaurant had a good crowd for a Monday night. We sat at the bar and ordered drinks and the bartender told us that the crowd was 75% transient boaters.

We sat sipping our drinks while looking at the menu. We were both hungry and decided to sit at the bar to eat. I have learned over the years that if you don't mind sitting at the bar you can generally get better if not faster service than if you were to sit at a table.

There were three couples in a group occupying the other end of the bar down and they appeared to be already wired for a festive night. By their dress and demeanor I told Nad that I had an idea that they were on the other powerboats that we saw in the marina when we pulled in. It wasn't long before my observation was proven right. One of the guys from the group looked over at us and asked us where we were from and I told him Lake City, Minnesota. I don't know why I said that but it just came out that way. I looked at Nad and winked knowing that he had already caught on.

He asked us if we were transients and I told him yes! As the conversation developed we found out that they were also transients and they were running 35' Formula's and they were heading south. When I told the guy that we were talking to that we were in a 47'

Fountain I could see his eyes light up. He left his group and walked over to where Nad and I were sitting.

He introduced himself as "Sparky". Their group was from Lansing Iowa and they were headed to the Gulf for an early spring vacation. I let Nad answer all of the questions that Sparky was asking about his boat. I just sat back to observe Sparky and his group. I'm not sure why but there was a feeling about this group and that we would see more of these people. Maybe more than we wanted!

Sparky told us that they were waiting on a table for dinner and asked if we would like to join them. I gave Nad a quick glance and he ever so slightly nodded yes. I was beginning to wonder if Nad had the same feelings that I did about these people. We would soon find out!

Nad ordered a round for the group and they asked us to join them at their end of the bar. We grabbed our drinks and joined their group. Sparky gave the introductions and we shook hands with everyone. Only one of the couples was married and we found out that there was a couple on each of the three boats in their group. They all looked to be in their late twenties or early thirties and The topic of conversation dwelled on Nad's boat. The Formula's that this group had had twin 496 engines in them. Nad was enjoying telling them about his triple 800 engines in his boat. I could see their eyes raise when he told them that his boat would run well over a 100 mph. I already knew that on a good day, a 35' Formula with twin 496's could hit around eighty.

The bartender got our attention and told us that a table was ready for our group. We followed the hostess to our table and I ended up sitting next to Sparky. Everyone was intently looking at their menu. Nad was on the other side of the table engrossed in a conversation with two of the girls. Sparky and I were having a lively conversation about the "Pro's &

Con's" of high-powered boats. I had to tell him about Winkin', Blinkin', and Nod III which seemed to moderately impress him.

As we were talking I began to notice some things about Sparky that seemed to strengthen my feelings that I had earlier about the whole group. Outwardly, Sparky gave every indication of being a regular user of cocaine. One of the dead give always is the habit of continually sniffing ones nose as if they had a cold. As we talked I casually observed the others in the group and noticed to some degree that they were all sniffing their noses in varying degrees.

The waitress came and took our dinner orders and I asked her to bring us another round of drinks. I was about to excuse myself from the table to hit the head when Sparky beat me to it. We both stood up and I followed him the men's head. Sparky went into one of the stalls while I took care of business at one of the urinals.

Eureka! As I was standing at the urinal I heard the telltale noise of Sparky doing a line in the stall. I gave myself a quick mental pat on the back for my astute powers of observation.

As I was washing my hands Sparky came out of the stall wiping his nose and brushing at his upper lip. I debated about making a comment but decided to let it go for now. I knew I would have ample opportunity to pursue the matter at a later time. I walked out of the head leaving Sparky behind and went back to our table.

In a couple of minutes Sparky also came back to the table at sat down. Our fresh drinks had been delivered and I held my glass up for a salute to our newfound boating friends. I wanted to tell Nad what had happened in the head but I would have to wait for the right opportunity. I knew in my mind that these people were going to be an asset to Nad and myself. They were about to become unwitting informants.

Our dinner finally arrived and the conversation seemed to fall by the wayside. Everyone was more interested in eating than talking for the time being. I had ordered the "Surf & Turf" dinner and was eating it with gusto. After about ten minute's small isolated topics of conversation started popping up.

One of the group had suggested a party on the docks. I thought it was a great idea and as well a great way to get to know our new found friends. We finished dinner and went back to the bar for another drink and to get a plan of action going for our party. It was around 9:00 and I figured we could still get a few hours of partying in before calling it a night.

We finished our drinks and headed down to the marina. Sparky wanted a look at Nads boat so we stopped there first. While Nad was showing Sparky and the other guys around I got into the liquor cabinet and started asking what people wanted to drink.

Most everyone wanted a beer so that made it a little easier for me. I passed out the beers and we went back topside. The girls were sitting in the bolsters and admiring Nads boat. I sat on the stern seat and enjoyed the view. After a while Nad and the others came up from below. Sparky was in awe of Nads boat.

The marina had a little patio with deck chairs so we all went to the patio and sat down and started telling sea stories. I had put all beers that we had a cooler brought them up with us. One of the other guys went to his boat and brought out a cooler full of beer so it looked like we were set as far as beer goes.

We finally got around to talking about the trip south and why everyone was going down to the gulf. Sparky asked Nad first and Nad told him we were on a joy ride and had no particular reason for going down other than to have some fun. I thought that was a good response and kept my mouth shut.

Sparky's group was going down also for fun and hoped to make a little money while he was down there. He was somewhat vague about it so I didn't pursue it. We told them that we were heading out first thing in the morning. They had also planned on leaving in the morning and Sparky asked if we wanted to go down together.

I looked at Nad and he shrugged his shoulders and said, "why not". I told them that we were going to running hot because we wanted to be in the Gulf by next Tuesday. They all said that was fine with them but for us not to wait on them if we really got up to speed.

Nad went down to the boat to get the charts so we could show them what we had mapped out for the trip. If nothing else, should we get separated we could always hookup at the marinas that we had planned on stopping at. We showed them where we would stopping for fuel and meals. They took notes and said it all looked fine to them.

I still hadn't had a chance to talk to Nad about what had taken place in the restaurant head. I figured it could wait until we got back on the boat by ourselves. It was a nice evening with the temperature around the low 50's. Around midnight we ran out of beer and decided to call it a night. We said good night to all and told them we would be up and about around 6:00 in the morning. We could have coffee and donuts then get underway. They agreed and we all went our separate ways.

When Nad and I got on the boat and were down in the cabin with the door shut I told him what had happened in the restaurant head. He looked at me in a surprised way. "Are you sure" he asked? "I am reasonably sure that he was doing a line of coke from the sounds that were coming from the stall" I replied.

I could see that Nad was thinking and he said, "wouldn't it be ironic if we all ended up in the same place?" I thought about what he had just said. Ironic would be one word that I would have used amongst others. The chances that we had run into a pack of "Mules" heading to the Gulf to make a pickup were a million-toone. I wasn't going to start making book at this time.

If they were still around in a couple of days we would probably know more. Nad and I agreed not to tell them that we were heading to Biloxi when we got to the Gulf. We called in a night and hit the bunks. Tomorrow was going to be another day.

Chapter 44

Nad and I were up and in the marina showers at 5:30. We put the coffee on before we went to the showers. As we walked back to the boat I could smell the coffee brewing. I'm glad I had the foresight to bring a pound of Blue Mountain along with us. We poured ourselves some coffee and went up to the patio.

Right at 6:00 Sparky's group started getting off their boats and heading for the showers. By 6:30 we were all sitting in the patio drinking coffee and eating donuts, Bagels, and English Muffins. We went over our plans for the days run. We were now at mile marker 582. Our goal for the day was to be at Adams Landing in Quincy, IL by nightfall. Quincy was at mile marker 327.2. That would be a run of about 255 miles.

We had ten Lock & Dams to go through. With the exception of Lock & Dam #14 to #15, all of the runs between Locks were around 30 miles. The run between 14 and 15 was about ten miles. If we were running the 255 miles without Locks and averaged 70 mph it would take us around 10-11 hours. With ten Lock & Dams to go through I was calculating our travel time to be around 1213 hours. That would allow us one fuel stop and put us at Adams Landing around eight that evening.

Everyone was ready to get underway and we headed for our respective boats and fired them up. All of a sudden the marina was filled with the rumbling crescendo of nine high-performance engines warming up. Sweet music to my ears.

At 7:30 we were all pulling out of the marina. Our first leg was a twenty-six mile run and as soon as we cleared the No Wake Buoys we throttled up. Nad was driving and I was the throttle man. We had our headsets on and Nad told me to get us up to 70 mph.

I didn't need to be told twice. I eased the throttles forward and the engines responded with their deep-throated roar. In a matter of seconds we were running at our desired speed. I looked back at the other boats and they were all in line behind us. We had agreed before we left the dock to monitor channel 72 on the VHF radio in case anyone had problems.

In twenty-five minutes we were looking at Lock & Dam #12. I had called ahead to let them know there were four powerboats coming their way. They gave us a favorable report on the barge traffic. We would not hit any barge traffic until we got down to Lock & Dam #17. That was good news for all of us. Lock & Dam #12 is normally an eight-foot drop but with the high spring waters it was only a two-foot drop and we were out of the lock in ten minutes.

I did some quick calculations and told Nad that we might have to run at 75 mph on a couple of the legs. He agreed and I called the other boats and gave them my thoughts and asked them if they would have any problems at 75 mph. All of them gave the go ahead. This run would be a thirty-three mile run and if we ran at 75mph we could cover it in less than 30 minutes. I eased the throttles forward and held them at 75 mph.

The boats running behind us had it pretty easy. They were all following in our wake, one behind the other. The advantage there is if we hit any other boat wakes our boat would flatten them out and the boats behind us would basically have smooth water to run on. The only exception being if we hit the wake of a larger boat then we would all have to slow down somewhat. At 47' we could hit larger wakes with less problems than the smaller 35' boats behind us. Because we were traveling mid-week we did not anticipate coming across many larger boats.

Once again the Lock was waiting for us. The Lockmaster from #12 had radioed ahead for us to tell them that we were coming and he said he would contact all of the locks to give them a heads up.

Lock #13 is normally an eleven-foot drop. Again, because of high spring waters that drop was reduced to a five-foot drop. We were out and underway again in less than fifteen minutes.

Things were looking good! We had a thirty-mile run to Lock & Dam #13 and we did it in about twenty-five minutes even. The rest of the lock through were pretty much the same. At Lock # 16 we were told that #17 had a barge in it for a northbound lock through. I told the group that we would keep the next run at 75 mph and we could stop at the Mississippi River Gas Dock at mile marker 455.4 and gas up while we were waiting for the barge to lock through.

Everyone was in agreeance and headed for our first fuel stop of the day. Right after we got up to speed coming out of Lock # 16 a couple of guys in a Ranger fishing boat came up beside Nads boat. They were smiling from ear-to-ear running with us at 75 mph. I could see their boat number on the bow and they were from Iowa. The driver of the boat was indicating to us that he wanted to race.

I held my finger up to the driver to indicate to him to wait a minute while I talked with Nad.

Nad was all for it! I called the other boats to tell them what was going on. They all laughed and I told them to be careful because the little fishing boat might get tossed out of the water. We were ready. I looked over to the fishing boat and signaled for the driver to give it his best. He had a 300-horse motor on the back of his boat with a Sea & Land Jack Plate. The motors sounded as if it had been tweaked a little bit but I couldn't see him getting over 90 mph with his boat.

I watch as the driver slammed his throttle forward and his boat eased ahead of us rather quickly. I waited until he was about a hundred feet in front of us and put our throttles to the wall. Nad yelled at me to hold on because he was going to arm his NOS system. NOS or Nitrous Oxide would momentarily increase our horsepower by 50%.

Nad headed our boat for the far right side of the channel. He knew that if we passed to close to the smaller fishing boat we would easily swamp him or cause him to lose control. I was ready and looked at Nad and he hit the NOS button.

There was a sudden roar and I could feel myself being thrown into the back of the bolster. The effect was like a slingshot. We passed the fishing boat like he was standing still. I looked at the speedometer and the needle was sitting on one hundred and forty miles per hour. We literally blew the doors off that guy. We could see him turning to the left to get out of the way of the other boats behind us. I looked at Nad and said, "I.O.W.A. Idiots Out Walking Around". We both laughed.

I brought the boat back down to 75 mph and I could hear all of the chattering from the group behind us. Sparky said he thought his boat had stopped because we had pulled away so fast. Everyone got a good laugh from it. I wonder if the guy in the fishing boat will tell his buddies about the race.

We pulled up to the Mississippi River Gas Dock a little earlier than we had planned due to the impromptu race. The dock crew tied us up and I told them the three boats behind us were coming in for gas also. We took on 135 gallons of gas. It was more than we anticipated but then it was worth the added expense.

We were all filled up and got right back on the river. We had a bout a twenty-mile run to Lock & Dam #17. I called the Lockmaster at # 17 and asked him how long it would be before the barge was locked through. He said the barge would be out of the lock in twenty minutes.

My calculations told me if we ran at 65 mph we would be there in about 18 minutes. I set the throttles at sixty-five mph.

We pulled up to the lock just as the barge was coming out. Our timing couldn't have been better. Once we got the green light we entered the lock. Lock #17 was a real short drop, maybe a foot if that. While we were locking through I yelled at the others to ask if they wanted to stop for lunch anytime soon. They said yes and I told them we would stop at North Pier Marina & Mr. Stiffy's Beach Club for lunch at mile marker 415.2.

The marina was right on the channel and we could tie up right at the restaurant. We locked through in less than ten minutes and we got right back up to 75 mph. Within fifteen minutes we were looking at Mr. Stiffy's Beach Club. In 30 minutes we were sitting at the bar having a drink and waiting on our lunch.

We finished our lunch and walked back down to the boats. The girls in Sparky's group wanted to know if they could ride with us the rest of the way. I had no problem with that nor did Nad. I looked at Sparky and he looked a little miffed. I told him to relax and he nothing to worry about. Hell, what can you do at 75 mph anyway?

We were only five miles from #18 and it was clear and waiting for us. We all got in the lock and one of the girls in the back grabbed the aft hand line and I grabbed the forward one. As we were waiting for the water to drop I suddenly heard a bunch of shouting and wolf whistling. I turned around and all three of the girls had taken their tops off and were flaunting their assets to the boys behind us. The Lock & Dam crew was getting a good view, notwithstanding Nad and myself.

The down river doors were starting to open and I told the girls they had better get their tops back on before we cleared the lock. The three of them turned around to face us and gave Nad and me a good look before they put their tops back on. The signal sounded for us to exit the lock and we shoved off. I knew these guys in the lock would remember us.

We had a 45-mile run to Lock & Dam #19 and 19 would also be a long lock through. IN normal water it is a 38' drop. It would probably take us about a half-hour to lock through. I got on the radio and told the group that lock #19 was in Keokuk, Iowa and it was there is a United States Coast Guard Station there. I told them that it would be wise if we went through there with our exhaust in the silent mode. I also told the girls that there would be no flashing at #19.

This leg was going to take us a good thirty-five minutes to run at 75 mph. I decide to wait until we were in lock #19 before calling Adams Landing to let them know that we needed overnight dockage for four boats. We cleared the lock and I set the pace again at 75 mph.

As anticipated lock #19 was waiting for us. We pulled into the lock and while we were waiting one of the lock guys told us they had heard about the girl's escapade in #18. I played dumb because I knew what he was hinting at. He wanted a cheap shot for himself. I smiled at him and said to myself, "no chance buddy".

Unlike most locks, #19 has what they call floating mooring bits that move up and down with the water level. If you had to hold on to a line for a half-hour you would get darn tired. In #19 you can tie off your lines and sit back and relax. It was about 3:30 when we pulled out of #19. We were actually ahead of schedule as far as time. I redid my calculations and it looked like we were going to make it to Adams Landing around 6:00. I got out the cell phone and gave them a call. They said they would be looking for us around 6:00.

The run to Lock & Dam #20 was just over 20 miles. We were there in short order but had to wait for a northbound lock through. There were five pleasure boats in the lock that were heading north. We had about a fifteen-minute wait before we could get into the lock.

Once clear of the lock we only had a 16 mile run to Adams Landing. Adams Landing in just off the river channel at the mouth of harbor. Quincy Bay as it is called is a natural harbor and is the largest on the

Upper Mississippi River. The approach to Quincy Bay is done from down river. If you try to approach the Bay from up river you stand a chance of grounding your boat in the shallows off Quinsippi Island.

We pulled up to Adams Landing at 6:45. They called on the radio and told us to tie up at the restaurant. We drew quite a crowd as we pulled up to the restaurant dock. We got the boats tied up for the night and everyone headed for the showers. By the looks of the crowd that we drew, it was going to be a fun night.

Chapter 45

After our showers we went up to the restaurant for something to eat. "Happy Hour" was in full swing. The was packed with locals and transient boaters. I could hear talk about our boats. A lot of emphasis was on Nad's boat. We found some seats at the bar, ordered drinks and told the bartender that we wanted to eat diner at the bar. He got some menus for us and told us what the nightly special was.

After our third round of drinks we ordered dinner. Dinner was good and the portions were ample. When I was done I ordered a Windsor-7 with a squeeze of lime and started a conversation with the young lady sitting next to me. Her name was Mindy. She was about 30 something and had long shiny black hair, which contrasted her green eyes. She had full pouty lips and a nice figure. I was already thinking about later!

Nad interrupted our conversation saying that he was taking some people down to his boat to give them a little tour. I responded with a nod and told him I might bring Mindy down later if she wanted to party with us. I was looking at Mindy when I said that and her expression made it clear that she was into a party.

I ordered us another round of drinks and asked Mindy directly if she wanted to go down to the boat and party with us. She said yes and I said when we were done with our drinks we could go down. It didn't take her long to finish her drink and we headed for the boat. The rest of the gang was already down on the dock and a party was in full swing.

I got Mindy and I a drink and I grabbed a couple of deck chairs for to sit in. I asked her if she was going to be warm enough and she said she was fine for the moment. I told her if she got cold to let me know and I would get her something warm to put on. Nad had turned on his stereo and the music was rocking the dock. It didn't take long for other boaters to join the party. In about a halfhour we had about forty or fifty people on the dock.

A few of the other boaters had come over to our dock in their dinghies and someone suggested a dinghy race using oars only. There were five dinghies and teams of two were selected. We set some fenders in the water about a 100' apart to mark the course. The first heat of five dinghies took about 4 minutes to complete. Anyone can run a dinghy with a motor on it but when you have to row it, that's a different story.

No one could go in a straight line. It was even harder when the person rowing was laughing so hard that he couldn't control the boat. The races went on until they were down to the final elimination race. There were 3 boats in the race and Nad was in one of the boats. Someone yelled go and they started rowing. Mindy and I cheered Nad and his partner on for all we were worth.

Nad had good lead on the other two boat then he lost one of his oars. By the time he had retrieved his lost oar the race was over. A local couple ended up winning the race. Fun was had by all. It didn't take long for people to start thinking what to do next. Someone suggested a drinking game and everyone was for it.

The game "Fuzzy Duck" was selected. To play this game someone kicks off by saying "fuzzy duck" to the person on their left. That person repeats the phrase and the process continues clockwise around the table until someone decides to say "Does he?". Now the direction of play is reversed and the phrase changed to "ducky fuzz". This continues around the table until someone says "Does he?" again, whereupon the direction changes and the phrase reverts to "fuzzy duck". The point of the game is to say "Fuzzy Duck" very fast. Anyone who pauses or gets the phrase wrong must drink the pre-determined quantity of beer or a shot. If anyone says "Does he?" twice in a row they incur the maximum fine and drink a double shot. There's nothing worse than a drinking game cheat.

The object of the game of course is to be the last one left in the game.

I went to the boat and got a bottle of Wild Turkey to use as the penalty shot drink. It is a 101 proof and will put the unwary down real fast. There was about 20 people playing the game. I opted out because I really don't get into drinking games were large amounts of booze are being consumed as part of the game. In about two hours the players were down to the last five. The longer they played the drunker they got. It was really getting funny to watch them. Within minutes two more were eliminated and the last three were definitely drunk.

It didn't take long for the game to end after that. One of the three said "he does" twice in a row and he couldn't handle the double shot of Wild Turkey. The final person out said the forbidden "Does he fuck" and the game was over. I said goodbye to Mindy on the dock and headed for bed.

Tomorrow was going to be a long one and I was ready for anything.

Chapter 46

Why does morning come so fast? I felt like I had just laid my head down on the pillow and the alarm went off. It was 7:30 and I just wanted to lay my head back down. Begrudgingly I got up and put some coffee on then grabbed my shower bag and headed for the shower. Nad was still sounding asleep so I tried to be as quite as I could.

The hot water from shower felt good. I stood under the water for about five minutes letting the water take the tension out of my body. When I got back to the boat, Nad was up and drinking coffee. I poured myself a cup and sat down at the dinette. "Nad, what happened to you last night", I asked? "I guess I had too much to drink to fast and I hit the bunk early", he replied. I told him about the "Fuzzy Duck" game and he laughed saying he wished he had stayed up to watch it.

I pulled out the charts to go over our trip for the day. We had about 327 miles to travel before we got the Ohio River and five locks to go through. Our plans were to make it to Kimmswick, Mo., which was about 150 miles down river. We had called Kimmswick Marine Service and made reservations the day before. The further south you get the warmer it gets. Warmer weather means more boats on the river and you need to make reservations ahead of time or you may end up anchoring out in the channel.

Nad went up to take a shower and I got the boat ready to go. Our fellow boaters were now out of bed with most of them heading the showers too. I saw Sparky and told him what our plans were for the day. He casually agreed and said they would be ready to go in about 30 minutes. By the time Nad got back from the shower we were ready to go. We waited until Sparky's group was ready then we started the engines to get them warmed up. It was a nice morning. The temperature was right at 51 degrees and the Marine Weather Radio was calling for a high in the mid 70's today. You could not ask for anything better. I heard the other boats fire up so I started up our engines. Within minutes we were back on the river. We made a quick run to Lock & Dam #21 in Quincy, IL just 3 miles down river. We were through in record time.

We had about 22 miles to travel to Lock & Dam #22 and we decided to make it a quick 22 miles. Nad was working the throttles and once we cleared the Dam wall he eased the throttles forward until we were showing 75 MPH on the speedometer. The water was calm and there was little or no wind. We did not have any traffic to worry about. I took a quick look behind and saw the other boat following up behind us.

In less than 20 minutes, we were looking at Lock & Dam #22. I called the Lock Master on channel 14 and he said we would have about a 15-minute wait before we could get a southbound lock through. I killed two of the engines and we just idled around above the locks until it was time to lock through. Lock & Dam #22 is in Hannibal, MO., home of Mark Twain. I kind of wished we had made plans to stop for a while to look around.

As if it were scripted for a movie, the upper lock gates started opening in about 15 minutes. I started up the other two engines and we headed for the lock. As we were in high waters, the drop was only about a foot. Again, we were in and out in a matter of minutes.

This next leg was going to be another short one like the one we had just gone through. It was another 22 miles to Lock & Dam #24 and once again we were there in and out in just under 20 minutes. While we were locking through Nad got on the radio to the other boats to ask them about their fuel. I was thinking and hoping they could make it to North River Road Marina at mile marker 257.7, which was just over 33 miles down river. Sparky's group said they had no problem with that but they would not be able to run fast. Nad told them we were going to make a run for it and we would meet them at North River Road Marina. Once we cleared the lock wall Nad pushed the throttles up until we were running at 100

MPH. I just love his boat at high speed. At a 100 MPH his boat feels better than a smaller boat doing 30 MPH.

We had to back off the throttles twice for some smaller pleasure craft but made the 22 miles in just under 30 minutes. At mile marker 257.7 we made our turn into the channel going to the North River Road Marina. Nad called the Marina to let them know that we were coming in for fuel and there would be four boats behind us.

They were waiting for us at the fuel dock. As we eased up to the dock and they grabbed our lines and tied us up. We were already fueled up by the time "Sparky's" group arrived. It took another hour to get all of the other boats fueled up. Everyone made a quick head call and we were on our way again.

Back out on the river we held the speed down to a modest 60MPH. It was a 16-mile run to Lock & Dam #25 and the lock was open and waiting for us when we got there. It was getting close to noon and we all agreed to stop at the Port of Winfield for lunch. I called the Port on the marine radio to let them know that there were five boats coming in and they said they would shuttle us to town for lunch. In less than an hour we were sitting in a cafe having lunch and talking about the days travels. The Port of Winfield is at mile marker 240.2 just below Lock & Dam #25 right on the channel. They are open year around and provide a shuttle service to boaters in to town.

After lunch we caught the shuttle back to the marina and reviewed our charts. We had about 90 miles to go to reach Kimmswick Marine Service dock and only two Lock & Dams to go through. The Melvin Price Lock & Dam #26 was about 40 miles down river and running at 60 MPH we could be there in about 40 minutes or so unless we ran into heavy river traffic.

In 45 minutes we were at the Melvin Price Lock & Dam. We had to wait about 20 minutes for a northbound lock through then they took us right in. The Price Lock & Dam is a 23' drop at normal water. The lock through took us about a half-hour. During the middle of the season waiting for a lock through in this area can take hours. The towboat traffic can be very heavy at times. About 5 miles below the Melvin Price lock is the confluence of the Missouri and Mississippi rivers. At this point the river becomes very turbulent from the currents of both rivers.

At mile marker 194.1 we hit the upper entrance to the Chain of Rocks Canal and 9 miles down river we came to the Chain of Rocks Lock & Dam #27. As luck would have it they were waiting for us to enter the lock. In under 30 minutes were on our way for the final 30 + mile leg.

Nad called the Kimmswick Marine Service dock on the cell phone to let them know that we were in the area. He told them we anticipated to arrive at the marina around 6:00 PM. I radioed the other boats and told them the marina had been alerted to our arrival and asked them how fast they wanted to travel. Sparky said 70 MPH should be okay for all. I reminded everyone that the barge traffic could be heavy but we would try to keep our speed around 70. I asked everyone to space out in case we had to make sudden maneuvers.

A 70-MPH run to the marina was not a dream. No sooner than we got up to speed we had to back out of the throttles. The traffic just kept getting worse. It took nearly two and half-hours to get to the marina. The dock crew was waiting for us and we all got tied up and secured for the evening. It was 7:00 pm and we all headed for the showers.

We met back down at the boats for a couple of cocktails and then headed up to the restaurant. It was a balmy evening and there were several people out on the lounge deck so we decided to sit out there. Our server came out and took our drink orders and had them back in a flash.

The marina Dock Master came by and talked with us for a while and I told him that we would be topping off our fuel tanks in the morning. He said he would be down bright and early to accommodate us. I ordered another round and included Brian, the Dock Master. As long as Brian was there I asked him if there was any excitement in town. He told us that there was a new stripper bar in town and the dancers were pretty sharp. I looked at the others and asked, "does anyone feel like going to a strip club after dinner?" Surprisingly it was the women that said something first. They wanted to go even if their men did not.

I do not like stepping in someone else's territory but these people had better think twice about letting their women go to a strip club with me. No one else said anything so I let the subject drop.........but only for a while.

We had a nice dinner and a couple of after dinner drinks. I brought up the subject of the Stripper Club again. As luck would have it just the women wanted to go. Nad was tired and the other guys wanted to service their boats. Okay..............fine with me. Four nice looking women and myself going to a strip club. This could prove to be an eventful evening for the five of us. It was only two blocks to town from the marina and the strip club was already jumping by the time we had arrived.

As luck would have it, it was amateur night The luck of course was on my side. I was thinking it would not take to much goading to get these girls up on stage. We found a table just off the right side of the stage against the wall in dimly lit area. A waitress dressed in a sexy teddy took our drink order. No one was dancing at the time so we able to have some idle chat. I figured I would start the ball rolling and see who

I could convince to get up on stage first. I reminded the ladies that first prize was $500.00. It was two of the ladies that had the most assets that jumped up to the plate.

The scantly clad waitress came by and I asked her what the ladies had to do to get in the contest. She handed me a couple of entry blanks and a pen, which I in turn gave to the Libby & Sue. Both of these girls, taking a guess, would each fill a 38-40 D-E bra. Both had real nice figures and they liked to get trashy. The girls filled out the entry forms and we gave them back to the waitress. She told us the contest would start in about 30 minutes. I ordered another round of drinks and started motivating the girls. They really did not need to be motivated. They were actually chomping at the bit to get started.

The DJ made an announcement that amateur night was about to begin. He introduced the first girl who should have stayed at home. Some people have no pride at all. This chick out weighed me by a 100 pounds and if one of her breast got loose it would have broken her jaw. There was a lot of cheering from one guy in the audience, probably her boyfriend or husband.

There were three more girls that got up and did their routine. One of the three was somewhat nice looking. Then the DJ called out Libby's name. We all stood up and gave her a big cheer as she walked up on stage. She got the attention of everyone in the club. The place actually went silent for a moment. Libby started dancing to the music. She started out with slow seductive movements sort of enticing the crowd of men that were there. She was wearing some very tight shorts and a tank top. She had long brown hair, a very pleasant face, very nice breasts, and an absolutely wonderful ass.

She slowly pulled off her top, which of course brought round of cheers. Dollar bills were already flying thought the air. Libby was by far the best dancer of the night………..so far. She slid the zipper down on her shorts and the crowd went wild. Even the ladies left at our table were getting excited. Libby slid out of her shorts revealing a bright red thong. At that point I was content. Even if she decides not to go any further I would have not complained at all. She was a very sexy woman. Libby was not anywhere near done. She was just getting started.

After a couple of minutes she released her bra and pandemonium set in. I saw $5 and $10 bills flying onto the stage. Libby's 38's showed no appearance of being ready to sag. They were real and they were proud. They just stood out there like troopers. The crowd started yelling started yelling, "show skin to win, show skin to win. "After a couple minutes she pulled down her thong and I thought the roof was going to cave in.

Everyone was on their feet and yelling at the top of their lungs. Libby had a custom trim in the mons area. It was trimmed in the shape of a heart and very short. We could tell that she was really getting into it. If I were to hazard a guess I would say that she already had over a $100 in tips laying on the stage. After a few minutes the music stopped and Libby slowly bent to retrieve her tips and clothes. She went back stage to dress and after a couple of minutes she came and rejoined our group. Sue and Libby counted up her tips and found out that she had made over a $125 in tips.

Three more girls got up and did their routine but could not come anywhere close to getting the response that Libby got. Sue's name was then called and she decided to back out of the contest. She said she didn't want to give Libby and competition. The crowd was a little displeased but what could they do. The DJ got all of the girls that had danced back up on the stage and stood behind them one at a time and asked for crowd response as to who the winner would be.

There was absolutely no contest. Libby won hands down. The DJ handed her five crisp $100 bills and asked her if she wanted to do another dance. What a lady........she was game. Once again she brought the house down and made another $100 in tips. Not a bad evening for her with over $300 in tips and prize money. We had another round drinks, compliments of the DJ. He came over and asked Libby if she was professional dancer and she answered no. He asked her if she wanted a job dancing at the club to which she also responded no.

We left the club and headed back to the boats at the marina. When we got back we could see the rest of the gang were still in the bar. We walked in and Libby went straight to her boy friend and told him what had happened at the club. He acted surprised that Libby would do something like that but I could tell he was really sorry that he missed it. After the gang had heard the whole story we settled down for some serious drinking. Boater Style.

I don't know where the time went but all of a sudden the bartender was yelling last call. Someone yelled out, "Party on the docks." That's all it took. Within 10 minutes the bar was empty and a party was going full fledged on the docks. I scoped in a buxom young lass that looked to be in her mid-twenties. I walked over and introduced myself. Her name was Kitty. I resisted the temptation to make a comment about her name. She had long blonde hair and stood about 5'8". She was a local and lived about 10 minutes from the marina. We made small talk and I got her a drink. She was a very cuddly sort of girl. She had no problem getting right up next to me and holding her breasts against my arm.

I asked if she had a boy friend and she replied no. I was still in good enough condition to take on a woman so I put the clamps on her. When the timing was right I asked her if she had plans on going home or if she was going to stay at the marina for the night. "Captain, she asked, are you putting the make on me." Like George Washington I could not tell a lie. "Yes I am,' I responded. She looked at me with her big brown eyes and asked if I would rather go to her place instead of staying on the boat. I thought that was an excellent idea and we put our plan into action.

I found Nad and told him what was going down. He kinda chuckled and something about a wheel getting greased. I didn't pay much attention but instead got on the boat and went below to grabs some things. I brought the things up and set them down on the back seat of the boat. Kitty was standing beside the boat and ask for a quick tour. I helped her aboard and took her below. She was obviously impressed and asked some intelligent questions about the boat. She chided that we were going to have a lot more room at her place later than we would on the boat. I was looking forward to it.

Chapter 47

I remember an old saying that I had heard a couple of times. "Give Me Head Until I'm Dead." I think I was about to find out the true meaning of that saying. When Kitty and I left the marina for the parking where her car was she came right out and asked, "Captain do you like oral sex?" I wasn't sure how to reply to her question. I mean, a not so recent President claimed that he did not have sex with his female Page. So maybe getting head is not sex, at least by his standards. I answered Kitty the only way that I could. That I did like oral sex, both giving and receiving. That seemed to set the mood for the rest of our time together. Viva la France!

Kitty dropped me off first thing in the morning. The docks were empty and it didn't appear that anyone was moving around on the boats. I walked down the dock to Nad's boat and climbed aboard. I climbed down below and found Nad curled up on the floor. Guess maybe that is as far as he made it last night.

I needed some coffee and I tried to be as quiet as possible. It didn't work. Nad woke up with a startled look on his face. I could plainly see that he was trying to figure out how he got on the floor. I laughed at him and asked him if he remembers anything from last night. He did not. Now that he was awake I busied myself with making some coffee. I knew Nad could use some.

I poured me a cup and went topside. A few people were starting to move about the docks. Sparky's head popped out of his forward hatch. I yelled good morning to him but he didn't seem to be in much better condition than Nad. He looked at me feebly, nodded his head and disappeared below.

I was ready for anther cup of coffee. I went below and Nad had climbed up to his bed and was already back asleep. I was thinking that we were going to get a late start based what had I had already seen this morning. I went back up on the dock and started walking around. Libby stuck her head out and saw me and waved. She asked me to wait so she get some coffee and join me. She was out in a flash with coffee in hand. We walked out towards the river to the end of the dock.

It was a start of a beautiful morning. Libby asked me how I enjoy my night with Kitty. I told that I enjoyed it without going into any detail. She seemed to be hedging for more information. When she realized that I was not going to give her any details she changed the subject. "What are the plans for the day," she asked. "Well Libby, I said, We will probably be getting started a little late this morning.

It appears some of you folks burned a little mid-night oil last night." I explained to here that we had one more fuel stop before hitting the Ohio River. "We will be stopping in Cape Girardeau at the River City Fuels Docks, I explained. It is just over 100 miles from here and it is the last fuel stop before hitting the Ohio River."

Actually after Cape Girardeau we had 51.9 miles to travel to the confluence of the Mississippi and Ohio Rivers. After we got on the Ohio River we had to take it slow. Spring floods on the Ohio brings literally thousands of deadheads out onto the river. In addition, we had to travel another 50 miles before we would be able to get any gas. That would be in Paducah, KY at the Ogden Landing Marina. If luck went our way we could make the Kentucky lock on the Tennessee River before night fall The Dam Kentucky Marina was right on the other side of the lock.

Heads were starting to appear up and down the docks. There were some sad looking faces poking out of the hatches of the boats. It seems I might have missed a nice party last night...........Well, only maybe! I yelled to those that were present for everyone to meet up at the restaurant so we could discuss the day's events. Nad stuck his head out the front hatch and told me to quit yelling. Yep! It was going to be a slow start this morning.

It was after nine before everyone was up and showered. By 9:30 everyone was in the restaurant. I had the charts on the table and once everyone had coffee I started laying out the plans of the day. I told them the same that I told Libby. If we got out of here soon enough we might make Kentucky Lake by nightfall. I explain the fuel situation and what to expect once we got on the Ohio River. I told them that we had about 107 miles to Cape Girardeau for fuel then another 90 + miles to Paducah, KY for fuel and then about another 25 miles to the Kentucky Lock & Dam. It was to make for a long day. Looking at this crowd I just couldn't see us doing 200 + miles today. I suggested that we make it to Paducah and spend the night there. That in itself would be a good day's travel. Everyone seemed to be in agreeance.

We finished up breakfast and headed down to the docks to get the boats ready to head out. Between last night and this morning, Brian the Dock Master had gotten all of the boats refueled. I'm not sure how he did it but he got it done. All of our boats were ready and Nad gave the high sign for everyone to fire up their engines. With in seconds nine fireballs were fired up and running. From Kimmswick we had a straight run for Cape Girardeau. About 57 miles and the river was wide open at this point and we were done with the Lock & Dams on the Mississippi River.

We were the last to pull away from the dock. We fell in behind the rest of the group and let Sparky take the lead. Sparky set a moderate pace at around 60 mph. Nad and I thought that was a good speed. As long as we didn't run into any heavy traffic we would be alright.

I called ahead to The River City Fuel Docks. They have sort of a unique situation in that their dock is just big enough for one boat. This is a fuel stop only. There are no marinas in this area. In fact once you leave Kimmswick there are no marinas until you hit Paducah, KY. I was calculating with five boats it would take around two hours to get us all refueled.

We pulled up to the fuel dock in Cape Girardeau an hour and a half later. I saw Pat the fuel attendant waiting on the dock for us. Sparky called on the radio wanting to know what to do. I told him just pull up to the dock and Pat would take care of everything. It took us just over two hours to get all the boats refueled.

While we were waiting to get fueled Nad and I were looking at the charts. I was showing Nad a spot about 35 miles down river that was one of the more dangerous spots on the river. From around mile marker 19.8 to about mile marker 10.8 this area is loaded with whirlpools. I remember only hearing stories about these whirlpools and until one year when I was bringing up a Houseboat from Kentucky for Fun'N The Sun. Right at mile marker 14.1 the boat, for no reason at all started spinning. I was running around 9 mph and before I could do anything the boat was doing 360's in the middle of the river.

The houseboat that we were on was a new 58' Thoroughbred with an 18' beam. The current or whirlpool in this case just grabbed the boat and there was nothing at the moment that I could do. After about the third spin I grabbed the wheel and started edging the boat towards the outside of the whirlpool and at the same time slowly increasing my power. It's very similar to swimming against a rip tide. Eventually I got out of the whirlpool.

The conditions have to be just right. The right depth of water and the right amount of current. The worst was around Island 29 or from mile marker 14.1 down to 12.2. I asked Nad if we should tell the rest of the boats about this area or just let them find out on their own. He kinda shrugged his shoulders as if to say, let them find out on their own.

Nad and I had just passed mile marker 16.2 and we were looking down stream at the boats ahead of us. They were a half mile ahead of us. We would be able to see if any of the boats got caught in a whirlpool. Unfortunately.......no whirlpools. There were some smaller ones but they did not really affect the control of the boats.

We were still running around 60 mph and had just a few minutes before we hit the confluence. I radioed to the other boats to remind them that we were going to slow down and group up at the CairoMississippi Bridge.

Chapter 48

We made our final turn of the Upper Mississippi River at Mile Marker 3.8, Greenfield Bend. As we came out of the turn we could see Cairo-Mississippi River Bridge, a half-mile ahead. We could see the other boats slowing down. Nad started pulling our throttles back and we began to slow down.

We all gathered under the bridge to go over some details prior to turning up the Ohio River just a mile ahead. I had listened to the Army Corps flow broadcast earlier. We were going to be bucking a nine mph current one we made out turn. I made a quick remark to be on the alert for deadheads floating in the water.

The current had swept us down river right to the confluence. We all got fired up Nad and I took the lead. We could now see the different colors of the two rivers. The Mississippi River actually appeared to blue in contrast to the water of the Ohio River. Because of the flow of the Ohio River and recent rains the Ohio was a very muddy brown color.

We all made the turn onto the Ohio River and right away we could feel the effect of the current. There was a lot of trash and wood floating in the water. I let Nad do the driving and I worked the throttles. Mt eyes were a little better than his and the last thing I wanted to do was hit a deadhead. We were just barely on plane and it really sounded like the motors were laboring.

We had 46 miles to go to the next fuel stop in Paducah, KY at Ogden Landing. We would be lucky to make this leg in two hours. At Mile Marker 964.5 we saw the construction project for the new Olmstead Locks. When that project is finished Lock & Dam 53/52 will be shut. Because of the high water we wouldn't have to go through Lock 53 & 52. That would save us some time.

We pulled up the Ogden Road Marina almost three hours to the minute from when we left Cape Girardeau. The marina being right on the river they had a long enough fuel dock to accommodate all five boats.

While we were filling up Nad and I got into a conversation about our new fellow boaters. I mentioned that I had only seen a couple of instances were they were using drugs. I was questioning Nad as too maybe we were barking up the wrong tree by hanging with these guys. Maybe they were just heading down to the Gulf for a vacation. Before any of them came up to our boat we had put a plan of action together.

All of the boats finally got fueled up we all met in the boathouse office to pay our bills. I asked the Dock Master if we had time to walk up to the Hotel, which was right above the marina. He wasn't sure if any boats were scheduled to come in but he go ahead and he would call up there if we had to move our boats.

We walked up the hill from the marina to Inn overlooking the river and marina. When we got in the restaurant we ordered a round of drinks and some sandwiches. While we were waiting I excused myself under the pretense of having to make a phone call. I went into the lobby were the pay phones and dial 800 information just make it look like I was making a phone call. I killed about 3 minutes and walked back to were everyone was sitting.

Sparky casually ask me first If I had gotten my business taken care of. I said yes and let it go at that for a moment. I waited until the right opportunity arose and got the attention of the group. I was about to put our "plan of action" into play. When I had everyone's attention I told them that I had called a buddy here in Paducah and Nad and I were going to spend the night here. I told them that I was going to score some pot.

Sparky was the first one in the group to react. "Pot?", he exclaimed. I responded with a muffled, "yeh." "Hell, he said, if you wanted some smoke all you had to do was ask. I enough with me to take of your needs and I'll be getting some more when we get to the Gulf."

Nad was sitting at a part of the table where I could wonk at so no one would be any the wiser. Sparky's response enlightened me. I know it wasn't much to base conclusions on but it was a step I the right direction.

I thanked Sparky but told him I still wanted to see my Buddy so we would stay here and I would get what I wanted from him. We finished our drinks and sandwiches, paid and headed back down to the marina. I was going to get an over night slip then say goodbye to the group. We talked about meeting them at Kentucky Lake City Docks some time tomorrow. In some early conversations we had talked about spending the night in Kentucky Lake.

We watched as they pulled away from the docks. Nad was the first to speak. Making sure there were no other ears in the listening range and said, "That was sweet Captain. I suppose you are gloating about right now." I quickly question, "gloating about what?" Nad proceeded to tell me what he thought I was thinking.

Nad I said, "It is still a little to early to make conclusions. If you remember it only started with a few words about some Pot." "Nad, we need to be thinking out of the box here. I think tomorrow if we hook up with Sparky and his group I'll really put the fire under him."

Nad nodded his head as if to agree with me. In the very short time that I have been with Nad I have learned to look for body language when either making a statement or asking a question. Looks tell all!

We grabbed our gear from the boat and headed up to the Inn. At the front desk we checked in and I booked us in a two-room suite. H-mmm with a Jacuzzi. After a week on the boat I wanted to kick back and relax. I remember back when I was working for Fun 'N The Sun. When the renters would come back from their vacations on the houseboats the first thing you would hear is, "the trip wasn't long enough." The second thing you would hear is, "I can't wait until I get home so I can jump in the Jacuzzi." The Inn was not home but that wasn't going to stop me from jumping in the Jacuzzi. If I played my cards right maybe I could hook up with a sweet young thing and really relax.

We got our keys and headed up to the Suite. It was a very spacious Suite. The sleeping were either ends of the Suite and the middle part was a commons area. I of course grabbed the suite that had the Jacuzzi in it. After all, Nad was not going to go out and try to pick up a woman.

We met back in the commons area after we had dumped or stuff in our respective rooms. I asked Nad, "what do you want to do now?" "The way I see it we can go down and have a couple of drinks then come back up and get ready for dinner or, get cleaned up then have a couple of drinks then go have some dinner?"

We both opted to go have a couple of drinks first after we looked at what time it was we figured it was just about "Happy Hour" at the Inn's bar. You've got to love it when a plan comes together.

The bar was a quaint little bar right off the main lobby. It was big enough to hold at least a hundred people and it was about half full. We worked our way up to the bar and luckily caught the bartender standing right there in between drinks. We both ordered our usual cocktails and of course I had to explain to our bartender how make a Martini. That one of the problems that you put up with when you get off the beaten path.

As I looked over the rim of my glass taking the first sip of my Martini my eyes fell on the most gorgeous thing that I had seen I the last........h-mm.....well.... Maybe the last 5 days. She was a tall one. Guessing, I'd have to say around six two or better. She had a totally proportional body to her height and was dressed to kill. She appeared to be alone and was headed right for me.

"Excuse me," she said softly, "is this seat taken?" "Not until you sit down." I flauntingly said. She looked right into my eyes. For a fleeting moment I was mesmerized by her stare, or was it glare? With out any hesitation I reached over and pulled the bar stool out for her sit down. She graciously thank me and I introduced myself to her and asked her what she would like to drink.

She introduced herself as Wanda and accepted my offer of a drink. When the Bartender got back down to us I ordered us both a drink. Wanda was drinking a Gin Ricky. An older drink but a very nice one. I of course ordered my second Martini. I had a very brief flashback to the Burlington Hotel in Alma, WI. One night I had consumed seven Martinis. After that they called me Captain Martini.

"Captain, she asked, what brings you to these parts?" "My buddy and I," looking over at Nad who was totally involved in some political discussion with two lawyers, "are on a jaunt down to the Gulf. "We are spending the night here at the Inn." "It's a small world, she said, I am also staying here tonight. I am in town for a consultation at the Hospital, I am a Doctor." You could have knocked me off my bar stool with a feather because she didn't look old enough to be a Doctor. Maybe a first year resident but .... She was a very attractive woman. I had guessed her age to be around twenty-nine maybe thirty. She was in fact thirtytwo and was in her fifth year of practice. She had beautiful long dark brown hair with brown eyes to match. They were very full and well made up.

She had high cheekbones and lips to die for. It was as if she was selecting each word that she spoke very carefully to exemplify the beauty of her lips. As I casually glance at the rest of her body, I could not see a flaw in it. This woman had some good breeding in her.

She had finished her drink and I immediately ordered her another one. She thank me and we started taking about ....well really nothing. She was from Iowa and worked at the University Of Iowa Hospital. That is were my younger brother had his heart transplant.

Nad was still engrossed with the two lawyers. I couldn't help thinking about the name, "Wicked Wanda". I think it cam from a Men's Magazine. I wonder if this Wanda is wicked? Wanda snapped me out of my momentary trance by asking if I had any plans for dinner. I told that I, and Nad had not made any plans for dinner. At that very moment Nad came over and I introduced him to Wanda and he begged forgiveness because he was going out to dinner with the two lawyers that he had been having a conversation with.

Timing is everything! "Wanda...........I'm yours," I thought to myself. Nad rushed off leaving Wanda and me an apology for not having dinner with us. I told him I was sorry he would not be eating with us but that we understood. What a bunch of crap. I was jumping for joy! I was going to alone with Wanda........Well........maybe.

"Do you know of a good place to eat?", I asked. She said yes but we would have to drive there. I told her if we can get there by boat I'll drive otherwise she was going to have to supply the transportation.

As we were finishing our drinks I told Wanda that I would like to go up and cleaned up a little. She said she would like to freshen up a little also. We agreed to meet in the lobby in an hour.

The Jacuzzi was going to have to wait for now. I jumped in the shower and took a long hot one. I knew I had an hour to ready so I may as well enjoy it. Done with my shower I put on a pair gray slacks and a black Italian cashmere sweater.

It was still warm outside but I grabbed a leather jacket just in case. I had fifteen minutes to wait until I was to meet Wanda in the lobby. I used that time to make a call to the Cities to talk with Carmen. I told her where we were and what had happened up 'til now. There was nothing new on her end so we said goodbye and hung up.

I was five minutes early getting to the lobby and Wanda was three minutes early. I had a feeling this was going to be a nice evening. Wanda had put on a chic little cocktail dress that clung to her every curve and exemplified her ample cleavage. She was ready for anything......I could tell.

I helped her with her wrap and we headed outside. She asked if I would like to drive and I told her that I had no problem with that. We got to her car, a sporty little Mercedes and I opened the door for her so she could get in.

Even as tall as she was I had to adjust the driver's seat. I like a lot of room when I drive. I back out of the parking spot and she told me which direction to head off in. We only had about 4 miles to go. The place we were going to was a little Italian restaurant right off the main drag. The name of the place was Anunziato's. As we were in Paducah, KY, I was not expecting much in the way of a fancy Italian Restaurant. Much to my surprise they had valet parking. I pulled the car up to the front of the restaurant and the valets opened our doors and we got out.

There was actually a doorman that opened the door for us and we walked into Italy. It was like walking through a time warp. One second you are standing on a non-descript street in Paducah, KY and the next second you are standing in a village somewhere in Italy. The looks, the smell, the people, everything said Italy. The hostess even spoke with an Italian accent. There were several people seated near the hostess podium waiting for tables. Our hostess said it would be about a half hour wait for a table. I told her she could find us in the bar when a table was ready for us.

We walked into the bar or Cantina as they called it and sat down at a table out of the main stream of traffic. Our waitress came and took our drink orders. I had my usual Beefeaters Martini with two olives on the side and Wanda ordered a Rob Roy. As I looked across the table at Wanda I couldn't help admiring her beauty. The lighting in the Cantina was low and seductive and her dark brown hair was reflecting some red highlights. Our drinks and we toasted to our meeting and to a good dinner. Feeling somewhat romantic I reached across the table and lifted her empty hand and put it to my lips. I gave her hand a soft kiss and looked into her eyes. She was looking right back at me. Her beautiful lips gave a slight hint of approval. How wicked was Wanda going to be?

Our trance was broken by the hostess telling us that our table was ready. I begrudgingly let Wanda's hand go and got up to pull her chair out. We followed our hostess to the dining room and she seated us at a cozy secluded window seat, gave us some menus and said our waitress would be along shortly. I gave a little chuckle to myself thinking that dinner was not the foremost thing on my mind at that very moment.

Lucia, our waitress was Italian through and through. She asked if we were ready to order and I told her that we were not ready but if she would get us another round of drinks we would be ready by the time she got back. As we looked at our menus I couldn't help but to wonder what the outcome of the evening was going to be. Was Wanda going to be wicked and shut me down or was she going to be wicked and wild.

Our waitress came back with our drinks and we told her that we were ready to order. Wanda opted for Veil Parmesan and I ordered Angel Hair Pasta with clams and a white cream sauce. I also asked the waitress to bring us a bottle of good Chianti Wine. With dinner and wine ordered we sat back and consumed our waiting time with small talk.

Wanda was from a small town in central Iowa, Fort Dodge. She was born and raised there. She attended The University of Iowa and got her degree in medicine. She did her internship at the University Hospital and went on into private practice with her father, a well known and one the top Orthopedic Surgeons in the mid-west.

Our conversation was interrupted by our waitress bring us our dinner. I was actually hungry and dug right into dinner. Alternatively, was it possible that I was in a hurry to consume the plate mussels in front of me. The food of the sex gods. Dinner was excellent and I told Wanda that her choice of restaurants was right on. We lingered over the remaining wine and talked about social issues. She had a good head on her and she made a lot of sense. She seemed to have an agenda to rid our country of it's social woes. It was starting to get a little deep for me even though I understood everything she was taking about.

She caught herself mid sentence and excused herself for monopolizing the conversation. I told her that no excuse was needed as I was enjoying everything she was talking about. We finished up the wine and I caught the eye of our waitress to let her know that we were done and we were ready to leave. She brought the dinner bill and I left it and a proper amount of money on the table. I got up and helped Wanda up and we headed out. While we were waiting for the valet to bring her car I asked what she would like to do for the rest of the evening. She looked at me blinking with her big brown eyes as if to say, "big boy....need you ask". I only hoped that my guess was right......and I was about to find out.

"Captain Art, she asked, didn't you tell me that you had a suite with a big Jacuzzi in it?" "Yes I did", I answered. "I think we should put it to some use tonight, if you're game". My foot must have on the accelerator because the car suddenly surge forward stud horse chasing a mare in heat.

She looked over at me smiling and said, "easy there big boy. We have all night. No need to rush". H-mmm that's easy for her to say. She broke my thoughts by saying, "Captain, as long as we are both leaving in the morning, and I have not unpacked any of my bags yet how would you feel about me getting my stuff from my room and bringing it down to yours?"

"Let it be, I said, hoping that she would understand what I meant. "Do you need any help", I inquired. She responded with a no just as we were pulling up to the hotel entrance. I pulled into a parking spot near the front door. I got and nearly ran around the car to get her door opened. Come on Captain, I was thinking to myself, slow down boy. Like she said, you've got all night. As we were walking towards the elevator I told here to go ahead and I would meet her in my room. I gave her my room key as I was going to go to the front desk and leave a message for Nad and I could ask for a new one.

I wrote out a message for Nad and ask the clerk to make sure that Nads message light was activated on his room phone. With that done I headed for my room. While I was at the front desk I had the clerk call room service to send up a bottle of nice champagne. There's just something about a beautiful woman, a bottle of Champagne, and a Jacuzzi.

As I was riding the elevator up to my room I got to thinking that this was the second Lady Doctor that I had met in about as many weeks. I made a mental note. H-mmm, Doctors, Lawyers, I wonder if there are any lady Indian Chiefs.

Once again timing is everything. Not five minutes after getting back to my room, room service arrived with the iced down Champagne. I went to the bathroom to start filling the Jacuzzi and heard Wanda entering the room. I shouted to her that was in the bathroom filling the Jacuzzi then asked her how hot she wanted the water. "Hot, she said, but not scalding".

I adjusted the temperature and went out to the main room. I opened up a bottle of Champagne and poured us each a glass full.

I handed one to Wanda and she immediately made a toast to a fun time in the Jacuzzi. I could deal with that. I refilled our glasses and told

Wanda that I was going to head into the Jacuzzi, She said she would be following me shortly.

When I got in the bathroom I stripped down and slowly slid into the Jacuzzi. It was hot but not scalding. I turned in the jets on laid my head back against the edge of the tub. I took a long swallow of my Champagne and closed my eyes. The rustling of clothes got my attention and I turned to look. It was Wanda and she just about to get in the tub herself. She had brought both bottles of Champagne with her. She climbed in the tub and I busied myself with refilling our glasses.

Wanda now in the tub slide over next to me and kind of snuggled up closely. I had turned the lights down and lit the candles that hotel had supplied. The mood was serine, the water was hot, Champagne was cold, and the woman was beautiful. What more could one want? From this point forward everything became a blur until I woke up in the next morning.

I woke up first and went to take a quick shower. I heard the shower door open behind me and Wanda slid in beside me. The shower was not made for two people but there just was enough room for the both of us. Wanda started washing my back and said, "Cap I want to thank you for a wonderful evening last night. I really enjoyed it because it had been such a long time for me." I turned around and looked in her eyes. She was telling the truth. I reached out and pulled her to me and gave her a long kiss.

We finished our shower and I got out first, dried off and got dressed. I slipped on a pair of shorts, a Polo shirt, and a pair of deck shoes. I got all of gear organized and packed up then to-ld Wanda that I was going down to the restaurant to meet Nad.

Wanda said she would be down shortly. I grabbed my gear and headed down stairs. I dropped my gear off at the front desk and was going to take of our rooms but the clerk said that Nad had already taken care of it.

I walked into the restaurant and saw Nad sitting at far wall over looking the Marina. I walked over and sat down at the table. Nad didn't look any the worse for wear. I asked him his evening went and he said he really enjoyed it. I knew he wasn't going to ask me how my evening was because he really didn't want to know. I poured myself a cup of coffee from carafe sitting on the table. It was good coffee. Strong, hot, and black.

As we were talking about our plans for the day, Wanda walked up and I pulled out a chair for her and poured her a cup of coffee. She greeted Nad and asked him how his night was with the lawyers. He told her what had transpired last night and Wanda mentioned that two of the lawyers were in her class in school. While they were talking my cell phone rang.

It was Sparky. He was calling from the marina in Kentucky Lake where we were to meet them later today. He started out, "Cap, we are going to go on ahead. Jeff's boat has a prop shaft leaking and there is a Certified Tech down river with the parts to fix it." It was at the marina that we were going to stop at on the Tenn-Tom. I told Sparky that we were going to be leaving in a little bit and we would catch up with them this evening.

We all ate breakfast and I grabbed the check, left a nice tip for the waitress and we headed for the front desk. Wanda offered us a ride down to the marina. We accepted and loaded our gear into her car. When we got to the marina Wanda walked down to the boat with us. She wanted to see Nad toy. When we got to the boat I helped Wanda on board and we went below. I sowed my gear then gave her a quick tour. Nad threw his down the hatch and said he was going to check the engines and get them fired up. Wanda was startled when the first engine fired up. She started to say something but I told her to wait because there were two more engines to start.

One after the other Nad started the engines. The noise was not deafening when you down below but you could definitely hear them and you could feel the vibrations. We went back topside and I helped Wanda off the boat. She said she was impress and wished she had more time to take a ride.

We said our good-byes and I gave her a soft lingering kiss. She stood back while I untied the dock lines and as I stepped aboard I pushed the boat away from the dock. Nad backed the boat out of the slip and turned the boat towards the river. I turned around and blew Wanda a kiss and she returned it. I gave her a final wave then turned around to take care of business.

Nad was already easing the throttles forward as the boat entered the river from the marina. Nad already had his head set on so I put mine on and told him I would take the throttles. We only had about twenty-two miles to go to the Kentucky Lake Dam. With any luck we could be there and through it within the hour. We discussed our speed and Nad said as long as we have fresh fuel let's go ahead and open it up whenever we could.

The thing is, once you make the turn to the Tennessee River the barge traffic can be really heavy. There are also a couple of blinds turns and I didn't like the idea of coming around a blind turn at high speed head on into a barge. I told Nad that I would use the radio to check for traffic whenever we needed it. With that I eased the throttles forward. We only had a half mile to go after leaving the marina until we made our turn onto the Tennessee River. I was still pushing the throttles forward when we made our turn. Once you make the turn the potential of heavy barge traffic is always there. This area is a loading area for barges. I made quick call on the radio using channels 13 & 16 to advise all traffic that we were heading down river at a high rate of speed.

There was no response. The speedometer was indicating ninety-five and I told Nad that I was going to hold it that speed. He agreed, then hit the switch for the "Silent Choice Exhaust". An instant roar was heard. Three, eight hundred horsepower engines with open exhaust was one of the most beautiful things to hear. To me it is not noise, it is music to my ears. I dialed in our speed and the distance to the Kentucky Lake Lock and the computer said we should be there within 23 minutes. That of course was providing we didn't run into any traffic and had to slow down.

We were about a mile from day marker 16.6, which is Calvert, Kentucky, and it is a large industrial complex and known for heavy barge traffic. I gave a call on channel 13 to any concerned barge traffic that we were running at ninety-five MPH and to give us a call with their location. One barge, the "Nancy J" responded and told us he was heading our way and he was almost a mile below day marker 16.6. He told us he was not aware of any other traffic in the area so just keep her coming. And that we did! We flew through the Calvert City Complex without even blinking our eyes. The banks of the river were loaded with barges being loaded with a variety of goods from chemicals to scrap metal. There were a few deck hands on the barges that waved at us as sped through the complex.

I gave a call the "Nancy J" to let her know that we should be seeing them shortly. No sooner than I had put the radio mic on its hanger we saw the "Nancy J". We had than enough room to pass by her. I got Nads attention and pointed to the wake that the barge was leaving. He acknowledge me with a quick nod of his head. Over the intercom he told me to hold on because he didn't want to slow down. The wakes were not big by any means but at ninety-five we were probably going to grab some air.

As we went passed the barge Nad turned the boat slightly to port to line up on the wake so we could hit them head on. The bow plowed into the wake and rose into the air and we went air born. Nad yelled at me to stand by the throttles because when we came down we were going to hit the prop wash from the barge. If you have never seen the prop wash from a loaded barge it would be hard to explain. Smaller boats have swamped or even overturned in the wake from the barges. Nad was worried about us high siding when we hit the water which could cause us to flip. Just as we hit the water I jammed the throttles to full and Nad yanked the helm wheel to starboard. The boat stayed right on track. I pulled the throttles back until we were at ninety-five again.

At mile marker 20.0 I called the Kentucky Lock and they advised us that there was no commercial traffic in the area. They were locking some pleasure craft our way and they would be ready for us in about fifteen minutes. I pulled the throttles back until we doing about twenty-five MPH. That would put us at the Lock at just about the time they said they would be ready for us.

As we pulled up to the lock we could see the doors opening up. In minutes the pleasure craft had cleared the lock and we nosed in to the wall using the port side of the boat. The lift in this lock was going to be around fifty-three feet or so. It would be better than a half hour before we were through. I called the Dam Marina and told them that we were locking through and that we would be stopping for a fast pit stop. They said they would be ready for us when we got there.

The lock gates opened up and we eased out of the lock. As soon as we were clear of the lock wall I pushed the throttles forward. Nad turned the boat to starboard and we headed for the breakwater just outside of the marina. As promised the dock crew was on the fuel dock waiting for us to pull up. Nad eased up to the dock and shut the engines down. I tossed the dock lines to the kids on the dock and they tied us off. They started filling the tanks right away. We were topped off in about fifteen minutes and we were ready to leave. Nad made a quick inspection of the engines and said everything looked good.

With that he started up the engines and when he was ready I signaled the dock crew to cast off our lines. We backed out of the fuel dock slip, turned around and head back out to the breakwater. Once we were clear of the breakwater I pushed the throttles forward and we were on or way again. Our plan was to head down to mile marker 115.5 and stop for fuel then head down to the Yacht Harbor Marina, which is on the Tenn-Tom Waterway in Iuka, MS. There we were to meet up again with Sparky and his group. It was only ten o'clock and if we held the boat at eighty MPH we should be at the Yacht Harbor Marina around one or two in the afternoon, which would include our gas stop at mile marker 115.5

I got on the radio and called for any traffic on channel 13 and 16. I gave our current location, speed, and direction for any concerned traffic. I did get a response from anyone. I switched the radio to the dual channel mode, which would let me know if any traffic was talking on channels 13 or 16. We zipped by a few fishing boat but that was about the only traffic that we were seeing at this time.

We made our gas stop at mile marker 115.5, Cuba Landing Marina and got back out on the river again. With only a hundred miles or so to go we calculated that we would be in the Yacht Harbor Marina within an hour and a half. Still running at eighty-five MPH we knocking the miles down fast. Just below mile marker 127.0 we heard traffic on the radio about a barge at mile marker 130.2. The barge was negotiating one of the narrowest parts of the river. The area is known as Lady Finger Bluff and the early steamboat Captain called it the "Narrows". I switched the radio to channel 13 and hailed the barge. The Captain answered back and I told him were heading his way and eighty-five MPH. He said he was a fifteener and he was pretty much taking up the whole channel. He recommended that we slow down and stay to the left side of the channel.

I pulled the throttles back until we were doing around thirty-five MPH and kept our eyes open. Within minutes we saw the barge rounding a bend in the river. I pulled the throttles back until we were at idle and Nad kept the boat on the left side of the channel. We slid past the barge and waved at the Captain and crew as we went by. Once we cleared his prop wash I pushed the throttles forward again and we went right backup to speed. We had one more spot in the river to negotiate and that was at mile marker 152.5. This spot is one of the sharpest turns on the Tennessee River. It is a hairpin turn and a smaller fast moving boat would have a little trouble at fifty MPH. We were going to take turn at eightyfive and hope that we didn't meet any traffic.

I gave Nad a heads up and he reset the trim on the lower units. The bow came down a little and you feel the keel biting the water. It was right hand turn and it came up fast. I had my hands on the throttles not that it was going to do any good if we had a problem. Nad was in deep concentration keeping the boat on track. This was like being in a car and taking a thirty-mile an hour turn at eightyfive. Only a car that was well prepared for that tight of a turn would make it through unscathed. Notwithstanding, the experience of the driver.

I had all the confidence in the world about Nads ability to handle his boat and I had become very confident with his boat. As we entered the turn it kept getting tighter and tighter. The boat was heeling to starboard and the starboard gunnel was just inches from the water. The "G" force was phenomenal pushing us both to the port side of the boat. Thank god for bolstered seats. They kept us from flying all over the cockpit.

Nad was really fighting the wheel trying to keep the stern of the boat from sliding out from under us. It was fight of pleasure because Nad had a grin on his face from ear to ear. It was all over in a matter of seconds. As we came out of the turn Nad trimmed the lower units back up for maximum efficiency. I looked over and smiled at Nad and he smiled back. Over the intercom he remarked, "I love it when a plan comes together". We had about sixty miles to go and we Looking at the charts quickly I reminded Nad that we had to keep our eyes open at mile marker 172.3 because of a ferry that makes numerous crossings each day. If the ferry was in the middle of the channel we were going to have to slow down again. If she was at the dock we could keep on going at our current speed.

As luck would have it she was dead in the channel when we got there. I pulled the throttles back and slowed down to an idle.

As we slid by the ferry some of the passengers waved at us. We waved back and once we were clear of the ferry I pushed the throttles forward again and took her back up to speed. With only forty miles to go, my calculations were showing we should make it in about a half hour. I grabbed the cell phone and Sparky a call. He answered right away and I told him what our status was and he said he would be on the dock with some people when we came in.

My calculations were right on! In thirty-five minutes we were pulling into the Yacht Harbor Marina. Sparky gave us a call on channel 16 and told us which slip to go to. We were going to be on "F" dock so Nad made a right turn as we entered the marina. "F" dock was the last dock on this side of the marina. We saw everyone standing at a slip and we took a chance that that is where they wanted us. Our assumption was correct and Nad turned the boat around so he could back it into the slip.

With the boat now tied up and shore power connected we automatically went into party mode. Sparky brought us up to date. Jeff's boat was due to be launched later today and the report was good.

A new seal on the prop shaft and he was be ready to go. Sparky told us that the marina had a nice pool with a swim up bar. The weather was nice in fact it was nice enough to go swimming. I didn't need a second more to think about it. I excused myself and went back on the boat and put on my swimming suit.

I came back topside and everyone was gone except Nad. "What happened to everyone", I asked Nad. "When you said you were going swimming everyone else decided to do the same thing. Give me a minute Cap and I'll go up with you". I said okay that I would wait for him and he went below to change clothes. I polished off the drink that someone gave me and was wishing for another but decided that I could wait until I got up to the pool.

I was checking out the marina when Nad came back up. It was a large marina with six docks and each dock had roughly a hundred slips. There were some pretty large boats I the marina so I was guessing that this was a first class operation. I looked up towards the main building that overlooked the marina. It was really well laid out and up on a small rise maybe three hundred yards behind the pool area was a rather large opulent house. It would better be described as a mansion. My immediate thought was that the owner of the marina probably owned the house. I made a mental note to find out.

We got up to the pool and it was fairly crowded with surprisingly all adults. I would later find out that the marina catered to single people and unless some Grandparents brought the grandkids down for the day, which was discouraged, there were no kids. What unique concept! I looked down to the dock where Nad's boat was tied up. Some of Sparky's gang were heading up the dock towards the pool area. I grabbed a couple of deck lounges for us and threw my towel down on one of them.

I was ready for a swim and a drink. All I had to do was get the two in order. We were at the deep end of the pool so I took a couple of quick steps and launched myself head first into the pool. The water felt good and was very refreshing. I swam around for a bit and shouted at Nad to jump in then headed for the bar. I swam up to the bar and slid up on a barstool. There were twelve bar stools around the bar that were actually in the water. There was another dozen on the landside looking down at the pool.

The bartender, or maybe I should say bartenders, was a very cute, early twenty something and I immediately ask her what her what her name was and ordered a drink in that order. Her name was Dina and she was the owner's daughter. She was twenty-two and going to college at "Ole Miss". I introduced myself and pointed over to Nad and told her that our drinks would be going on the same tab. I told her which slip we were in and she said she would take care of everything.

Nad eventually swam over to the bar and ordered himself a drink. Sparky's people were showing up and the quietness and peacefulness of the pool when I had first arrived was now gone. I told Dina that we knew the people from Sparky's group but that they were on their own. She nodded with acknowledgment. It wasn't long before everyone was in the pool and things were getting crazy. Sparky's group already had a head start on us and they were getting crazy.

The sun felt good on my back and the drinks were going straight to my head. I asked Dina if they served any food out here and she said yes then gave me a menu. We hadn't eaten since breakfast so everything on the menu looked good. At this point I wasn't worried about Sparky's group as they had been here for a day already. I figured if they missed lunch it was their problem. I ordered some appetizers for both me and Nad and ordered myself a Monte Cristo sandwich. I gave Nad the menu so he could order something for himself. With that out of the way I ordered us another round of drinks.

I caught Dina in a slight lull and started asking her some questions about the marina. The big house up on the hill was owned by the owner of the marina, which just happened to be Dina's mother.

Her father had died last year and left everything to the mother. Dina directed my attention to the marina. "Captain, do you see that fifty-five foot Carver at the head of "C" dock, she asked. I nodded yes and she said it belong to her mother also. I had to laugh when she told me the name of the boat. "AFTICA".

Her father had bought the boat right after they purchased the marina. The boat had been appropriately named. "AFTICA" stood for, "ANOTHER FUCKING TOY I CAN'T AFFORD". Apparently Dina's father made sure that he had insurance on everything to make sure that in the event of his untimely demise, the marina, boat, and the house would be fully paid off. I asked Dina where her mother was and she said that she was around somewhere and would probably be down at the pool sometime today. I couldn't wait! If Dina looked anything like her mother that meant that her mother could be a knock out.

The booze was flowing freely and Dina had her work cut out for her with this crazy group. There was a lot of splashing and screaming going on as well as a bikini top or two that seemed to just fall off. Some of the boaters from the marina even got into the mix. No doubt about it, it was going to be a fun night tonight.

The ringing of a phone behind Dina got my attention. Dina answered the phone and when she was done she turned to me and said, "Captain Art, that was my mother Angel. She said there is a fax for you in the office and you can go up there to get it or she will bring it down when she comes down to the pool". I thanked her and told her I would go up and get it just in case I had to send an answer back right away. I finished my drink and told Nad I was going up to the office. I swam over to the pool ladder, climbed out and went over to our deck chairs and dried off, slipped my shirt on and headed for the office.

I walked into the main building and asked a gentleman where the office was. He pointed and I headed in that direction. I walked into the office and told a young lady sitting at a desk that I was Captain Art and that there was supposed to be a fax up here for me. Suddenly from a back office a feminine voice called out. "Joanne if that is Captain Art send him into my office please". "Yes Ma'am Joanne shouted out". Joanne turned her head towards a doorway but I was already a head of her. I walked towards the door but before I got there the Angel had appeared. I mean Angel appeared.

I was guessing right at six-foot tall, long auburn hair, green eyes, and a body to die for. She was a well-managed, early forties woman. She had a voice of authority and carried herself thusly. She offered me her hand at which I did not hesitate for one second to extend mine. With the self-introductions over she invited me into her office. She pointed to a chair and I sat down as she walked behind her desk.

"So, she started out, you are the infamous Captain Art". I looked at her questioningly, "I have already heard all about you", and she handed me my fax. I looked quickly at the fax and saw that it was from Chad my lead dockworker at my marina. I scanned though it, shrugged then mumbled something under my breath.

"Bad news", Angel asked? "Not in so many words, I answered. The owner of the marina that I run was on the docks and had some words with one of our boaters. The boater is a little pissed off and he is threatening to leave and take a half dozen of his friends with him. The owner, I continued, is not a people person and as long as I am there I can keep him off the docks in the marina".

"I know all about him, Angel said. We have known Nafe Williams for years. My husband went to college with him and I agree with you he is not a people person". It's a small world I was thinking to myself. Almost fourteen hundred miles from home and I run into someone that knows someone. Angel looked at me and smiled, "I spoke with Nafe just before you came up here. When your fax came in I thought I would give him a call and say hi. He told me all about you". "All", I exclaimed. "Well maybe not all but a lot. He actually speaks very highly of you".

Way to go Nafe I thought to myself. You're a putz but you had something nice to say about me. I made a mental note to thank him when I got back to the marina. Angel was talking to me and I was still in a little bit of a trance regarding the conversation regarding Nafe. "Excuse me Angel, I begged, I was thinking about the marina. I guess I need to call up there and see if I can put this fire out". "You're welcome to use my phone if you need to" she offered. I thanked her and said that I would call the marina later from my cell phone.

Angel asked me what brought me down this way and I told her that Nad wanted to take a trip down the river and asked me to go with him. She asked me about Sparky and his gang and I told her that we had met all of them on the river and we sort of traveling with them. "Captain, let me caution you about those other people. They have been here before and I don't trust them. I have a suspicion that somehow, someway, that they are all involved with drugs".

"Really, I said acting totally surprised. I haven't seen any indication of drugs around them since we ran into them above St. Louis". She couldn't have known that I was totally bullshitting her or she would have called me on it. "Thanks for the information, I said. I'll keep my eyes open from now on. We are supposed to run down river with them all the way to the Gulf. Maybe I should rethink that".

Now I was really throwing out some crap but I couldn't tell Angel what was really going on and take a chance of blowing our cover. I had to change the subject before I accidentally let something slip out. Besides I don't make a good liar because I always forget what lies I told then I get caught. If you tell the truth and it really happened that way you will always remember that.

We talked a little while longer then I asked her if she was coming down to the pool. She said yes that she would be down as soon as she finished up in the office. I told her I would spring for a drink when she got down there. She said okay and I left the office after giving her a courteous handshake. I walked out of the office and headed back down to the pool. I had a lot of stuff going through my head and some of it I needed to deal with right away.

When I got back to the pool there was something going on. People were yelling and Nad was trying to get my attention. Several people seemed to running down to the docks. Nad jumped the enclosure around the pool and waved to me to follow him. I picked up my pace and went around the pool heading towards the dock. As I was running down the gangway I could see Sparky's boat heading out of the marina. That at first didn't give any cause for concern, that is until I looked again and Sparky was standing on the dock. As I came up to Nad's boat he was already in and firing up the engines. Sparky was yelling about some "SOB" that drove off in his boat. Quickly assessing the situation I figured that Nad was firing up his boat to give chase. That seemed logical to me because Nad's boat would be the only one in the group that could catch Sparky's boat.

When I got to the boat I jumped in and went straight to the throttles. I yelled at Sparky to untie the boat and jump in which he did. Nad pulled the boat out of the slip and turn towards the river channel. I was tempted to open the throttles right there but as we were still in the marina it might cause a little havoc with the other boats in their slips. I don't think any of us were worried at that moment about catching up with Sparky's boat. I started pushing the throttles forward once we had cleared the marina.

Once we were on the river we knew that the person driving Sparky's boat could go only one of three ways. If he headed South or down river that would be a dumb move on his part because he would hit a Lock & Dam in about thirty miles. If he turned North he had two choices. Once he got back to the Tennessee River he could go East or he could go West back into Kentucky Lake. The first thing we looked for once we got on the river was water disturbance in the form of a wake. He wasn't more than a minute ahead of us so we should still be able to see the wake that was left behind.

He was heading South. Dumb on his part in fact doubly dumb! First for stealing Sparky's boat and two for heading South. There are no tributaries on this part of the river for him to get off the river. That means that in thirty miles or so he is going to hit the Jamie Whitten Lock and Dam. What a fool!

I had pushed the throttles forward and we were running at a hundred and ten MPH. Sparky was in the navigators position and all three of us had our headsets on. We had two more slight turns to go through then we would be on a straight part of the river for about five miles. I was guessing once we got around the last turn we should be able to see Sparky's boat. Bingo! My hunch was right. Not three miles ahead of us was Sparky's boat. "Okay guys, I shouted into the headset mic, hang on I'm going full throttle. The power came on instantaneously and within seconds we running at a hundred forty MPH. The distance between the two boats was closing rapidly, very rapidly.

Nad kept his boat right in the wake of the boat ahead of us. He told me to keep the power on because he was going to hit the wake from the other boat at full throttle. That meant at the speed that we were now going when we hit the wake we would go air born and literally pass this guy while we were I the air. I told Sparky to hold on. He already was. For dear life!

Even though my acquaintance with Nad has been short lived at this point I had learned in the beginning to trust him. We were coming up on the boat in front of us at nearly twice his speed and Nad was showing no signs of turning or telling me to pull the throttles back. He was pushing that envelope of trust real hard. We kept getting closer and closer until what seemed like a crash was immanent he shouted for us to hold on.

One quick turn of the wheel to the left and we shot over the wake. I mean we shot over it. We were about twenty feet in the air as we passed Sparky's boat. At first the guy driving the boat seemed to be totally oblivious to us. That is until we were passing him in the air. The looked on his face was of pure shock and terror.

We landed in the water not twenty feet in front of him and I immediately pushed the power back on. Nad steered his boat directly in front of Sparky's boat and I pulled the throttles back to equal his speed hoping the guy would realize the error of his way and shut down. Nope! He was not shutting down. I kept pulling the throttles back hoping if we slowed down he would slow down. Again no. He just pulled out around us and tried to pass.

I shouted at Nad to get closer to him as if he were going to ram him. Nad nodded and eased the wheel to the right and the gap between us started closing. We were within three feet of the guy and we were using hand signals telling him to shut down. Oh!......this guy really dumb. He had know idea who he was messing with. I shouted to Nad to back off a little because I was going below real quick.

I unplugged my head set and went below straight to my duffle bag. I unzipped it and there was what I was looking for. My trusty gun. I pulled the gun out of the holster and headed back topside. When I was plugged back with communications I told Nad to get beside him again. I switched positions with Sparky and told him to listen to Nad for any throttle instructions. He nodded in an affirmative motion. Once again Nad pulled right behind the guy and this time whipped the boat to the starboard side of Sparky's boat which would put him on our port side.

We got right beside him and point my gun right at him and pulled the slide back injecting a round into the chamber. I wanted this guy to see me do this. Maybe it would intimidate him enough and he would stop the boat. It wasn't happening. He looked over at me, smiled then flipped me off and turned the boat away from us. Nad was on it and stayed right next to him. I shouted to Sparky asking him which part of his boat that he wouldn't mind getting a hole in it. He looked at me in disbelief! "Where, I shouted again, we don't have time to talk this out. I'm going to fire one round in the air and if he doesn't stop I am going to shoot at him or at the boat very near to him". Sparky wasn't liking this all but he really didn't have a choice. His fuel tank was full and this guy could dick around with us for a couple of hours before running out of fuel. Then you had to think about possibility of the guy screwing the boat itself up.

Sparky shrugged his shoulders and shouted, "wherever". I told Nad to get a little closer and to stay on top of this jerk. When got close I made sure the guy was looking at me and I fired a round into the air. We were close enough for him to hear the report of the round going off. It didn't seem to faze him. He just pulled away from us again. Again Nad was staying on top of him and we got back beside Sparky's boat and I point the barrel of the gun directly at guy.

He looked at me as if to say, "I dare you." To bad this guy never had the chance to get to know me. People who know me don't dare me. I was looking for something on the boat to shoot causing the least amount of damage. I looked past him and saw that the windshield, where it wrapped around was in two sections. If I hit the rear section which was only about a foot long it could easily be replaced.

I motioned for the guy to stop the boat once again and I was ignored. I shrugged my shoulders giving the guy the look of, "Okay you asked for it" and fired the gun. He jumped when he heard the gun go off and immediately looked to see if he was hit. Then he looked to his left and saw that entire rear section of the windshield was gone. Common sense 101 just kicked in. He started pulling the throttles back.

Nad had let his boat fall behind just a little after I fired the round. We were now behind Sparky's boat and the guy was bringing the boat to starboard getting out of the main channel closer to shore. It seemed like a perfectly prudent thing to do. Both boats were still pointing down channel but almost at a standstill.

Suddenly the guy gives Sparky's boat a little gas then jumps from the boat swimming towards the shoreline. What a move on his part. He has distracted us sufficiently to make his get away by swimming to shore. We had no alternative but to go after Sparky's unmanned boat. Between Nad and Sparky they quickly brought Nad's boat alongside Sparky's close enough so I jump from one to the other.

It was a leap of faith. Actually it wasn't that bad because we were only moving around twenty MPH. Once on Sparky's boat I went to the helm and pulled the throttles back and disengaged the drives. Sparky then climbed over himself and started looking around the boat to if anything was missing. Other than the left side of his lower windshield being shot out everything looked okay and I moved so Sparky could get at the helm and jumped back over to Nad's boat. We turned the boats around and headed back to the marina.

As soon as we pulled into the marina people started heading down to the dock. We got both boats tied up in the slips and shut them down. Nad immediately pulled out his ignition keys and I saw Sparky do the same thing. Once was enough. It is not uncommon for boats to get ripped off on the coast but it is highly unusual that some one steal a boat on the river. We checked around the docks and no one had seen a thing and of course no had any idea who the guy was that took Sparky's boat.

When things had settled down Sparky came over, "I owe you guys big time for what you did. Let me know what I can do for you". "Don't worry about it Sparky, Nad said, it's boaters helping boaters. I am kind of glad it was your boat because we would have never caught him if it had been my boat". We all laughed!

It was getting to be about five and it time to start thinking about something to eat or at least make some plans for dinner. I threw the question out to the group as to whether or not to do some grilling or go up to the restaurant. The restaurant won out. With that everyone went to their respective boats to get changed for dinner. Angel was standing near by and I called out to her and asked her what she was doing for dinner. She said had no plans so I asked her if she would be my guest for dinner. She said yes and I figured it was the least I could as I never did get a chance to buy her a drink at the pool. I told her I meet her in the bar at seven.

I went to our boat and went below. Nad was mixing a couple of drinks and I was glad. I could use a little bracer about now. It had turned out to be an exciting afternoon. We were kicked back sipping our drinks when there was a knock on the boat. I stuck my head through the hatch and saw that it was Sparky. I told him to come on down and have a drink with us. He jumped on board and came below. "What would you like to drink Sparky?", Nad asked. "A beer would do me fine right now", he said. He continued, "how would you guys like to do a little line of some nice blow?" I looked at Nad then back to Sparky, "sure why not. It's been a hell of a day and it looks like we are going to party tonight so we may as well let it all hang out".

Sparky quickly cut out three sizable lines of coke then handed me a straw to use. Great I thought, I get to be first. I had a feeling that this stuff was not going to be the same thing that one would get on the street. This was going to be a little better quality. I quickly snorted half of the line up each nostril then licked my finger and got the rest of my line off the mirror and rubbed it on my gums. I was right! It was some good shit.

With that out of the way Sparky said if we wanted anymore all we had to do was ask. He figured he owed it to us. I thanked him and told him we would meet him in the bar later and he left saying if we were still on the boat when he headed up to the bar he would do another line with us. I said that was okay with me.

After he was gone Nad immediately broached the subject. "What do you think, he asked. Is he just a guy that likes to do his coke or is he the one that is going to lead us to our goal?" "I guess we'll have to just wait and see Nad, I said. I know this is the second time he has shared with us so it's still just a little early to make a judgment call". With that I pulled out a little booty and my "one hitter" to work up a little appetite.

It was about a quarter to seven and Sparky was once again knocking on the side of the boat. I jokingly told him come on down and take care of us. I was still buzzed from the effects of the first line he gave us. Oh well.......what the hell. It's all for the cause. He cut up some more healthy lines and we made short work of them. Checking the mirror for any residual on my nose I made the announcement that I was heading to the bar to meet Angel before dinner. Nad and Sparky followed me in tow.

The bar was already pretty crowded when we got there. Some of Sparky's gang was at the bar so we grabbed some bar stools and slid in. I ordered my usual Beefeaters Martini, straight up, with two olives on the side. I wasn't sure how the Martini was going to effect me after having done a couple of nice lines. One thing for sure, it was the making of a very long night. After everyone had their drinks I brought up the subject of our travel plans. We hashed it around for about fifteen minutes and decide to get underway in the morning when everyone was back to life. I had mixed emotions about that.

I felt some soft hands slowly sliding over my shoulders and around my neck. They were accompanied by a very pleasant fragrance. I was only guessing but I knew it had to be Angel. I turned around on the bar stool and met her face to face. She gave me a smart little kiss and asked for a drink. I didn't bother to ask her what she was drinking. I figured the bartender would know that, being she was the owner of the place. A couple of minutes later the bartender place a Manhattan down on the bar and I passed it to Angel. I would have never guessed her to be a Manhattan drinker.

Angel asked how many people were going to come up for dinner from our group. I got Sparky's attention and asked him if he knew how many of his people were going to have dinner. He said all of them were coming up so that would be ten of them and two us plus Angel. I looked at her and said, "same as the Last Supper". She looked at me for a second then caught on. I ordered the two of us another round. Angel told the bartended to let the kitchen know that there was going to be group of fourteen people for dinner. I corrected her and said thirteen. She smiled and said, "fourteen because my daughter Dina will be joining us. We can't have Nad eating alone". I started to say some thing but decide it was best left unsaid.

Diner was fun but basically uneventful. I had to complement Angel on the dinner. Everything was done just right and the portions were perfect not withstanding the service was impeccable. I wonder if that had anything to do with the owner sitting at the table with us. Nad and Angel's daughter Dina were just chatting away like they had been friends for years and the rest of the group were trying to get a Fuzzy Duck game going. I asked Angel if she had ever played Fuzzy Duck and she said no so I gave her a brief version of the rules and she said right off that she didn't want to play because she didn't like drinking games. I told her that I glad that she had said that because I also didn't like drinking games.

Angel suggested that once they get the game started that we slid out of the place and go down to her boat for a drink and a tour. I told her I was up to that and I would love to have a tour of her boat. Angel ask me if she should be worries about Nad and her daughter. "Angel, I said, if it were handed to Nad on a silver platter he would still turn it down. He is totally dedicated to his wife so you needn't have any worries about that". Angel seemed to be a little relieved.

The Fuzzy Duck game was now in progress and Angel and I slipped out without anyone the wiser. I couldn't help noticing how nice the evening was as we walked down the dock to Angel's boat. The air was calm, the humidity was low, the temperature was just right, and I had a beautiful woman at my side. Man! These are the things that movies are made from. We were at Angel's boat and I let her go ahead as we boarded her.

The interior lights were already on and they were preset to a romantic level. I have always loved Carvers. Having owned a couple of them myself I could appreciate this one. I had expected to see more of a feminine interior and was surprised by the almost neutral decoration. The carpet was in the beige family and all of the seating such as the couch and chairs were Corinthian Leather with a slightly darker tone than the carpet. The usual nautical decorations were strategically placed throughout the salon area. We walked forward to the lower helm area and I could appreciate the array of electronics that "AFTICA" was equipped with. I had to ask Angel about her proficiency of operating the boat. "Let's go for a moonlight ride and I'll show you, she said. I looked at her and asked her if she was serious. She was and I knew that she was when she reached out and started to engines.

"Captain are you wondering why I started up the engines without prechecking everything"? I told her I was just a little concerned about it but I make it a habit of not telling people how to run their boat unless they are totally stupid or they are about to do something that is going to affect me or someone around the boat. She smiled at me and said, "I have to be honest with you. This was all planned and I was down here earlier and got things ready. My goal was to get you down here and seduce you, either here in the marina or out on the river. Which would you like?"

WOW! Talk about forthrightness, aggressiveness, or whatever you want to call it. This woman, figuratively speaking, already had me in bed. I was duly impressed. I looked her and asked, "when do we get underway?" She looked at me with batting eyelashes and responded with, "as soon as you get on the dock and get the lines off." There are something's that I don't need to be told twice and this was one of them. I was already enjoying the cruise and we were still at the dock. I made an about face and headed for the dock.

I cast off al the dock lines and stepped aboard. My feet were no sooner on the swim platform, which is the normal boarding point on this boat once you leave the dock, and she engaged both drives and we slid out of the slip. Once clear of the slip I walked around the boat securing all of the fenders. We were out on the river by the time I got back to the helm station. Angel was busy with the electronics and I could see looking at her computer that she had this area of the river well charted and she was fixing to use the autopilot system. Her system was not unlike mine. Once she had captured a GPS fix she switched on the autopilot and the computer took over. The radar and computer would take over everything.

"Would you like a drink Captain or would you like to get naked and have some wild uncontrolled sex?" I must have looked flabbergasted because she chuckled a little. "Angel, I asked, are you asking me what I'm thinking or are you asking me to give me a choice?" She smiled, "I could care less what you're thinking". My shorts fell to the deck. After that point I'm not exactly sure what happened.

It was over in a second, a minute, five, ten, fifteen minutes. I don't know how long it was but I do know she had complete control and she was not giving it up until she had finished with her agenda.

You have to love a woman like Angel. She's the kind that pulls you up the mountain and pushes you off the top. The choice is not yours it is all hers. She literally collapsed on top of me and again I was content not to upset the applecart.

After a few minutes she began stirring and I could feel the perspiration between our bodies. It was a good feeling! She looked at me and asked," Do I need to give you an apology?" "For what", I asked. "Good, let's do it again".

The Bust

Chapter 49

I was dreaming of Angel when I woke up. It was fun evening and we cruised the river until around midnight. I had to tell her that she was a very capable person operating a large boat and the she could crew for me anytime she wanted. Right now however all I wanted was a cup of hot strong coffee. I'm glad I had the foresight to bring some Blue Mountain coffee with us on the trip.

Begrudgingly I climb out of the bunk, slipped on some shorts and a tee shirt and busied myself making coffee. I knew the coffee grinder was going to wake Nad up but it didn't matter because he needed to get up anyway. Coffee was on and brewing so I jumped in the shower for a quick hot shower. By the time I got out of the shower the coffee was done and Nad was up. He was a little slow in getting up which sort of told me what kind of an evening that he had. I poured both of us a cup of coffee and handed him his.

"Did you have a little fun last night?", I asked. He looked up at me and rolled his eyes a little and mumbled that he would never play Fuzzy Duck again. I could only conclude that he was not the winner. I went topside while Nad got up and got ready. It was a nice morning and the morning air felt good. It was a little humid already but not unusual for this part of the river. The sky was clear and the temperature was around seventy degrees. I was still topside when Nad came up. He was looking a little better than when he first got up.

We talked about the night before and found out that my suspicions were right about Nad not being the winner playing Fuzzy Duck. Nad also surprised me by telling me that Sparky had talked to him last night about a moneymaking proposition. I was all ears but Nad said that was all the information that he had. I asked him what he thought it meant and he said he just wasn't sure. I didn't want to get my hopes up but I was certainly hoping that it had something to do drugs. Mainly Cocaine!

I looked at my watch and it was seven o'clock straight up. Other people were starting to stir on the dock. I was hoping that Sparky and gang were going to get up at a decent hour. I wanted to get underway as soon as possible. The next couple of days were going to be very tedious. We had a bunch of Lock & Dams to transit, in fact nine of them in less than a hundred and fifty miles. There was a possibility that we would not get through all of them today, a very good possibility.

From the Yacht Harbor Marina it was 76.8 miles to Jamie Whitten Lock & Dam which would be the first lock that we go through on the Tenn-Tom. After that we would hit a Lock & Dam every few miles. The Locks operate a little different on the Tenn-Tom than they do on the Upper Mississippi. Down in this area they tend to use horn signals for communication between the Locks and the boats. Three long blasts from a boat tells the Lock that the boat wants to transit the Lock and the Lock responds with three long blasts when the Lock is ready. If the lock responds with four or short blasts that means you are going to have to wait.

There is a lock schedule also. It is primarily for weekends and holidays. Some of the locks will open on request and others open on either even or odd hours. There is a slight twist to this schedule. If you let the Lock know that you are going all the way to the Gulf you are exempt from the schedule and they will let you through on demand, of course you need to remember that commercial traffic always has priority. I would be pleasantly surprised if we made over a hundred miles today. Everything depended on the amount of commercial traffic.

A parade of people were going back and forth from their boats to the showers. Sparky stop on his way to the shower and we talked briefly about the day's travels. He agreed with me and we said we would talk once we were on the river. He wanted to get to the shower because he was the last one from his group to get ready. Nad started going through his "pre-flight" routine getting everything checked and ready. Everyone was full of gas and ready to go.

I was just going below to get another cup of coffee when Angel showed up on the dock. "Good Morning Captain", she said with a chirpy voice, did you sleep well last night?" "Very well thank you", I answered back. I was hoping that you would come down to the dock before we left so I could thank you for last night". "I should be thanking you, she said, you took care of some pent up emotions. I don't suppose that your going to be back through here in the near future are you?", she asked. "Angel at this moment I can't answer that question. As soon as I know I will definitely let you know", I told her.

She looked a little sad but I knew she would get over it. Dina, Angel's daughter showed up and stood beside her mother. They were a beautiful pair. Dina asked where Nad was and I told her he was below getting some coffee. I asked her if she wanted a cup but she declined. Moments later Nad came back up. There was a smile on his face when he saw Dina. Could it be possible that Nad...........No, I thought to myself, not true blue Nad. As a gentleman I was not going to ask him but if he was to volunteer any information I would be all ears.

The first boat fired up and then as if it had been choreographed the rest started up one after the other. We were the last to start up. We had to say good-bye to the Mom and Daughter team. Angel told us to get on the boat and her and Dina would get the dock lines for us. I gave Angel a kiss good-bye and told her I would keep in touch. Dina did get a hug from both Nad myself.

One by one the boats eased out of their slips. Somehow we ended up being first in line so headed out to the channel to wait for all of the boats to get out of the marina. Once everyone was on the river I eased the throttles forward. I radioed Sparky and told him he could take the lead and we fall back to the rear. Everyone passed us up and Sparky set the speed at fifty-five MPH. In roughly thirtyseven miles and thirty-five minutes we would be at the first lock. Other than a few fishing boat and a couple of houseboats the river was quiet.

We heard Sparky calling the Jamie Whitten Lock and telling them that there were five boats all heading to the coast. The lockmaster told him that they would be ready for us when we got there. He also said that he would call ahead for to the other locks to let them know that we were coming. This would greatly help us as all we had to do was radio each lock and they would give us a status update. We didn't have any real plans set in stone for this leg we could not foretell what the commercial traffic was going to be like. Somehow I doubted that we would make all nine locks today.

We pulled up to the Whitten Lock and they were waiting for us as promised. Once we all got up to the wall the lock gates closed and we started to lock down. This was going to be around an 80' drop to the other side. It was all over from start to finish in about thirty-five minutes and we started up the boats and headed out once the lower gates were open.

I did some quick calculations and assuming that we got through the next six locks as quickly as we did the first we would make the marina in West Point, Mississippi before dark. I called the group on the radio and had everyone go to channel 72 to discuss the matter. The conversation was interrupted because we had arrived at the next lock which was G.

V. "Sonny" Montgomery Lock and they also were ready for us. This lock was only going to be about a 30' drop as were the next five locks so it would go quickly.

Once we were out of the lock we went back to channel 72 to finish our conversation. We ended up all agreeing to try and make the Old Highway 50 Marina in West Point but if we got held up at any one lock we would stay at the marina in Aberdeen, Mississippi for the night. The remaining locks are only five to ten miles apart with exception of the Aberdeen Lock which is about fourteen miles from the Amory Lock.

Things were looking good and we were making good time. We got through the John Rankin, Fulton, Glover Wilkins Locks smoothly. It was about 12:30 and I was getting hungry. I didn't have a whole lot of dinner the night before and of course breakfast this morning was out of the question. I knew I was going to have to wait until we pulled into a marina for the night before I could get anything to eat. It was my own fault! I told Nad in the beginning that I didn't see any need to bring supplies on board because we were going to be stopping on a regular basis for gas and overnight dockage. Oh well! This wouldn't be the first time that I have missed a meal and I'm sure it won't be the last. It was around 2:30 when we hit the Aberdeen Lock & Dam and the Lockmaster told us we were going to have about a forty-five minute wait to lock through. Running some fast figures through my head I figured it would be 3:45 before we got through the Aberdeen Lock. We had another seventeen miles to go to get to the Old Highway 50 Marina in West Point and that would put us there at around 4:45. I was figuring that the West Point Marina would be an ideal stop for us.

Once we were cleared to enter the Aberdeen Lock everything else was like clockwork. We were in and out on our way almost to the minute of what I had calculated. I had called a head by cell phone to the marina and they said they had room for us for the night. They could put four boats in slips and the fifth would have to tie up at the restaurant. I told Nad over the intercom that we should get ahead of the other boats and tie up at the restaurant. He agreed and with that I pushed the throttles forward. We started catching up with the other boats and within seconds we were starting to pass them all.

Sparky wanted to know what was going on and I told him about the docking arrangements. He gave a little laugh and said "go for it". It always seems to amaze me how close I can come to predicting time and distance. Right at 4:40 I was calling the marina to let them know that we were about to leave the river channel and enter their marina. The fuel dock answered right back and asked if we were going to need gas. I have to admit that that piece of logistic got by me. I quickly called the other boats and we were all going to need gas. I called the marina back and told them we would be topping off our tanks before tying up for the night.

We pulled up to the fuel dock first and I jumped off the boat to get her tied up. The dock personnel were waiting for us and they jumped right on Nads boat and started to top off the gas. First in, first out and that's way I like it. I paid for the gas and got the boat untied and we headed for the restaurant dock. I knew I wanted this tie up because there was a deck over looking the dock and there were a lot of people have drinks and dinner on the deck.

Nad slid up to the dock and again I jumped out and tied the boat up. "Nice boat", I heard a feminine voice exclaim. I turned around and looked up to the deck above us. She couldn't have been more than eighteen but was built like a woman. I thanked her and she asked if she could come down and take a look. I told her that we didn't have time right now but if she was still around later I might be able to accommodate her. Actually I was trying to blow her off hoping she was here with Mommy and Daddy and they would leave and take her with them. Little did I know that she was going to bugging me half the night.

The weather was still nice and the temperature was hanging around 78 degrees. The only I didn't like about being down south was the humidity and it was probably at 90 percent right now. I went below and changed my shirt then came back up. One at a time Sparky's boats were getting into their assigned slips. We decide to wait for them because they would have to walk right by us to get to the restaurant.

There was a fairly good crowd of onlookers on the deck eyeing Nad's boat. Some of them were asking questions about the boat like how much did it cost, how fast did it go and the like. I let Nad field all of the questions as it was his boat. I just sat back and listened and watch Nad at work. He is very proud of his boat and he is always happy to tell people about it. Unlike myself, Nad would not embellish things about the boat like the speed or horsepower. Now myself on the other hand, I would have told them that the boat goes two-hundred miles an hour and it has three engines that have twelve-hundred horsepower each just to see the look on their faces.

Sparky's group wasn't wasting anytime on getting into the party mode because everyone was walking up the dock towards us with a drink in hand. I jumped on board quickly and grabbed a couple of beers for Nad and myself. We stood around on the dock for a while recapping the days events. Sparky got me off to the side and told me to go below and said that he would take care of me. I knew exactly what he was talking about.

I climbed on the boat with Sparky behind me and we went below. With deft he quickly laid out a couple of lines for me and Nad then went back topside. Instead of doing the line I brushed it all off into the sink. I had had enough of this stuff and didn't feel like doing anymore. I was about to head back topside and Nad came down. I told him what I had done and he said good because he was going to do the same thing. I went ahead and went back topside while Nad took care of business. I thanked Sparky for the treat, unbeknownst to him what we had done with it.

Nad was back up on the dock and I was ready to go get something to eat and drink. "I don't know about the rest of you, I said, but I am hungry and thirsty. I am heading for the restaurant". With that I turned and started walking up the gangway leading to the deck above us. When I got up to the deck I looked around to see if there was a place for all of us t sit down. A waitress came by and asked, "Ya'll here for dinner or drinks"?

We were in the south Ya'll. I never thought I would miss the southern drawl but it sounded nice coming from her mouth. I asked her if she could get seating for ten people. She said if we would wait just a moment she would take care of us. She went over by the rail over looking Nads boat and brought a couple of table together. When she had finished she looked over to me and motioned us to sit down. We ordered a round of drinks and she brought us some menus. Apparently everyone was as hungry as I was. Everything on the menu looked good. It always does when you are hungry. It's like going to the grocery store on an empty belly. You are going to buy way more stuff than you really need. I was having a hard time making up my mind on what to eat. Our waitress came back with our drinks and I asked her for a recommendation on what to order for dinner. She said everything was good but the special tonight was whole pond raised Catfish with fresh Vidalia onion slices, homemade Hush Puppies, and Cole Slaw. That hit a button. I will eat Catfish up north but you just hold a stick to it compared to how they do it down south. I asked her for a glass of unsweetened ice tea with the meal also. I like a good glass of ice tea with a slice of fresh lemon once in a while.

I got the rest of the groups attention after all of the dinner orders had been given to the waitress. I wanted to get a timeline on the rest of the trip. I asked Sparky what their schedule was and he said that they didn't really have a schedule and we certainly didn't. We all knew that we had about three hundred and thirty-eight miles to go before hitting the Gulf. I was thinking we should do it in two days and I asked if anyone else had any input. Everyone seemed to be happy with that.

"Sparky, I asked. Are you guys going to a marina once you get down there"? I had to ask the question because up'til now we hadn't discussed it. It was only because of my suspicions about Sparky and his group that I wanted to stay with them for as long as we could. He may be just a user of cocaine and comes down here to buy quantity. On the other hand he and his group could be major mules bringing large quantities up to the cities. In any event we were going to try and stick with them.

"Yes we are Cap, he answered. We are going over to Biloxi once we hit the Gulf and we'll be staying at Johnny's Marina. You guys are welcome to come with us if you want. When we get a little closer I'll let them know that there will be another boat with us". I looked at Nad as if I needed his approval before making a decision. Nad said it was okay with him because we really hadn't thought that far ahead. That was a good answer coming from Nad but then it was the truth for the most part. We really hadn't thought about where we were going once we hit the Gulf.

Our initial goal was to try and hook up with someone that we thought was involved with drugs and we found that in Sparky. Secondly we had to try and find out who or where the source was coming from. I was hoping that Sparky would fulfill all of those needs and at this point I was about 90% sure he was going too. It was just a matter of time.

We finished dinner and went to the bar to have a couple of drinks. There was a fairly good size crowd in the bar, mostly local people. Nad got into a conversation with a guy who had a boat in the marina. For some reason I didn't feel like socializing so I feigned sleepiness and said I was going down to the boat to turn in early. Actually it was a good time to get a hold of Carmen and give her an update on our situation. I said good night to everyone and headed down to the boat.

I gave Carmen a call and gave al of the information that we had up to now. I also told where we were going once we hit the Gulf. I suggested to her that she have someone do a little investigation on the marina that we were going to. I told her if she had a contact down in the Gulf she might want to have someone go to the marina and get some boat registration numbers and run them just to see where who was there and where they were from. She thought that was a good idea and said she would get right on it in the morning and get back with me if she found out anything conclusive. We talked a little bit longer on a more personal subject. Carmen wanted to know if I was going to come back up river with Nad because she wanted to fly down and come back up with us. I told her at this point I didn't know what we were going to do. We left it that and said good-bye. I called it a night and hit the sack.

I woke up with a start not knowing why. I looked over to Nad's bunk and he was sound asleep. I put my head back down and listen for anything unusual. I heard nothing out of the ordinary. I looked at my watch and it was showing 6:20 AM. What the hell I figured I may as well get up and put some coffee on and get cleaned up. I started making some coffee and Nad woke up. I said good morning to him and asked him late he had stayed in the bar. He said he had come down about an hour after I did hoping that I was still awake so he could talk to me about a conversation he had with Sparky.

"Sparky wanted to know if he and his wife would swap boats with me for the day, he started out. They have been thinking about buying a new boat but were unsure what they wanted. They had been eyeing my boat, he continued, and just wanted to give it a try for a day". "Interesting, I replied, did you buy in to it or do you think he has an ulterior motive"?

"By the way he talked I took him seriously. I think he really is looking to buy a new boat. It doesn't matter to me one way or the other if he takes the boat for a day. It's not like he is going off on his own, I mean we'll all be together". I shrugged my shoulders and said it was his call. My mind was already working to see if I could read something into Sparky's request. Naturally with my mind I came up with several plausible answers of which some made sense and others didn't. I poured Nad a cup of coffee and helped myself to my second cup. Nad was slowly climbing out of his bunk so I decided to topside.

Once again it was a beautiful morning! I sat down on the rear seat leaning against the starboard bulkhead with my feet up on the seat. It was still quiet except for the lapping of the water against the hull of the boat and an occasional fish jumping out of the water. For a moment I was mesmerized by my surroundings. I laid my head back against the gunnel and shut my eyes trying to clear my brain of any extraneous activity. My solitude was suddenly interrupted by Sparky. "Sorry Captain, he said. Were you sleeping"? "No Sparky, I answered. I was just relaxing and enjoying the day. How about some coffee", I asked. He said yes and I told him to come aboard and have a seat while I went below.

I came back with a fresh cup of coffee for the both of us. I handed Sparky his cup of coffee and then I sat back down where I had been sitting earlier. "Say Cap, Sparky asked. Have you talked with Nad yet this morning"? "Only briefly. He mentioned something about us swapping boats for the day because you are thinking about buying a new boat and you've kinda taken a shine to this one". "That's right, he said. I have always wanted a Fountain and now I am in a position where I can afford it. Do you have any objections"?, he asked. I was very candid with him, "It's Nad's boat and if he wants to swap for the day it's fine with me". He smiled and said something about not being able to wait to get started.

About then Nad came topside. "I overheard you guys talking about the boats, he said. I guess if we are going to do it I should give you a run down on everything". It made sense to me so I butted out and left the two of them alone. I decide to take a walk on the docks and take a look at the boats in the marina.

When I got back to our boat Nad and Sparky were just finishing up. Sparky's wife was on board with them and the rest of Sparky's group were standing around on the dock. Sparky and Nad climbed off the boat and headed for Sparky's boat. I jumped in behind them just so it would seem that I was interested in the whole thing. Nad wasn't going to have any problems with Sparky's boat because he used to own one just like it.

However, even though a boat may seem similar, each boat has it's own little nuances. Sparky went over these little nuances with Nad while I watched. It only took about ten minutes to over everything. Once that was done we got off the boat and went back to Nad's boat. There was a lot kibitzing going on about Sparky taking Nad's boat. All good natured of course. Everyone seemed to be in the mood to get underway. I followed Nad below to get our bags. Just something that we might need for the day. While we were below I told Nad to make sure there was not anything incriminating laying around. There should not have been anything anyway but I just wanted to make sure.

We grabbed our cell phones and I grabbed my gun and put it right on top of the things in my bag. With that done we went back topside. Sparky had gone back to his boat to get some stuff from his boat. I threw a question out to the group to see if anyone had brought a video camera with them. Jeff piped up and that they had and I asked if we could borrow it so we take some video of Sparky in Nad's boat. No problem he said and ran quickly back to his boat to get it. When he brought it back I told him that I would replace the tape at my earliest convenience because Nad wanted to keep it for himself. My immediate motive was not for that but it was a good excuse to get them on film without anyone being any the wiser. It might prove beneficial to have what everyone looks like.

Bags had been switched and everyone was on their respective boat waiting for the high sign to fire up. Nad stayed with Sparky just to get the engines started up. I went to Sparky's boat by myself and got it fired up. I was waiting for Nad to cast the lines off for Sparky. Once Sparky was out of the slip Nad trotted down to Sparky's boat and jumped aboard after he cast all of the dock lines off. Nad told me to go ahead and take the boat out which I was more than happy to do.

Once everyone was on the river we fell into the formation which had been agreed upon before we left. Nad and I would pick up the rear and Sparky of course would be leading the pack. I told them that we might zipped to the front just so we could get a good shot of everybody with the camera. I also told the girls that flashing would be allowed.

The first lock of the day was only four miles down river. It was the John C. Stennis Lock & Dam. Appropriately named after Senator John C. Stennis, who also has an aircraft carrier named after him. Sparky had set the pace at a slow fifty MPH. With only four miles to go it would take just a few minutes to get there. We could hear Sparky on the radio talking with the lock. The lock gave us an all clear and said they would be ready for us when we got there.

After the Stennis lock the next one was the Tom Bevill Lock & dam and after that one we would have about a fifty mile run for the next one and likewise for the one following. We got through the Stennis lock in record time. Once we were out of the lock Sparky kept Nad's boat at an idle because the lockmaster told him that we were going to be held up at the next lock due to commercial traffic. It was only two miles down river so we were going to take our time getting there. I got on the radio and told all the boats that we were coming forward to get some video shots.

When I got the video camera ready I told Nad to speed up and stay on the starboard side of the other boats. I got on the radio real quick and told the other boats that we were going to be coming by on a pass. I went to the back of the boat and kneeled down on the rear seat. I could have figured it was going to happen! The girls were going to flash us as we went by. One by one we went passed the other boats capturing everyone on video. When we got to Sparky we went on passed him then made a port turn in front of him so we could head to the back of the pack again.

I kept the video going the whole time we were heading to the back of the pack and again getting some nice shots. As Nad was turning the boat to fall in behind the others my ears detected a rattling sound like something had come loose. I went back to the front of the boat to set the camera down and told Nad that something was loose in the back of the boat and I was going back to check it out. When I got back there the sound was gone or least I couldn't hear it. I yelled at Nad to make a couple of sudden turns thinking maybe the turning would make the noise reappear.

Nad yanked the wheel quickly in both directions and I heard the sound again. It seemed to be coming from one of the Scuba Tanks that were in the rack on the starboard side of the boat. I reach over and shook one of the tanks. It was solidly mounted so I didn't think it was the source of the rattling. I grabbed the second tank by the valve and shook it and I was pleasantly surprised. There was movement in my hand. In fact, the top of the tank was actually loose. I couldn't figure out why it was loose. It is a one-piece tank.

It starts out as two pieces during the manufacturing process. The bottom part is a cylinder and the top part which is half round is welded to the bottom part. Unless the weld broke, which is virtually impossible, that would be the only reason for the top to have any play.

I twisted the top counterclockwise and it stared turning. I kept turning the top and I could see threads appearing. After turning the top about five or six complete revolutions it came off. You could have knocked me over with a feather. I looked down into the tank and was a pile of money packed into the tank. It appeared that is was all hundred dollar bills bundled in $10,000.00 packs. The tank was so full of these packs I couldn't begin guess how much money was in there. If I were to hazard a guess I would probably say in the hundreds of thousands of dollars.

I took one the packs of bills and walked back to the front of the boat and showed it to Nad. His eyes opened wide and he just stared at the money unbelievingly. "Where did you get that", he asked. "It was in one the tanks back there and the tank is full of money", I answered. I looked at Nad and said, "I think we just got an answer to one of our more important questions. These guys, or at least Sparky has got to be involved in drug trafficking. I was still having a hard time believing what I was looking at. My curiosity had me wondering if the remaining three tanks were also full of money.

At this point I didn't want to push my luck. I put the money that I had taken out of the tank back then picked up the top of the tank to screw it back on. For no reason at all while I had the top in my hands I grabbed the valve and twisted it to the open position. To my surprise there was the sound of high-pressure air coming from the valve. I turned the top over to look inside and found that a plate had been welded inside the top.

It became very clear on what I was looking at. The tanks or least the one that I was holding, had the tops cut off, then they were machined to put threads on both the top and bottom sections of the tank. This would allow the top of the tank to be screwed on as I had found it. The machining was done in such a manner that one could not detect any seams. As for the top of the tank it was very clear also. By welding in a plate or false bottom and welding it to "ASME" (Associated Society of Mechanical Engineers) standards they could pressurize the top part of the tank with up to 2,250 lbs. per sq. in. which was the normal pressure for a full single seventy cu. ft. tank. Anyone opening the valve would hear the high-pressure air rushing out which would be perfectly normal not giving it another thought. I drew quick diagram of the tank for future reference.

I screwed the top back on the tank twisting it as hard as I could. I was hoping that it was tight enough so it wouldn't come loose again. The last thing I wanted to do was raise any suspicion that we had been snooping around Sparky's boat. After securing the tank I went back forward to discuss it with Nad. He was still shocked about the find. I had to admit that this was a totally ingenious way to hide drugs. There was still the question of where, when, and how the money was exchanged for cocaine.

I screwed the top back on the tank twisting it as hard as I could. I was hoping that it was tight enough so it wouldn't come loose again. The last thing I wanted to do was raise any suspicion that we had been snooping around Sparky's boat. After securing the tank I went back forward to discuss it with Nad. He was still shocked about the find. I had to admit that this was a totally ingenious way to hide drugs. There was still the question of where, when, and how the money was exchanged for cocaine.

We discussed our options and agreed that once we were tied up tonight that I would call Carmen in the cities to let her know what we had just discovered. We needed to talk with her anyway to let her know where we going once we hit the Gulf.

We had reached the Tom Bevill Lock & Dam and we were going to have about a half hour wait according to Sparky. Everyone put their fenders out and we all rafted together letting the boats drift with the current until we got close to the dam then we would start one of the boats and eased back up river a ways then let the boats drift back down. Sparky asked if we wanted to swap boats back and I looked at Nad and he motioned yes with his head so we made a quick swap back to our respective boats. I can't say that it felt good to be back on Nad's boat but I was at least relived a little by not having to stay on Sparky's boat any longer.

Sparky thanked Nad for letting him run his boat for a while. You could tell that Sparky was duly impressed. Little did Sparky know that were also duly impressed by what we had discovered on his boat. I smiled inwardly knowing that it was a very good possibility in the very near future, I mean very near, that the only thing Sparky would be doing with boats is making models of them in prison.

The lock gates finally opened up and it took better than ten minutes for the barge to clear the lock so we could get in. While we were locking through we discussed our plans for tonight. We had about fifty miles to go to the next set of locks. After that it was another fifty miles to the first available marina. We decided after going through the Howell Heflin Lock & Dam we would stop at the Demopolis Harbor at Mile Marker 216.7 for the night. That would leave us around two hundred and sixteen miles to get to the Gulf. With only two remaining locks after the Heflin Lock to go through we calculated that we could be in Biloxi by late tomorrow afternoon.

The down river lock gates opened up and we were gone. With Nad's boat still in the lead that meant that we would be setting the pace. I got on the radio and asked everyone how fast they wanted to go. We all agreed on 70 MPH and with that I eased the throttles forward. The Lock Master was unable to give us a traffic report on any upcoming commercial traffic so we were going to have to keep our eyes open. We were figuring our travel time right at an hour baring the meeting of any commercial traffic. I called ahead to the marina to let them know that there was going to be five boats coming in later that afternoon.

At Mile Marker 245.8 we hit commercial traffic. The barge was blocking the entire channel and we were stuck until he was finished making up the containers that he was picking up. I got a hold of the barge Captain and asked him how long it was going to take him to get made up. He said it would probably take an hour for him to completely clear the channel. I got a hold of the other boats to let them know that we were being held up for about an hour. I remembered a beach that we had passed about a half mile back and made a suggestion that we go back up and beach the boat for a while. Done deal! I called the barge Captain and asked him to give us a call when he was clear of the channel. He said okay and turned the boats and headed back up river.

We got to the beach and we were happy to see that it was a deepwater beach and there was little to no current. One by one we brought the boats into the beach. Once all the boats were shut down we hit the beach. Jeff started throwing out cold beers to everyone and I caught two of them then gave one to Nad. It actually tasted good at that moment too one who rarely drinks beer. Sparky also brought out some other treats which Nad and I hesitantly ingested.

Our waiting time passed by quickly. I had brought my hand held radio onto the beach and the barge Captain was calling to let us know that he was about to clear the channel. It was time to get back on the boats. I was getting to enjoy the warm sand and was thinking about stripping down and getting a little sun just before the Captain called us. Oh well! I made a mental note to pay attention in the future.

We were back on the river and heading south again. We had around thirty miles or so to cover before we got to the marina. Nad's boat was in the lead so we kept the speed at fortyfive MPH. It was a little after two o'clock and we would be at the marina no later than three o'clock. We had to slow down one more time at Mile Marker 222.3 for a barge but fortunately he was not blocking the channel. Sometimes if you go by a barge to fast and create a large wake they get a little upset. I have always found it better to slow down especially when you are in a narrow channel.

The Demopolis Harbor is right on the river about a quarter of a mile below the junction of the Warrior River at Mile Marker 216.7. It was ten minutes until three when we pulled in. Nad pulled into the fuel dock so we could get that out of the way. Sparky's group was going to get topped off later. After we were filled up we went to our assigned slip and tied the boat up. Nad wanted to do some minor PM (Preventative Maintenance). I thought about calling Carmen but I didn't want to take a chance of being on the phone if anyone from Sparky's group came down to the boat. I decided to wait until later. I knew we would go up to the bar and I could wait until then saying that I needed to check on my people at my marina.

It felt good to know that tomorrow, baring any unforeseen problems, that we would be in the Gulf. We only had two more locks to go through and one of those was only three miles below from the marina. Depending on what time we got out of the marina in the morning and how hard we pushed we should certainly make the Gulf by mid afternoon. I leaned over the engine compartment hatch and could see Nad crawling around. I asked him if he needed any help and he said he was about done. I decided to go below and take a quick shower.

Done with my shower I made myself a drink and went back up top. Nad was sitting on the dock reading what appeared to be an owners manual. I got his attention and asked what he was doing. "It looks like one of my blower drive belts is about to go", he said. "Do you carry a spare one, I asked, or are you going to have to order one?" "Order one, he responded, I can call them today and have it shipped wherever I want. The good thing about this is that it's the middle engine and if I have to I can shut it down".

I wasn't going to second-guess Nad. I had all of the confidence in the world that he knows what he is talking about. Nad stood up and stretched then said he was going below to get cleaned up. I told him I would be sitting up here relaxing. I went below quickly to mix a fresh drink and when I came back up a couple of Sparky's people were walking by. I said hi to them and asked if they were heading up to the bar. They said yes and the rest of the group would be coming up shortly. I told them that Nad was getting cleaned up and we would be up as soon as he was ready.

When Nad was ready we walked up to the bar. Things were relatively quite especially Sparky's group. My guess was that the trip was starting to take a toll amongst other things. We pulled up a couple of chairs and sat down with the group. Other than idle chit chat nothing was really being said. Nad got engrossed in a conversation with Jeff and was telling him about his blower belt deteriorating. I sat there trying not to get involved with anyone. I was trying to think up a suitable way to excuse myself so I could make a call to the cities. What a stroke of luck! My cell phone rang and it was Chad, my main dock worker. I started talking to him then excused myself from the table. I don't know about these other people but it runs me up the walls having to listen to someone talking on a cell phone.

Outside I was able to take care of business with Chad then make a quick call to Carmen. I brought her up to date then told her about the find on Sparky's boat. She couldn't believe my story about finding the money in a diving tank. I had to explain it to her a couple of time before she completely understood what I was saying. "Carmen, we are going a marina in Biloxi called Johnny's. We should be there sometime tomorrow afternoon. Can you get someone down there to start checking the place out? I would suggest that they start with getting as many registration numbers off any boats that are there and start running them"

"Captain, she responded, I am already on it as we speak. I have a couple of DEA people here and they will contact their people down there". I told her about Nad's boat about to have problems and that that should be the only thing that would keep us from reaching the Gulf tomorrow.

I felt good talking with Carmen. She was a sweet woman and I actually sort of missed her. She definitely had a lot going for herself. I went back inside the bar and saw that everyone, but myself was ordering something to eat. I sat down quickly and grabbed a menu. Before our server was done with the others I had made my choice. Deep fried Catfish with all the trimmings! After ordering dinner I decided it was time for a Martini so I told our server what and how I wanted it. Beefeaters, straight up with two olives on the side. She said she would make it herself. When she brought it to me I told her she could go back to the bar and start making another one because by the time she got back I would done with this one.

True to my word, I was done with my first Martini by time she got back with my second one. The thing about drinking Martini's you always hope that the next one is as good as the last. Shelly, our server made sure that it was. I was done with my second Martini and had ordered a third when dinner arrived. I was feeling a good buzz and I was glad that dinner was here. Not standing on ceremony I dug in. I was hungry and the Martini's weren't helping stave off my hunger.

Looking around the table it appeared that everyone was just about as hungry as I was. I was the first one done with dinner and I ordered a nice double snifter of cognac. I knew this was going to finish me off. Three Martini's and a double cognac plus a day on the river. Yep! I was going to hit the bunk early tonight. Much to my surprise many of the others felt exactly like me and said they were going to turn in early also. We were looking at a two hundred mile plus trip tomorrow. Before we left the bar we discussed the next days plans. We all agreed that we should get underway early in the morning certainly no later than eight o'clock. We would need to have at least one fuel stop and best shot we had was at Mile Marker 118.9 which is the Camp Rd. Marina right above the Coffeeville Lock & Dam. From there we would have a straight shot to Johnny's Marina in Biloxi.

Everything seemed to be in order and I got up and said good-night to everybody. As I was walking down to the boat my brain was going into overload. The next couple of days could prove to be very trying if not potentially dangerous, especially for myself and Nad. We were about to enter a totally different environment, the underworld of drugs. Without any explanation Glen Frey's song, "Smuggler's Blues" popped into my head. The words were vivid in my mind and they spoke the truth. I began to hum the opening words of the song, "There's trouble on the streets tonight, I can feel it in my bones". It's seemed a little funny that I would suddenly remember a song that came out way back in 1984.

When I got on the boat I went below and pulled out my gun. I decide to give it a quickly cleaning and oiling because I wouldn't have time to do it later and I wanted to make sure it was ready to go…just in case. I was just finishing up when Nad came aboard. "Getting a little nervous Captain?", he asked. "Just getting prepared, I responded. I don't want to wait until the last minute". He smiled then chuckled a little and walked over to where he had his gun stashed and pulled it out. "Getting a little nervous Nad". He looked at me and we both laughed.

Sleep came easy and fast for me. I vaguely remember some more of the "Smuggler's Blues" lyrics going through my head as I fell asleep. "Ev'ry name's an alias in case someone squeals. It's the lure of easy money, it's gotta very strong appeal". It was a fitful sleep!

I woke up with a start. Nad was already up and was in the process starting the engines. I sat up quickly and immediately laid back down. I must be getting old I thought to myself. My head was throbbing a little from last night. I only had three Martini's and a little Cognac. I still remember the night in Alma, Wisconsin at the Burlington Hotel when I was given the nickname of "Captain Martini". The night that I drank seven Martini's.

Reluctantly I climbed out of the bunk and slid on some clothes. Nad had made some coffee so I poured myself a cup and went topside. The dock was a bustle of activity. All of the boats were running and in the last stages of preparedness to get underway. I said good morning to Nad and walked to the rear seat to sit down. My head still had a few cobwebs in it and I just wanted to sit for a while. Nad turned around and asked me if I was ready to go. What the hell I thought! So much for sitting and resting. I made a feeble attempt to nod yes then got up to take care of the dock lines.

The night before we had decided to run a steady sixty MPH on this last leg. One reason was to conserve fuel and the other reason I just couldn't remember. We pulled out of the slip and head for the river. Once we were on the river I called the Demopolis Lock & Dam to find out if they would be ready for us once we go there. The Lock Master said they had a barge that was in the process of leaving the lock as we spoke. If we didn't get there to soon he would be ready for us. As we had only three miles to go to get to the lock so we kept the speed down to twenty-five.

We met the north bound barge about a quarter of a mile or so above the lock. I called the Lock Master to let him know that we were ready to lock through whenever he was. He answered back that he was ready and we could enter the lock. The Demopolis Lock has about a forty foot lift so it was going to take every bit of about three quarters of an hour to lock through.

My guess on timing was right on. In forty-five minutes we were underway again. We eased our speed up to sixty MPH and sat back for the almost hundred mile jaunt to our gas stop. It was a nice day but looking south I could see some massive thunderheads in the sky. I brought this to Nad's attention and he said he had been looking at them also. I switched the radio to the weather channel to get the weather report. It didn't sound good. They were calling for severe thunderstorms this morning until around noon. This kind of sucked! Other than a few showers on the way down, our trip was a good one, weather wise. I called Sparky on the radio to ask him if he listened to the weather channel this morning. He said no but he would do it right away. He called back in a few minutes and I could hear the tone of displeasure in his voice. My guess was we would be in the middle of the storm within the hour.

I'm getting way to wise in my old age. Within the hour the storm hit. It wasn't just any storm. It was a full fledged gale. The Emergency Weather Broadcast automatically came on with an update for the storm.

The computerized voice droned on, "….winds exceeding ninety MPH, flooding rain and damaging hail are possible. Several tornados have been spotted in an area from Silas, Alabama, north to Demopolis, Alabama. I looked at Nad with a shrug in my shoulders. We just left

Demopolis and we were heading for Silas. We were heading right for the storm. I got on the radio and asked the group if they wanted to stop so everyone could put up their canvass. It was unanimously agreed too and we pulled the throttles.

The wind was already picking up and it was not an easy job putting up the canvas, especially on Nad's boat. It took about a halfhour to get the job done and it was none to soon.

The storm hit with a fury. The wind was coming straight up the channel which was a mixed blessings. At least we could nose into the wind and it would be easier to keep the boats under control. Sparky's group, with their smaller boats were going to have their work cut out for them. As the wind picked up the waves got bigger. Within minutes we were heading into six foot seas being pushed by sixty to seventy MPH winds. It was not a comfortable feeling and I could imagine what the other boats were going through. We were at the mercy of the weather. There was no place in this area for us to get shelter and besides the fact it would be ludicrous to make an attempt to enter a marina in this kind of weather.

I was glad that we had stopped to put up canvass. It would have been totally miserable without it. Jeff's voice suddenly blasted out on the radio. With the smallest boat in the group, he was taking on water. He said his bilge pumps were barely keeping up. This was not a good time to be taking on water, I thought to myself. Jeff's boat is seaworthy enough but in these conditions once the boat gets heavy with water it can swamp in a heartbeat. We needed something just short of a miracle and we needed it now!

I yelled at Nad that I was going below to look at the charts. I knew there were not any Bluffs in the area that we could hide behind. I also knew if there was a sharp bend in the river, that we could get on the lee side of the bend at it might afford us a little protection.

It was a job getting down below with the violent pitching of the boat. I nearly landed on my ass a couple of times. I grabbed the charts and started looking for our current position. The last Day Marker that we had seen was 194.3 so we couldn't be to much further than that. I found what I was looking for. If we were where I thought we were, we were about a half-mile from a sharp turn in the river. The possibility was there if the topography was good. The charts don't show topography, only land mass.

I went back topside and told Nad what I had found. I called Jeff on the radio and told him about my findings. I told him if we or he could make it just a half-mile we might find a little calmer water. Jeff answered back and I could tell he was not a happy camper. He said he didn't know if he could make a half-mile right now. "Jeff, I said, you have to at least try to make it. We'll drop back and stay behind you but you have to try and make it to the bend".

Visibility had dropped to nearly zero. If it wasn't for the silhouette of the shoreline we would be "SOL".

Nad made a quick turn which of course was not a pleasant feeling, even in his boat. Turning a boat with a relatively narrow beam sideways in six foot seas will never fell comfortable to me. One moment I was looking at the sky and the next moment I was looking at water. Nad put his bow on the backside of a wave and did his best to hold it there. Even trickier is to maintain control in following seas. We got abreast of Jeff and made a turn in behind him. It was very plain to se that his stern was heavy with water. There was little to no rebound from buoyancy and every wave that crashed over him made him a little heavier.

It may have been minutes but it seemed like it had been hours when Sparky yelled on the radio that he could just make out the bend. Our headway through the water could not have been more than two to three MPH. Sparky said he was about four hundred yards from the bend and it appeared to be a little calmer. I'm sure that was good news to Jeff. I asked Sparky if he could see the shoreline yet and he came back that he couldn't see the shoreline but he could make out a tree line. There was a pause then Sparky came back with the news we wanted to hear.

"We are in the lee of the shoreline", he shouted. There is still a strong wind but not near as bad as it is in the channel and there is enough room for all of us to drop the hook. That was good news and I'm sure Jeff was relieved to hear it. It took us another ten minutes to get into the lee and it was a great deal calmer than in the channel. We let the other boats drop their hooks before we dropped ours. Satisfied that they were solidly hooked I worked my way up to the bow and pulled the anchor out of the anchor locker. Almost sliding off the bow of the boat I threw the anchor out as far as I could then let us drift back on it until I thought we had sufficient scope in the anchor rode.

When I thought we had enough rode out I tied the line off and gingerly worked my way back up to the cockpit. I took a sighting on the shoreline to make sure that we weren't dragging the anchor. For the time being it looked as if the anchor was going to hold us. I felt good about it because I had increased the scope from the standard 7-to-1 ratio to a 9-to-1 ratio which in layman terms means, for every foot of water depth I let out nine feet of anchor rode.

We kept our eyes on Jeff boat and after about a half-hour we see that his boat was riding higher in the water. I could also make out exhaust bubbling up from behind his boat which meant he didn't lose his motor.

It was nearly an hour before the storm blew over enough to where we felt good enough to venture back out on the river. Nad was nominated to "test the waters" because he had the biggest boat there. Nad maneuvered the boat so I could weigh anchor. I let the anchor drag a little in the water to get the mud or "Loon Shit" off of it before I stowed it in the anchor locker. Out on the channel the wind had dropped dramatically as did the waves. I radioed back to the waiting boats and told them to pull anchor and let's get the show on the road.

In a matter of minutes we were on our way again. We still had to hold our speed down but at least we were making a little headway. I mentioned to Nad that if we didn't get an opening in this weather soon that we would end up spending another night on the river. He nodded in agreement and extended his crossed fingers, for good luck.

In all we blew about two hours of good travel time but we could make it up after we made our fuel stop. Ahead of us I could see the clouds starting to break up. The wind was steadily dieing down as were the waves. Every few minutes I was adding more throttle as the conditions would allow. In about a half hour we were back up to speed. In just over an hour, again baring any unforeseen circumstances, we should make the Camp Rd. Marina.

It was just over an hour by the time we got to the marina but that was close enough for Government work in my book. Our spirits were brightened by the sun coming out again however, I didn't like the humidity that came with it. We pulled up to the fuel dock and started fueling up. The owner was on the dock and told us we just missed a major storm. I corrected him and told him that we did not miss the storm, in fact I told him, we almost lost one our boats.

With all of the boats topped off with gas we got back underway right away. We had right at a hundred and eighteen mile to go to get to the Gulf. Sparky wanted to run at seventy MPH so we told him to take the lead. Nad wanted to drop to the back of the pack because of his blower belt. He had checked it while we were fueling and he said it was getting worse and he didn't want to be in the lead when and if the belt broke. The sudden loss of power could result in a sudden loss of speed and a good chance of the boat behind us could run into us. We fell behind and waited for the other boats to get up to speed. Sparky leveled off at seventy MPH.

I was really getting to love the intercom system on Nad's boat. One has to realize the tremendous amount of exhaust noise being emitted from three massive blown engines. The intercom system allows the occupants to converse back and forth, plus the system allows you to also tap in the VHF radio and a cell phone if you want. The headset has a boom mic that has an adjustable noise canceling feature so if you are talking to someone they are not hearing the roar of the engine exhaust.

I had to thank Nad for installing the system because without it I would have missed the call from Carmen. Had we missed Carmen's call we would have been directly in harms way when we arrived at Johnny's Marina. "Captain, she started out. You can't show up at the marina in Biloxi. The ball is already rolling. If you remember, yesterday when we talked I had a DEA agent here with me in my office. I passed on your information to him and he got the ball rolling on his end. Things happened real fast". I started to interrupt her but held off letting her talk.

She continued, "apparently the DEA has had their eyes on this place for some time but could never get any conclusive information even with informants in the marina. You know as well as I do that timing is everything and your information was right on time.

Within minutes after I talked with you yesterday DEA agents infiltrated the marina and actually observed the shipment arriving at the marina. They are not sure how much cocaine arrived but a conservative estimate was placed at somewhere around three thousand pounds of the stuff". Again I wanted to interrupt her because questions were forming in my mind. Unbeknownst to her she was answering some of my questions so I relented and let her continue to talk.

"It seems that the marina has a dive shop that caters to the local diving enthusiasts. This shop in itself is a fairly good size operation and they worked with impunity for years. They have an excursion dive boat that can handle up to 50 divers and all of their gear for a day, several compressors, including one on the excursion boat, to charge the diving tanks. Anything that anyone could ever want in the way of diving equipment was sold in the shop. From all outward appearances it is a first class sport diving operation".

I had to interrupt, "Carmen, I said interrupting her, how did the cocaine get to the dive shop"? "That part they are not sure of at this time, she answered. There are several theories but at this time there is nothing definitive. After it is fully investigated we may get more information on that subject but for right it is very important that you do not show up at Johnny's Marina. Do what you have to do or say what you have say, just don't go to the marina".

Her instructions were very clear! I passed on the information to Nad and asked him if he had any ideas. We needed to come up with a plan of action almost immediately. I knew there was a reason that I liked Nad because he always seems to be quick on his feet. "I've got it, he suddenly declared. Sparky already knows that one of my blower belts is about to go. All we have to do is convince them that the belt went south but at the same time is created other problems. We don't have to wait for the belt to go. I can take it off anytime and say that we threw a belt. Give me a minute and I'll come up with some thing".

We were making good time and we were just passing the mouth of the Alabama River at Mile Marker 45. In a few miles we should start hitting more traffic on the river and that would slow us down. That would give us more time to concoct a plausible story unless we thought of something before then. My mind was racing trying to think this whole thing through. Suddenly Nad interrupted my thought process.

"Cap, he said excitedly, here's how it's going down. When we're ready you're going to call Sparky and tell him we have problems. It only takes a minute to remove the blower belt. I have an extra distributor cap that I am going to break into pieces. We will tell Sparky that we threw a belt and when it went it hit one of the other engines distributor cap and busted it. Because we'll supposedly be down to one engine we won't be able to keep up with them". It sounded good to me and I knew Nad could pull it off. All I had to do was play along with whatever Nad said.

Nad said we would wait until we were actually in Mobile Bay. There was a marina on the Dog River called Tiny's Marine Supply. They handle these types of boats and it be natural for us to want take it to the nearest place for repair. Besides, they couldn't expect us to try and make it all the way to Johnny's Marina on one engine.

I heard Sparky's voice on the radio. "Alright people, we are coming up on some traffic so we are going to have to back out of the throttles. I'm going to slow down to around forty MPH. Everyone, including us, acknowledged Sparky's transmission. We immediately started slowing down. We were just entering the upper end of Mobile Bay and there was a lot of commercial as well as recreational traffic on the river.

Nad got my attention and asked me if I was ready to start our plan of deception. I nodded yes and he told me to take the wheel. After we had switched places he told me how the plan was going to work. "Cap, he said. When I tell you I want you to pull the throttle back then kill the port and center engines. Leave the starboard engine running and keep it in gear but at idle. It is going to be a little hard to steer but you shouldn't have any problems". I was listening to every word he said. "I am going to pull off the blower belt from the center engine then I am going to step on my spare distributor to break it. Once I've done that, he said continuing, you call Sparky on the radio and tell him that we are broken down. If they are paying attention they might realize before we call them that something is up once we start slowing down".

I was following his plan so far. "Before they get back here to us I will have parts in hand to show them. What I'm not sure of at this point is what comes next so just pay attention and follow my lead". I said okay and watched Nad as he walked to the back of the boat. He pushed the button that opens the engine hatch then he turned to me and made a motion with his forefinger across the front of his neck indicating that he wanted me to shut the engines down. I pulled all three throttles back, disengaged the center and port engines then shut them down.

Nad with tools in hand began to pull the blower belt from the center engine. The radio crackled and it was Jeff who was the first boat directly in front of us. "Hey Captain, he asked, are you having problems?" "Yes, I answered back. We threw that bad blower belt and the port engine shut down at the same time. Nad is back there taking a look at it right now".

Jeff came back, "I'll tell the other boats and we'll turn around. See you in a short", he said. With only one engine running and at idle I was able to talk with Nad. I told him that Jeff had called on the radio and the others boats were turning around heading back towards us. He smiled at me and held up a distributor in his hand then dropped it on the deck. Deftly he stepped on it and it broke into four or five pieces. He picked up the pieces and laid them on the top of the port engine. In a matter of minutes the other four boats were at our side.

I shut down the starboard engine and the other boats shut their engines down also. Now we were drifting with the wind and current but at least we could talk. Sparky was the first one to say anything. "What happened, he asked. Nad, had been leaning into the engine compartment stood up with the blower belt in hand and said, "we threw the belt but that's not all. When the belt went it took out the distributor cap on the port engine". Nad reached into the engine compartment and pulled out the pieces of the distributor that he had broken and held them up for everyone to see.

"That sucks, Sparky exclaimed. Now what", he asked? Nad shrugged his shoulders like he was without an answer. Without hesitating I piped up, "do you guys know where the nearest marine repair facility is? Everyone was looking at each other questioningly. Sparky was the first to answer and he played right into our hand. "Yeh, he said. There is a place about five miles from here. It's called Tiny's Marine Supply and they do a lot of work on our type of boats. Do you want us to tow you in there?". I looked at Nad and he responded right away. "No, he said. I think we can make it in by ourselves but we sure aren't going to make Johnny's Marina today. The best case scenario is all we'll need to replace is the blower belt and the distributor then we'll be good to go and we can meet you guys at Johnny's tomorrow sometime".

Sparky agreed to the plan and before the group left us I got Sparky's cell phone number under the pretense that we would call him if we were going to be delayed. I chuckled to myself thinking that a delay was given and they would be getting a call. At the last minute Jeff said he would follow us to the mouth of the Dog River to make sure we got there. We didn't have a problem with that and said okay. With that they fired up their engines and waved good bye, all except Jeff.

Nad got behind the helm and fired up the starboard engine after closing the engine room hatch. He put the engine into gear and adjusted the trims tabs to help him control the boat. We limped along at about ten miles an hour. Any faster could be damaging to the steering system. It took a couple of hours for us to reach the mouth of the Dog River and once there we told Jeff that we had everything under control and he go ahead and catch up with is group. Jeff and his wife waved good-bye as they turn away from us.

Just as they were leaving I heard my cell phone ringing in my headset. It was Carmen again. First she asked if it was okay to talk and I said yes it was but first brought her quickly up to date. She seemed to be overjoyed that we had effectively ditched the other boat and were now operating on our own. "Captain, she started. Here's the plan. Can you guys make Pensacola before nightfall?" "Yes, I answered, if we take the GIWW, which is the Gulf Intracoastal Waterway". "Good, she said. I want you guys to head immediately for Pensacola and when you get there I want you to call the phone number that I am about to give you. The person that you will be speaking with is a DEA agent and he will give you directions to the Pensacola Naval Base. They will be waiting for you and when you get there they are going to load you and Nad, along with Nad's boat on a C-130 and fly you guys home". Your job is done!

I was at a loss for words. For some reason I didn't think it was going to end this way or so quickly. We talked a while longer then she hung up. I started telling Nad about the conversation and all he could say was, "you gotta be shitting me"! I had to chuckle a little after hearing his verbal response. Getting to things at hand I asked Nad what he had in mind with the blower belt. He sort of smiled and said no problem. We needed to fuel up before heading out for Pensacola and while that was being done he could replace the blower belt. I looked at and said, "assuming this Marine Supply has a replacement, right?" "Not worried about it, he said smiling, I have one".

I called the marina on the cell phone and told them we were coming in for fuel and to make a small repair then we would be gone. I used the cell phone because I didn't want to take a chance on using the radio in the event Sparky and gang were monitoring it and were still in range. The marina told us to come on in and they would take care of us. Within an hour we gone and on our way for Pensacola.

I had to be honest with Nad because I have never traveled on the GIWW before. The distance itself was only about twenty something miles according to the charts. What I wasn't sure about was how fast we could legally travel. My past experiences down this where straight out to the ocean after departing the Tenn-Tom. It was still early afternoon so we had plenty of time to get where we had to be before nightfall. The GIWW was well marked and we had no problem understanding the different navigation aids. We were actually able to take the boat up to any speed that we wanted but not wanting to throw caution to the wind we decided to keep it at forty MPH.

It wasn't long before we were near the area that we needed to turn off to get in to the Naval Base. Using my cell phone I called the number that Carmen had given me. A gentleman answered and I told him who

I was and he said he had been expecting my call and they were looking at us this very moment. At first I didn't understand what he was talking about but then he asked me if I could see the Navy rigid inflatable boat crossing our bow at this very moment. I said yes and he said follow it. That was it and he hung up. I told Nad to turn in behind the inflatable and follow it.

He looked at me like I had lost it. "Do you see that 50 caliber on the stern? I'm not sure we should be messing around with these guys. I think they are Navy Seals. He was right but I told him those were our instructions so go ahead and get behind them. Nad yank the wheel suddenly and aimed his boat right for the inflatable. The inflatable was equipped with twin 225 Honda 4-Stroke Outboards. The person driving hit the throttles when he saw us pull in behind him. I was really impressed with the quick response of the twin Hondas.

The inflatable was running at sixty-five MPH with us right behind. It was a little faster than I would run an inflatable but then I suppose these guys know what they are doing. Nad suddenly got a wild hair and decided he wanted to have some fun with the Navy. He reached over and jammed all three throttles to the wall. His boat lurched forward like it had been shot out of a slingshot. In a split second we were abreast of the inflatable and in a split second later we had two 50 caliber machine guns trained on us. One of the guys in the inflatable motioned for us to slow down and fall in behind him. Oops! I pulled the throttles immediately and we fell in behind them. I looked over at Nad and he had a sheepish look on his face. I could well imagine what he was thinking.

The inflatable slowed down and we entered a lagoon that was well hidden from prying eyes. One of the guys in the inflatable pointed towards a dock and motioned for us to go to the dock. We eased up to the dock looking straight into the barrels of five M-16's. I was thinking for a second I was glad we were invited and I quench the thought of asking them if the guns were loaded. I assumed these guys were guards and one of them told us to remain on the boat until so and so got there. He said the guys name but I couldn't understand what he was saying.

In a few minutes a suit walked down the gangway and approached the boat. He introduced himself as Tom Nagy with the DEA and showed us his credentials. He said everything was ready for us and they were ready to start loading the boat. It kind of caught both Nad and myself by surprise. There was no messing around here. It was all business. Nad was still trying to figure out how they were going to pull his boat. We were about to find out.

We pulled away from the dock and made our way the boat ramp. There was a boat trailer being back into the water by a military Hum-V. As got closer I heard Nad say, "what in the hell is going on! That is my trailer!" I looked at him and said it must look like his trailer. He looked again and said, "nope, it's my trailer". I was as dumbfounded as he was but we were in bed with the Government and they can pretty much do what they want. Nad eased the boat up on the trailer and it was cinched up with the winch. The Hum-V didn't seem to have problem pulling Nad's boat out of the water. Once we were out of the water I yelled down to one of the guards and asked him if we could get off the boat without getting shot. He smiled and said we could get off.

I saw Agent Nagy and walked over to him. "What now", I asked. He looked at me as if he was thinking of something to say. "I understand you guys did a fantastic job out there on the river, he started. We want to thank the both of you for what you've done. You will probably find out later but it looks like this is going to be a major bust and more than likely one of the biggest that we have had in a few years. As far as you guys are concerned, your job is over and as soon as they load your boat on the plane it's ready to go. That of course means you're going to have to get on also", he said chuckling. "Is it okay if I make a quick phone call the guys we came down the river with", I asked. "I would just a soon that you didn't", he answered.

I didn't want to get in a pissing contest with him but I had to explain to him my reason for calling. After I explained that Sparky was probably expecting a call from me he relented. I called Sparky and told him that there were major problems with Nad's boat and we would not be coming to the Johnny's Marina. I told him that Nad had flown back home to bring his trailer down and we were going to haul it back up north. Sparky said he was sorry to it and even sorrier that we couldn't get together and talk about the business proposition that he had for me. I made it sound like I was bummed out for missing a good deal but maybe we could hook up on the river again and talk about it.

I knew full well that the chances of seeing him or them on the river again were going to be slim to none. Sparky and his cronies were about to become guests of the Federal Government, I think the term is, "Cross Bar Hotel". I said good-bye and hung up. I turned to talk to Agent Nagy just as Nad walked up. "I am done with the boat", he said. "Good, Agent Nagy said, you guys will be escorted by the guards to the plane. As soon as the boat is on board you guys are history around here".

Agent Nagy signaled to one of the guards and he came over and escorted us to a waiting vehicle and we headed for the plane. We were driven right out on the airstrip to the waiting plane. We saw the boat disappear into the belly of the plane as we drove up. We got out of the vehicle and we were escorted to the plane by a couple of guards. I we walked up the rear ramp to board the plane it suddenly dawned on me that this plane was huge. Huge, being an understatement. I knew these planes were big but until you have a chance to get on one you really have no idea of the size. Nad's boat looked like a little fishing boat.

We were met on board by a couple of Navy officers that told the guards that they were excused. They introduced themselves and said they were going to be our pilots today. "Captain Art, Commander Ellis, our pilot said. It is a real pleasure to meet you. I remember your name being mention when I was in flight school.

You and Tom Turpin made quite a name for yourselves in Vietnam". I thanked him for the courtesy and told him it was all Sea Stories and left it at that.

They took us to our seats and gave each of us a set of heads phones so we could hear everything that was going on. They told us to have a seat and get strapped in because we were out of here in about ten minutes. It seemed longer than ten minutes when we heard the jet engines increasing in speed. The plane started moving and we taxied to the runway. With the brakes locked the pilot increased the power to a 100% and released the brakes. Even as big as this plane is, you were pushed back in the seat from the acceleration. In seconds we were airborne and on our way home.

Epilogue

Three months later.

For the most part everything was back to normal. It took me almost a week to re-establish order in the marina after I got back. The owner went down during my absence and went bananas on the docks resulting in the entire marina up in arms. I knock a hundred dollars off everyone's dock fees for next year and that seemed to calm everyone down, except for the owner. He was really bent when I told him what I had done. I told him he had two choices, and empty marina, or a hundred dollar discount. His choice and he mumbled about it but in the end, he would get over it.

I've seen Nad a few times since we got back from the Gulf in fact I took him and his wife Lisa out on Winkin', Blinkin', & Nod III for a day cruise with Kathy my new First Mate. I met her out cruising around on the bike one day. She was on the side of the road with a slight mechanical problem and I stopped to see if I could help. I got her bike up and running in a few minutes and invited her to lunch and the relationship took off from there. Yup! We are getting along pretty good and she is a regular down on the docks. Ya gotta just love Biker Chicks!

Sparky and gang are in the Governments "Cross Bar Hotel" for quite a while. I kinda felt sorry for the wives because they are doing a little time at the "Hotel" also.

Nad and I were invited up to the Cities to the Federal Building in Minneapolis and received plaques for our Civic Service to our country and the war against drugs. The end result of what Nad and I started was really impressive.

Our three weeks of undercover netted some spectacular results. There were over three hundred drug related arrests from suppliers, traffickers, dealers, and some end users. The DEA people recovered four thousand pounds of pure cocaine and confiscated over three million dollars in cash. We did find out that Johnny's Marina was the kingpin of cocaine in that area of the country. They had a sweet thing going on. It seems that they had a contract with a cruise line to supply them with diving equipment and filled air tanks.

When one of the cruise ships was in the area they would contact the dive shop and the dive shop would take out a hundred or so supposedly full tanks for them in exchange the equal amount of empty tanks. The empty tank of course were not empty but were full of cocaine. It was a simple exchange program. This apparently had been going on for some time.

When Nad and I were flying home from the Gulf, courtesy of the U.S. Government, we amused ourselves calculating how much money these druggies were knocking down. We will probably never know if our figures were right but I am willing to bet a dollar to a donut that we were damn close.

Here is how we figured it. Each diving tank would hold about thirty pounds of cocaine. This of course is rated as pure. Once it gets to the dealer it is cut by at least fifty percent. You now have sixty pound of not so pure cocaine. When it gets to the street dealer its cut again by fifty percent, sometimes more but I will use fifty percent as the main figure. Anyway, you now have one hundred and twenty pounds of about twenty-five percent purity cocaine.

When you multiply a hundred and twenty pounds by sixteen, the number of ounces to a pound, you get one thousand, nine hundred and twenty ounces. When you multiply the ounces by grams, which there are twenty-eight grams to an ounce you get fifty-three thousand, seven hundred and sixty grams. As near as we could tell a gram of cocaine sells for one hundred dollars on the street. You can crunch the numbers yourself. The bottom line is staggering.

Glen Frey was right! "It's the lure of easy money, its got very strong appeal".

Oh! "Toad" Turpin. He's a somewhat lucky young man. He was sternly admonished by the Federal Judge because of his evident stupidity to allow himself to duped into the situation that he was in. He did not get off without a little suffering on his part. For once he learned that Daddy's money couldn't help him. The Judge sentenced him twelve months and one day in a minimal security facility which is not bad considering he was looking at a possible ten to fifteen years. Following his incarceration he will have three years of supervised probation and one thousand hours of community service with the DARE Program.

I am getting Winkin', Blinkin', & Nod III warmed up. Great River Harbor in Alma, Wisconsin called and wants me down to help train house boaters next year. I thought Kathy and I would go down and visit for a couple of days and see our friends, Paul & Marrietta at Pier 4, Mike & Marie at the Burlington Hotel and of Hale & Janet at the Great River Harbor Campground & Marina.

See you there!

"As a small man,
I act tough to compensate for my
lack of manhood" -LR

CPSIA information can be obtained
at www.ICGtesting.com
Printed in the USA
FSHW012000041119
63767FS

9 781543 474510